Without pausing  reckless thought _____ _____, Hero moved over and threw back the blankets.

"Here," she said. "As you pointed out, it's the only warm place."

For once, the easygoing Kit appeared startled. "No, I'll be fine in front of the fire."

Hero shook her head. "It's the only sensible solution."

Kit looked right at her, that dark and dangerous glint in his eyes. "I don't think sharing a bed is a good idea."

Hero shivered at his low tone, husky with promise, and she knew she was on treacherous ground. She had no business encouraging any closeness between them, but neither did she want him to lie freezing upon the filthy floor.

"Huddling together might be the only way we both fend off illness," Hero said. "And I don't see a problem because, as you so often point out, you are a gentleman."

Kit's mouth twisted at the reminder, and he put a hand to his split lip, with a grimace. "Even a gentleman has his limits."

\* \* \*

### *The Gentleman's Quest*
Harlequin® Historical #980—February 2010

*the*
# GENTLEMAN'S
*Quest*

# DEBORAH
# SIMMONS

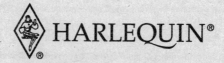

TORONTO • NEW YORK • LONDON
AMSTERDAM • PARIS • SYDNEY • HAMBURG
STOCKHOLM • ATHENS • TOKYO • MILAN • MADRID
PRAGUE • WARSAW • BUDAPEST • AUCKLAND

Recycling programs
for this product may
not exist in your area.

ISBN-13: 978-0-373-29580-7

THE GENTLEMAN'S QUEST

www.eHarlequin.com

**Printed in U.S.A.**

**Other works include:**

HQN Books

*The Brides of Christmas*
"The Unexpected Guest"

For Kim Neer Lindsey, Tami Kaplan Wright, and Karen Brown Irvine, in memory of the wonderful summers we spent together at Linden.

# Chapter One

Hero glanced out of the window of the coach, but saw no sign of Oakfield Manor in the gathering gloom. The bad roads had caused delays; she had been confined in the conveyance for too long. Across from Hero, her companion stared ahead stoically, undisturbed by the stuffy, small space of the old-fashioned vehicle and the ruts that bounced Hero about. As usual, she couldn't help wondering whether Mrs Renshaw was with her strictly as a chaperone or as a spy, to make sure she concluded Raven's business satisfactorily.

Resentment flared before Hero tamped it down out of habit. She knew what was expected of her. No doubt Christopher Marchant would be old and shriveled and balding and smelly. And randy. And she would have to lean close, displaying her low-cut bodice. With a little cajoling, she usually escaped with the prize and her person intact, if not her self-respect. But she had learned long ago that such luxuries as pride were for the wealthy and secure, not for someone like her.

Any doubts that the world was a grim place could be easily vanquished by a glance at the windswept moors, the barren trees and darkening clouds outside. If Hero did not know better, she might think Raven had managed the weather, as well as everything else, and the idea unnerved her.

Another rut threw her against the worn and cracking leather interior, and she realized they had turned onto a sparsely graveled drive in little better condition than the road. She had only an instant to wonder whether they were at last approaching their destination when she was thrown again, harder, and grabbed uselessly for a hold. But it was the arrival of Renshaw in her lap that alerted Hero to the fact that something was amiss.

The imperturbable female uttered a surprised grunt, while her weight stole Hero's breath. When she was able to ease out from under her burden, Hero realized the coach had halted, tilting to one side. She cursed Raven and his ancient vehicle with its ancient fittings, for they likely had lost a wheel here in the middle of nowhere.

Scrambling to the door, Hero managed to jump out onto a thicket of grass, but there was little comfort to be found outside beyond escape from the stifling interior. Pulling up the hood of her cloak against the gusting winds, Hero took stock of their surroundings, and her heart sank. They were off the main road, black clouds chased across the sky, and a rumble of thunder in the distance presaged the coming storm.

Hero shook her head against the sense of doom that threatened and made her way gingerly to the rear of the vehicle where the coachman and footman were muttering amongst themselves. Even Hero could see the wheel was broken, and since both men were eyeing it stupidly, she could only fear the worst.

"If you can't fix it, one of you will have to go for help," Hero said, raising her voice against the wind.

They turned to her, their reluctance obvious. The village they had passed through was a long way back. "'Tweren't much traffic on that roadway, miss," the coachman said, scratching his head.

"There must be more there than here," Hero said with a glance at the overgrown drive. Were they even on the right path? Should she send one of the men ahead? If one went ahead and one behind, Hero would double the chances of their rescue. But that would leave her alone with Renshaw, two women in a broken vehicle on unfamiliar lands, not far from the infamous moors, with foul weather looming.

The thought gave even Hero pause.

Yet what could possibly threaten them in this barren landscape? Anyone with sense, including the residents, would be safely inside, prepared to ride out the tempest. Hero had a pistol in her reticule, and Renshaw had not been chosen for her feminine accomplishments. Wide of girth and taller than many men, she was armed with a cane she carried solely for protection.

Still, wariness was Hero's watchword, and so, in the end, she sent the footman forward, leaving the grizzled coachman to keep watch, while she climbed back inside the coach to wait as best she could. But the wind set up an awful moaning, and Hero wondered whether the vehicle would collapse entirely, falling upon its side and crushing its occupants.

Although Renshaw made no move to follow, Hero exited once more, and as she leaped down to view the scene around her, she considered the length of Raven's reach. Surely it did not stretch this far from his fortress, yet the situation smacked of his design. Was it a test? As she had so often in the past, Hero wondered if she would ever escape from the Gothic nightmare that she seemed so often to inhabit.

It was then that Hero heard something above the distant thunder and bluster. A glance toward the coach showed it swaying slightly, the coachman seeming to doze upon his crooked perch, but the horses had pricked up their ears. Whirling, Hero looked down the drive that disappeared into the growing gloom, but she could see nothing.

Then it seemed as though the sound was coming from ahead, and Hero turned around. Surely, the wind was playing tricks upon her, for now all was quiet behind, while she could hear a horse approaching from the other direction. Walking past the coach and the horses that tramped uneasily, she peered into the dimness. For someone weaned on tales of haunts and odd happenings, Hero felt an uncharacteristic trepidation.

And then she saw him.

Drawing in a sharp breath, Hero wondered whether her dormant imagination had conjured the sight, for he seemed to come straight from one of Raven's Gothic novels. A dark figure atop a black horse, cape billowing behind him, he rode as if born of the storm itself, fast and hard and directly toward her.

Hero was so transfixed that she did not even move and might have been trampled had the horse not stopped neatly. The figure dropped just as neatly to the ground, and only then did she feel he might be real, not a product of some unwitting fantasy, for he stepped toward her with a murmur of concern.

For once, Hero could not answer, having been struck dumb by his appearance. Tall and wide shouldered, his dark hair whipping about a face so handsome that Hero had never seen the like, he seemed the very embodiment of every young girl's dream of rescue.

But Hero was no longer a girl, and she knew that no one could help her, unless it was only to give her shelter from the approaching storm. Indeed, he was shouting something to that effect, and before Hero realized what he was about, he had taken her arm. Mounting easily, he reached down to lift her up in front of him.

Hero could only gasp in startlement as she felt her carefully constructed world spinning out of control. Before she could speak, he tucked her side against his hard chest, drew one strong arm around her and kicked the horse into movement.

Hero opened her mouth to protest this stranger's complete usurpation of her authority. Such nearness made her uncomfortable, and the warmth of his touch had an unwelcome effect upon her senses. But then he flashed Hero a grin, and she was struck speechless once more.

As Hero gaped, witless, at the face only a few inches from her own, she realized she had never been this close to anyone in her life. It was unnerving, and yet she had to resist an urge to touch the lock of dark hair that blew across his forehead, matching eyes the color of chocolate.

They held her own for a moment, then glanced upward, and Hero followed his gaze to where thick drops began hailing down upon them. Despite his efforts to hurry her to shelter, the storm had come, yet it was nothing compared to Hero's personal tumult as he pulled her close.

Heart pounding, dizzy and disoriented, Hero had the strange sensation that she could deny this man nothing. And that wild thought was more frightening to her than any Gothic horror.

Once deposited into the hands of Mrs Osgood, a cheery, apple-cheeked housekeeper, Hero felt more like herself. Obviously, the situation outside had worked upon her nerves until she was overwrought, imagining her rescuer to be some kind of superior being with an unexplainable effect upon her. Although Hero was not the overwrought kind, the only other possibility was too terrible to consider.

It was with some relief that she realized, through Mrs Osgood's chatter, that she had reached her destination and that she had only to meet with Mr Marchant in order to conclude her business. Who her rescuer might be, Hero refused to wonder or care. Yet, at the claim, her body shivered as if in denial.

She tried not to remember the feel of his hard form, wet garments slick against her own, as he helped her from the horse and into the house. A small Gothic, complete with battlements, its dark facade so evoked Raven that Hero again wondered what he had wrought, only to dismiss her suspicions.

Augutus Raven might have access to an astonishing variety of resources, but he could not control the elements. And Hero could hardly be surprised by the style of the building, considering Raven's penchant for such facades. Many of his fellow antiquaries shared his delight in the old and cold and moldy, probably because they were old and cold and moldy.

Not that Oakfield was moldy, but it looked sadly in need of improvement. Still, the fire was warm, and Hero was glad to be given her own room, with Renshaw nearby. As she bathed, dressed in dry clothes and brushed her hair by the fire, the incredible encounter with the handsome stranger gradually faded away. And by the time Hero went to join Renshaw downstairs, she was firmly focused on the task ahead.

That focus was only sharpened by her surroundings, for the housekeeper showed her into a rather threadbare library. Ignoring the gloom of the poorly lit room, Hero eyed the mostly empty shelves and the packing crates that were scattered about. *Was Mr Marchant selling all of his books?*

If so, Raven might be interested in a bulk purchase. You never knew what nuggets were hidden away, undiscovered and undervalued by their owner. Hero moved toward one open box and glanced inside. Some Latin and Greek volumes were piled in no particular order, and she was leaning down to read the titles when she heard footsteps.

Plastering a smile on her face, Hero turned in greeting, only to stare in astonishment at the man who stood in the doorway. Without his cloak and gloves he looked even more beautiful than she remembered, and Hero blinked in dismay. *Surely this was not her host?*

"W-where is Mr Marchant?" she asked, cursing her faltering tongue.

"I'm Christopher Marchant, at your service," he said, bowing slightly. Then he flashed her that winning grin, and Hero felt unsteady upon her feet.

She knew better than to dismiss all antiquaries as the grasping old fools they were often portrayed. Still, she rarely dealt with elegant, free-spending sorts like the Duke of Devonshire. And she certainly had never met any like this man.

Too late, Hero realized she was gaping, and she hurried to recover herself. Panic threatened—how was she to proceed when her heart was hammering and her wits scattered? But she could do nothing else.

"Thank you," she said, with a nod of her head. "I am Miss Hero Ingram, and this is my companion, Mrs Renshaw. I have brought a letter from my uncle, Mr Augustus Raven. I believe he corresponded with your father in the past."

Hero stepped forward to present the missive, while giving the man an opportunity to ogle her bodice. But unlike her usual hosts, Christopher Marchant was not ancient or shriveled or randy. And Hero doubted that anyone who looked like he did would be impressed with her small bosom, no matter how low cut her gown.

"I beg your pardon for barging in upon you like this," Hero said, reciting her usual patter. The lonely old men she most often dealt with were so flattered by her attention that they did not object to her doing business on behalf of her uncle, if they would even call it that. Most would label the transaction an arrangement between friends or acquaintances, among fellow collectors.

However, Mr Marchant was…different, and Hero wondered whether he would look askance at her sudden appearance at his remote residence. "I was in the area and thought to make a stop for my own convenience. You will forgive me?" she asked, her standard simpering sticking in her throat.

"Of course, please sit down," he said, with an easy gesture. His open and engaging manner further confused her, for the men she was accustomed to dealing with were often as secretive as Raven, hiding their thoughts behind pinched faces.

"I'm afraid the house is still at sixes and sevens," Mr Marchant muttered, his smile faltering. For a moment Hero thought he would say more, but he simply glanced around the room as though just realizing its disarray.

He did not appear to notice that Renshaw was seated in the most shadowed corner, which was just as well, for Hero could not depend upon her usual tactics. Thinking frantically, she decided to take a direct approach. "Are you selling some of your collection?"

Mr. Marchant looked at her rather blankly before glancing about. "Oh, you mean the books? No, we recently moved in, my sister and I, and have not yet arranged everything."

"Well, if you should wish to save yourself some of the trouble, I know someone who might well take these out of your way," Hero said, gesturing toward the crates.

Mr Marchant nodded, though he showed no interest, which was puzzling. Here, inside Oakfield, he seemed distracted, and Hero noticed shadows under his eyes. Was he ill? He certainly looked robust and not much older than she, but perhaps a long night of carousing had left him the worse for wear. Isn't that what handsome young men did, gamble, drink and seduce women? Hero could only guess, for her dealings with such were few and far between.

"If that's why you've come, I'm afraid I can't offer you any hope on that score," Mr Marchant said. "They were my father's, you see." Sadness flashed briefly across his features, and Hero cursed Raven's greed. How many times had he swooped down upon a grieving relative to break up and sell the precious volumes the deceased had spent a lifetime lovingly acquiring?

"I'm sorry," Hero said, and she meant it. But when his dark gaze met her own, she felt as though he were looking right into her, and she glanced away, unwilling to let anyone, especially this man, see her. Suddenly, she wondered whether he could tell how he affected her, and she straightened, determined to reveal nothing of herself.

"Certainly, I can understand your feelings," Hero said, briskly breaking whatever connection had been between them. If Christopher Marchant's only attachment to his father's collection was sentiment, then he shouldn't care about any of the individual items, which made her task that much easier. "I would not want you to part with so treasured an assembly, but perhaps you could spare one volume?" she asked.

At her words, Mr Marchant's open expression turned closed, making her wonder if he was as uninterested as he seemed. *Was he aware of what he possessed and its potential value?* Any collector would know that a book long thought lost would start a bidding war.

Hero gave no outward sign of her thoughts, though the change in Mr Marchant made her uncomfortable. *Did he realize she had hoped to dupe him?* He had seemed genuinely welcoming, but now there was an edge to the man, the kind that made her wary.

On occasion even the old and withered antiquaries were immune to her charms. Some miserly creatures were intent upon holding on to the meanest title even if it meant going without supper. But Hero did not intend to return to Raven empty-handed, so she chose her next words carefully.

"Perhaps you are aware of interest in the volume, a text by Ambrose Mallory?"

To Hero's surprise, Mr Marchant's handsome face darkened with anger, and she hastened to avoid any outburst that would destroy her chances entirely. "I'm afraid once word is out, there is no stopping them," she said, with a shrug of apology.

But he was not placated. Instead, he looked astonished by her comment. "You cannot mean to tell me that there are more Druids out there, intent upon evil?"

*Druids?* Hero kept her expression steady as she realized her host might not be in his right mind. Even as she shied from the possibility, she wouldn't put it past Raven to send her here, knowing of his condition. It was just the sort of twisted jest that amused Raven, who might hope to gain a bargain, as well.

Floundering, Hero cast about for some sort of reply and tried a conspiratorial smile. "Not Druids, sir, but something far more dangerous," she said, leaning forward. *"Bibliomaniacs."*

But Mr Marchant was not amused. Surging to his feet, he turned toward the doorway, and for one startling moment Hero thought he might forcibly evict her. She felt a tremor of fear. *Or was it excitement?* But Mr Marchant appeared to regain control of himself as he strode toward one of the deep-set windows.

Rain was lashing against the panes, pounding as fiercely as Hero's heart, and the very air crackled, like that which presaged lightning. She was on the edge of her seat, ready to make her escape, if necessary. Yet at the same time, she had to fight the urge to go to him, for he seemed in need of comfort.

When he finally spoke, he did not turn toward her, but gazed out at the storm. "The book you refer to is gone, burned in the conflagration that took my garden and stables. I cannot help you."

It was a dismissal, but Hero ignored it. Her mind was too busy working. *Was he telling the truth?* Books were often lost to fire or water, but it would not be the first time she had been handed a Banbury tale to divert attention from a prize—or to gain a higher price from another bidder. Perhaps Mr Marchant knew that some bibliomaniacs would go to any lengths to acquire an item, handing over outrageous sums for the rare and coveted.

Word had it that Snuffy Davie paid about twopence for a book that eventually sold for £170 to the Regent himself. Those with the means, such as the Duke of Devonshire, filled whole rooms, even entire houses, with their acquisitions. It was definitely a mania, one that Hero could not understand.

Although Mr Marchant had seemed indifferent at first, perhaps he was stricken, as well. *Was he playing her, as she had tried to play him?* Hero eyed him closely. "If that is true, then it is a sad loss to the collecting world, as well as to yourself."

"Hardly," he said. "My sister nearly died, and that accursed book was to blame."

With that, his gaze met hers, and Hero swallowed hard. Again, she felt out of her element. This man's grief and anger threatened to reach out and touch her, something that she could not allow.

Hastily breaking eye contact, she sought to regain control of the situation. "I'm sorry," Hero murmured. "But I believe I have some information that might be of interest to you, if you would hear me out?"

He turned to look out at the rain again, reaching up to run a hand through his dark hair, and Hero found her own gaze lingering on the thick locks in need of a trim. His clothes were those of a gentleman, though not of the most expensive materials, but his form was such that he could probably wear anything to his advantage. And Hero found his simple breeches and coat far more appealing than the London dandies with their gold embroidered waistcoats or Raven's friends with their old-fashioned wigs and silk breeches.

When he said nothing, Hero decided to press her

point. "You see, with that copy burned, any other would be the sole surviving edition, a very valuable volume indeed. And my uncle has reason to believe that another exists, perhaps in this very house—"

Mr Marchant cut her off. "I certainly hope not," he said. He turned his head to send her another probing glance. "Are you even aware of what you are seeking? This book that you want tells how to augur the future from the death throes of innocent people. And my sister was to be one such victim."

Hero sucked in a harsh breath. Was that the subject, or was Mr Marchant delusional? Hero cursed Raven for giving her so little information, but the thought focused her attention on her task. Druids and auguring, whether real or not, had little to do with it.

"I'm sure my uncle has no interest in the text," Hero assured her host. "It's the rarity of the work that makes it collectible." Without waiting for Mr Marchant's response, Hero pulled the paper Raven had given her from her reticule and held it toward him.

"My uncle found this in another book he acquired. Since all copies of the Mallory were thought lost until recently, he was most interested, of course."

For a long moment, Hero waited, hand outstretched, but Mr Marchant did not stir from his position.

"Perhaps I have not made myself clear," he said. "I have no interest in this work except to destroy it."

Now he was talking madness. "I can hardly believe you, the son of a scholar, would condone suppression of the written word," Hero said, hoping to shame him.

But he did not argue. Desperate now, Hero stammered out a protest before catching herself. She took a deep breath, then eyed him levelly.

"I assure you that Augustus Raven has no intention of letting anyone even see the book, except to admire its position in one of his presses. His collection is vast and varied, but it is the singular editions he particularly treasures, the pages being of no consequence, as long as they have not been gutted."

Mr Marchant simply shook his head, and Hero's heart sank. "Perhaps you don't realize the kind of sum Raven would consider paying."

But even that did not move him, and Hero tried to make some sense of his stand. It would be just her luck to find the only man in England with some sort of conscience. Usually, she was a good judge of people, but even she could not take the measure of Christopher Marchant. Was he a lunatic? A fool? That rarest of all creatures, a man without a price? Or had he simply received a better offer?

Hero studied him closely, looking for a telltale sign, a hint of how she should proceed. But she could see no hidden meanings, no deep dark secrets she could use against him, no weaknesses she could exploit, no promise of further negotiation. Or was her judgement clouded by the man himself?

Finally, he turned away from the windows to face her. "I would not send you out in this storm, so you are welcome to remain here for the night."

At his words, Hero didn't know whether to be relieved or not. Her instincts told her to abandon her mission now, while she could, and to run from this man who had such an effect upon her. But Raven's will was stronger than her own, and he had sent her here with a purpose.

Hero nodded her agreement, knowing that she would try again at supper, at the very least, at breakfast at the very latest. And if all else failed, she could search the place herself.

Kit pulled off his neckcloth with a sharp jerk, tossed it aside, and sank into a chair to stare moodily out at the darkness. But even he realized that he spent entirely too much time looking out into the gloom, and he forced himself to turn away from the window. Instead, his gaze was drawn across his bedroom to the decanter he now kept on a chest of drawers. There was nothing wrong with a glass or two to help him sleep, he told himself.

But he knew his sister Sydony wouldn't agree. She would not approve of his behavior, the nightly drinks and the brooding that she would say was not like him. *But he didn't feel like himself.* He hadn't since the fire.

He was the one who had brought Sydony here, insisting that the property willed to him from a greataunt was good fortune. And he had reveled in his new role as a landowner, ignoring her misgivings and suspicions. He'd even begun to wonder about her sanity when she prattled on about Druids and mysterious lights.

And then he'd nearly lost her. If it hadn't been for their old friend Barto, who had not ignored Sydony's suspicions, Kit would have woken up in a ditch, stupid and useless, his sister dead, his garden usurped by cloaked killers.

Kit shook his head at his stupidity. Of the two siblings, he had been the cheerful one. Syd certainly wasn't dismal, but she had always seemed more conscientious, perhaps because she had assumed control of the household after the death of their mother many years ago. Meanwhile, Kit had drifted through life with a casual contentment—until the fire.

Ever since he'd been unable to move forward, to tackle the rebuilding with his usual enthusiasm. He felt as though he'd been kicked in the gut and, angry and hurting, he questioned everything, especially himself.

Surging to his feet, Kit moved to the chest and poured himself a glass of wine. Just for another night, he told himself. Because of her. He took a big swallow and frowned at the wry twist of fate that had brought him a guest.

Visitors to Oakfield were infrequent, if not nonexistent, so he had been surprised when Mrs Osgood reported that a servant had arrived on foot from a broken-down coach. Racing against the storm, Kit had hurried out, only to come across a beautiful creature standing fearlessly against the wind, one hand holding the hood of her cloak against her streaming hair. *Just as though she were waiting for him.*

He had been so desperate for companionship that he had imagined… Hell, Kit wasn't sure what he was thinking when he saw her, probably that she was some sort of answer to everything that ailed him. And when she fitted so well against him, his hopes seemed confirmed.

Kit shook his head. Whatever conquests he had made had been left behind in his old neighborhood, while the female population around here stayed well clear of Oakfield and its owners, out of long habit. So he could hardly be blamed for letting his imagination run away with him when presented with a young woman who was as articulate, intelligent and opinionated as his sister, while making poor Syd look like an antidote.

But then he'd found out what she was about, this Miss Ingram. *Hero.* Kit swirled the name around on his tongue and found it bittersweet. If she had come for any other reason, he would have welcomed her into his home, perhaps even into his life. Instead, he had studiously avoided her company.

It had not been easy for a man so isolated to forgo such an opportunity, especially when his visitor was no ordinary female. Kit's mouth twisted wryly at that understatement. Unusual and intriguing, Miss Ingram was a puzzle that begged closer study. But more than that, she somehow had managed to stir him to life, as nothing else had.

Kit couldn't help remembering his first sight of her, standing like a beacon in the gloom, as though she could hold back the darkness. Tossing back the last of his drink, he shuddered. Looks could be deceiving, as he well knew, for it seemed that Miss Ingram had brought the darkness with her.

A knock made Kit lift his head, and for one wild moment, he wondered whether the beautiful siren had come to plead her case here and now. Drawing in a harsh breath, he surged to his feet and ran a hand through his hair. But when he opened the door, it was only to greet the new housekeeper.

"Pardon me, sir, but the coachman is downstairs, wishing to see you. I told him you'd gone up to bed, but he said it was important," Mrs Osgood added with a hint of disapproval. Obviously, she did not think much of the staff bothering her master at this hour.

But Kit nodded without hesitation, for Hob was his friend Barto's man and coachman was the least of his duties. Hurriedly placing his empty glass on a nearby table, Kit closed the door and followed the housekeeper downstairs. This sudden summons from Hob could not be good.

But what? Kit wondered. Those responsible for the fire presumably had all died in it, and the maze and book that had drawn them here were gone. Yet Barto had insisted that Hob stay on at Oakfield, and Kit had agreed, if only to placate his old friend.

Now he felt a new sense of foreboding as he slipped through the darkened house. Was his home doomed to disaster? Cursed? Kit had never believed in such nonsense, but he had never believed in murderous cults, either. His mood was bleak when he entered the dimly lit kitchen, where Hob stood waiting. With a nod toward Mrs Osgood, who disappeared into the servants' quarters below, Kit stepped forward.

"It could be nothing, sir," Hob said, as though gauging his temperament.

But Kit knew that Hob would not be here if he did not have a valid concern. "Go on."

"Well, it's their coach, sir, the one that arrived today."

"You mean Miss Ingram's?"

Hob nodded. "I gather it belongs to her uncle, Mr Raven, but she's the one who uses it the most, according to the coachman." He paused to eye Kit soberly. "We got a new wheel put on easily enough, but when we looked at the old one, well, it wasn't any ordinary break."

"What do you mean?"

"I mean it looked like a saw had been taken to it."

"What? You're saying someone deliberately tampered with the wheel, assuring it would fail?" Since his own father had died in a carriage accident, Kit was well aware of what could have happened, and he felt a sharp surge of anger. "Why would someone do such a thing? And who? Some stable hand intent upon a rich prize?"

Hob shook his head. "It's an old coach, worn and uncomfortable looking, hardly what one would expect from a wealthy man like Mr Raven."

"From what I understand, he's something of an eccentric," Kit said, then he glanced sharply at Hob. "Perhaps the break was not intended for Miss Ingram, but for her uncle."

Hob shook his head. "This was done recently, sir, and they're far from this Raven Hill, where they make their home."

"But if whoever did this wasn't drawn to the coach, then what do they want?" Kit mused aloud. He didn't like any of the possibilities, least of all the answer he got from Hob, who eyed him with a frown.

"Perhaps they want something inside it."

# Chapter Two

Kit's mood was dark when he returned to his room. The candles he had left burning flickered as he swung open the door and closed it behind him. Without conscious thought, he reached for his glass, but it wasn't where he had left it. Glancing around, he found it had fallen to the floor, which was probably a good thing, for he needed his wits about him. He set the empty glass on the table and sank into his chair.

In the silence that followed, his gaze drifted to the empty seat opposite, and he realized that he missed having a sounding board. His old friend Barto's advice would be welcome now, as would Sydony's. Although the siblings had been apart before, this was the first time in his life that Kit had lived alone. And he'd better get used to it, for Sydony would be marrying Barto soon.

Kit had been so pleased at the news that he had not given a thought to the day when his sister would be gone, both she and Barto far away. But now that day loomed before him, and Kit glanced at the glass again before he caught himself.

He had a good home, which he planned to improve, property he hoped to make prosperous, and money he could draw upon to do both. So what if he was alone? He would just have to make more of an effort to meet the locals. Surely the gentry would come around, and there were some young people among them, for Kit had seen them at church.

The ladies he had chanced upon there, however, paled in comparison to the one who was under his roof. So why wasn't such a beautiful and intriguing creature married? Perhaps she was betrothed, Kit mused, but not many men would let her travel over the countryside making deals for her uncle.

As a rule, her gender did not conduct business. Although there had always been rich and powerful females who exerted their authority, often behind the scenes, a young woman usually did not call on gentlemen, even with a chaperone in tow. Perhaps Miss Ingram simply had been traveling in the area, as she claimed. Yet she spoke of her uncle's concerns so knowledgeably that Kit suspected this wasn't the first such errand she had undertaken.

He tried to remember all that he knew about Augustus Raven, but it wasn't much. The man styled himself after Horace Walpole, a dilettante of the past century who had authored *The Castle of Otranto*. As far as Kit knew, Raven had never dabbled in writing, but just as Walpole was famous for his Gothic home, Strawberry Hill, Raven had his own elaborate fortress called Raven Hill.

Unlike Strawberry Hill, it was shrouded in mystery, as was its owner. Augustus Raven was a collector, that much was known, and apparently, he had no compunction about having his niece acquire for him. And now he had put her in danger.

Kit frowned. At one time he wouldn't have given Hob's report a second thought, but he had learned the hard way not to ignore warning signs. The fact that someone had deliberately caused Miss Ingram's coach to break down so close to Oakfield was not a likely coincidence. And he could come to only one conclusion.

The wretched book had to be responsible.

It had drawn her here, as it had others before her, most notably a man named Malet, a latter-day Druid who had sought the text for some arcane ritual involving the maze behind the house. Both had been built by Ambrose Mallory, a mystic responsible for the writings that were wreaking havoc more than a hundred years after his death.

Had someone survived the conflagration? Or were there others out there who had not been caught in the blaze? Barto had the wealth and connections to investigate, but so far he had discovered nothing more than what they already knew, and Kit had begun to believe the whole business was over.

Until now. *But why Miss Ingram?* Kit shook his head. Whether someone thought she had the book in her possession or had information that would lead to it didn't matter. There were people who would stop at nothing to get their hands on that deadly nonsense.

Kit ought to know. They'd killed his father.

And after what Sydony had gone through, Kit wasn't about to let Miss Ingram meet a similar fate. Although he had pressing matters that required his attention at Oakfield and wanted nothing less than to be thrust back into the dark doings that haunted his new home, Kit had no choice.

He had been asleep on his watch once before, but he did not intend to let it happen again.

When Kit went down to breakfast, he found that his guests had already eaten and were waiting in the library. Although Mrs Osgood would have shown them there as a matter of course, Kit couldn't help wondering if Miss Ingram had been rifling through his father's books.

The thought sent anticipation buzzing in his veins, an antidote to the brooding melancholy that was his daily companion. But Kit was not willing to give it up easily, and he told himself that in the light of the new day, he would find his visitor wanting. Surely, no woman could be as beautiful and interesting as he had made her.

And yet, when he entered the library, Kit felt the same pleasure he had the day before. The pale light seemed to cast a glow upon her, just as when he had first seen her standing in the drive. And something about her pose, seated demurely by a window, hands folded in her lap, made his lips curve, for it did not seem a natural one.

Had she already rifled through the books or had she guessed at his suspicions? Kit wondered, not for the first time, what went on behind those eyes. They were a caramel color, as unusual as the woman herself, but told him nothing of their owner. Did she feel what he felt when he looked at her? Her impassive features argued otherwise and reminded Kit of the seriousness of the discussion ahead.

He looked around the room for Mrs Renshaw, only to find her seated at a distance that would make conversation difficult. But the stout female seemed to be nodding off anyway, so he did not bother to include her.

Turning his attention back to Miss Ingram, Kit spoke before she could begin reciting the usual pleasantries expected in such a social situation. "Show me what you have," he said, as he took a seat near her. "About the Mallory."

Kit saw a flicker of surprise, quickly masked, and he wondered how this woman had come to be so self-possessed. Sydony's feelings were always apparent, even if she wasn't voicing them, but Miss Ingram said little unless it related to her errand, and revealed even less. Showing no expression, she handed him a torn piece of paper.

"It is part of a letter from Mallory to one of his disciples," she said.

The paper obviously was old, and Kit handled it carefully. Although the hand was strong, the ink had faded and was difficult to read. Still, he could make out most of what remained.

*I write to entrust you with this copy of my life's work to hold for safekeeping. Speak not of it to anyone, but secrete it well away from all prying eyes, so that the historical truths therein might be preserved. I have hidden a copy here, but, as you may have learned, the rest have been seized and destroyed. I blame the cursed printer who—*

"Historical truths," Kit muttered in contempt.

"Apparently, all other editions were destroyed because they were deemed sacrilegious, and Mallory was labeled a heretic," Miss Ingram explained. "He died shortly afterward, purportedly poisoned by one of his own."

Kit frowned at the thought of the murder, hopefully not done under this roof, although most likely deserved. "And who did he send this to?" Kit asked, trying to decipher the name.

Miss Ingram leaned toward him, an intent look upon her face. "Martin Cheswick, an ancestor of the Earl of Cheswick. Raven acquired some books, including the one in which this fragment was found, after the current earl's father died."

Kit nearly whistled at the idea of such a personage being connected with Mallory. Then again, every family had black sheep in their histories, including the Prince Regent himself. "But that's where you should be looking, not here," Kit said, returning the paper to her.

Miss Ingram frowned. "It speaks of two copies."

"But the one that was hidden here burned," Kit said. And that would be that, if not for the broken wheel. He could shout out to the skies that the volume was gone, but someone obviously thought Miss Ingram knew better. Were they looking for the piece of correspondence or the book itself?

"Who knew that you were coming here?" Kit asked.

Again, there was but a brief flicker of surprise before Miss Ingram spoke. "Raven, obviously."

"Perhaps some of his friends or associates, as well?"

To her credit, Miss Ingram did not balk at his questions, but answered with a trace of irony. "Mr Marchant, I assure you that Raven does not discuss uncompleted transactions with anyone. That is why I alone am here, without a host of others clamouring to outbid me."

"But you were lucky to reach Oakfield at all," Kit said, "considering that the wheel on your coach was carefully sawed so as to cause it to break."

This time there was no mistaking her startlement. And even the distant companion roused herself from her slumberous slouch. Perhaps she was not as uninterested as she appeared.

"What are you saying?"

"My coachman replaced the wheel, but there's no mistaking that the old one was cut."

Kit was so used to talking to Syd that he realized not every gently born female would take well to such news, and he braced himself for some kind of fainting spell or hysteria. But Miss Ingram again proved she was not typical of her gender. Evincing no fear or horror, she eyed him evenly.

"But why would anyone want to cause such an accident?"

"I would guess for the same reason you are here," Kit said. "Perhaps they've heard of your uncle's interest in the Mallory and think that you might acquire it or might know something that would lead them to it, such as what you just showed me."

Miss Ingram frowned. "I don't see how anyone could know about it when it has been hidden for years."

Kit shrugged. "Perhaps your uncle had occasion to mention it to someone, or the former owner of the book in which this was found might have spoken of it."

"Mr Marchant, Raven does not easily share his secrets," Miss Ingram said, yet there was a certain hesitation in her speech that made Kit wonder, especially when she refused to meet his probing gaze. Augustus Raven might be a man of mystery, but he was not particularly quiet about his possessions. Kit could well imagine a boast falling on the wrong ears.

"The fact remains that someone has gone to great lengths to stop you, and if you had not nearly reached Oakfield, you might have had unwelcome company."

That made her blanch, and Kit pressed his point. "Miss Ingram, it has been my experience that the kind of people who seek this text do not take well to disappointment. If they think you have something they want, they will kill you to get it."

Miss Ingram paled, but did not falter. "That seems a bit extreme, even for a bibliomaniac."

"For your protection, I insist upon escorting you home."

Miss Ingram cocked her head, as though considering the suggestion. "That is very kind of you, Mr Marchant, but if someone is seeking this paper or the book it mentions, they will not be satisfied until they get it."

*Undoubtedly.* "But you'll be safe once returned to

Raven Hill," Kit assured her, even as he felt a twinge of uncertainty. Hadn't his own property been invaded? His own sister attacked? But what else could he do, especially for a woman who was no relation? By all accounts, Augustus Raven was wealthier and more powerful, his famous house practically a fortress.

Miss Ingram shook her head. "If these people are as dangerous as you suggest, there is only one real option." She leaned forward, her caramel-colored eyes glinting as she looked at him intently. "We must find the remaining edition. Once Raven has it in his possession, no one will have cause to pursue me."

Kit was taken aback both by the suggestion and Miss Ingram's apparent determination. What she proposed was the kind of wild escapade that he and Syd and Barto might have planned in their youth, but not something that reasonable adults would undertake, especially strangers.

Kit had never followed the strictest codes of propriety, but traveling around the country with a woman who was no relation to him, even with a sleepy chaperone accompanying them, did not seem like appropriate behavior.

"I don't think your uncle would approve," he said.

But Miss Ingram showed no sign of demurring. She straightened in her seat and gazed at him directly. "Raven approves of any means that gets him what he wants."

It was the challenge glinting in her eyes that made Kit waver. Instead of hiding away, sunk in the dismals, he could do *something*, maybe even hunt down those connected with the bastards who murdered his father, threatened his sister and now stalked Miss Ingram. But as tempting as that notion was, Kit knew he could hardly chase suspected killers while protecting her. And he would not use a woman as bait to draw them out.

"It wouldn't take long," she said. "Cheswick isn't that far from Raven Hill."

"Cheswick?" Kit echoed. *The ancestral home of the earls?*

"Yes, just as you said."

"*I* said?" Kit was used to being confounded by his sister, but Miss Ingram was taking the practice to new extremes.

"You said we should look to the recipient of the letter for the Mallory."

Kit groaned at that logic. "I simply meant that the book wasn't here, but had been sent away. You can't hare off to Cheswick based on a hundred-year-old scrap of paper sent to a long-dead relative of the earl."

"Why not? Where else should we start?"

She was so serious that Kit could only stare in amazement. "Do you realize how many times that book could have changed hands?"

"If it had surfaced, the collecting world would know of it," she insisted.

Kit shook his head. "The fellow who received that missive might have hidden it or sent it away. Had he any sense, he would have destroyed it. Or it could have been confiscated with all the others."

"Maybe," Miss Ingram said. "But maybe not. The only way to find out is to look."

Again, Kit felt a leap of excitement at the dare, at

the opportunity to move against the dark threat that clung to his home. But he did not see how banging on the Earl of Cheswick's door would solve anything.

Perhaps once he got Miss Ingram safely home, Kit would ask Barto for an introduction to the earl. As Viscount Hawthorne, Kit's old friend moved among the *ton* and might even know the fellow nobleman. A few discreet inquiries could be made, though Kit doubted the book would ever be found. And as far as he was concerned, it could stay lost for ever.

Kit shook his head. "I'm just a gentleman farmer, not one of the desperate characters you described, driven by book madness." *Or worse.*

"But you must know more about the Mallory than anyone," Miss Ingram protested.

"I can't even tell you what the book looks like because I never saw it—none of us did," Kit said. "Which makes going after it a fool's errand and perilous, as well. You can pursue the letter's history through the proper channels, if you wish, once you are home, where your uncle can watch over it—and you."

For someone who had argued so passionately for her preferred course, Miss Ingram seemed to accept his decision with equanimity. Straightening in her seat, she gave him a slow nod of resignation, and Kit was too glad she had seen reason to question her response. Instead, he leaned forward.

"Now, here's my plan."

Since Mr Marchant's scheme required some time to organize, Hero took the opportunity to look through the house once more. Although Gothic, it was small enough to be made into a cozy home without much work. And as she walked through the rooms, Hero began imagining improvements, not the sort that Raven undertook, but the kind that would make it comfortable, inviting…

Hero shook her head at such fancies. What Mr Marchant did or did not choose to do with his property was none of her concern. Her only concern was acquiring the Mallory, and that was what she was doing, wasn't it? Hero conveniently ignored the small voice that told her she should have fled, broken wheel or not, refusing Mr Marchant's offer to escort her.

By ceding to him, hadn't she proven her fears were valid, that she couldn't refuse him? Hero shook her head, unwilling to consider any such possibility. She was only doing what she had to, and if he insisted on coming along, why not make good use of him?

Stepping into a parlor at the back of the house, Hero realized it was probably a later addition to the original structure, for tall doors led onto a terrace. Although it had been raining yesterday, she could see the rear of the property more clearly now through wisps of fog.

The sight was not heartening. The blackened stubble that stretched behind the house gave credence to Mr Marchant's story of a recent fire. Although Hero had questioned the servants about it, they claimed to be newly hired and ignorant of the facts. But something had burned back there. Had the book been destroyed, as well? Hero had only Mr Marchant's word on that, and she had learned long ago not to trust anyone.

And that included a man who could trip her pulse with one look. No matter how straightforward he might seem, Hero knew that his casual air could be deceiving. Christopher Marchant was smarter than he looked and far more observant. Despite his often heavy-lidded gaze, he was awake on every suit, and no matter how appealing he was, Hero could not afford to let down her guard.

As if to prove her point, Hero felt, rather than heard, him move behind her, and her heart pounded in response. Such quiet steps might be those of practiced stealth, she reminded herself as she tried to calm her clamoring senses.

"What do you think of the house?" he asked.

The question was not what she expected, and Hero turned to face him, an automatic response upon her lips. "It's very nice."

He sent her one of those probing looks that usually made her uncomfortable, but this time Hero did not dissemble. "Perhaps it could use a little work," she admitted. "Some paint, wallpaper and bright fabrics to lighten the atmosphere wouldn't be amiss. I'm sure whatever your sister has planned will be lovely."

Mr Marchant glanced about him, as if at a loss. "I don't know whether she got that far, and now she's gone. She'll be getting married soon."

"Oh," Hero murmured. "Congratulations."

Mr Marchant did not comment, for he was still studying the room, with its heavy curtains and even heavier furniture. "It needs a feminine touch," he said, and for some reason Hero's heart skipped a beat. He did not mean *her* touch, she told herself. She was definitely not the feminine ideal, for she could not watercolor or sketch or play the pianoforte. And a gentleman would have little use for whatever skills she did possess.

"You don't think the place gloomy beyond redemption, do you? Haunted by the history of its original owner? Far too eerie to ever be livable?"

Hero choked back a laugh. "Eerie? You can't know the meaning of the word," she said. "I live at Raven Hill."

"Oh, sorry," Mr Marchant said. "Your uncle does have a reputation for being eccentric."

That was putting it mildly. However, Hero had no intention of discussing Raven or his home, and she hurried to change the subject. "Shall we be leaving soon?"

Mr Marchant nodded, but his expression grew rueful, as though he were disappointed by the turn of the conversation. Had he hoped for more personal information? Hero had never met a man who evinced interest in something other than himself and his acquisitions. Indeed, such behavior was so unusual that she couldn't help wondering what had prompted that interest.

Was it curiosity for curiosity's sake or something more sinister?

Now that his plan was implemented and they were on the road, Kit felt a bit easier. If things went as he hoped, whoever was interested in Miss Ingram would be far away by now, traveling in the opposite direction behind Augustus Raven's old-fashioned coach.

Hob had agreed to drive it, taking a circuitous route along the moors and on to Burrell, where he could leave it with a fellow who owned an inn. Hob had wanted to continue on, making his roundabout way to Piketon, where they could exchange vehicles, but Kit was leery of dropping the charade too soon.

There was no reason why Miss Ingram and her companion couldn't ride in his more comfortable carriage all the way to Raven Hill, their driver and footman at the reins. Augustus Raven could easily send someone to fetch his coach, and should he not be willing, Kit would hire someone to do so.

Kit's main concern was Miss Ingram's protection, and if he managed to spend more time with her in the process, that was simply an additional benefit. But once she was safely delivered, Kit did not see how he could further their acquaintance, for they did not move in the same circles.

Miss Ingram was no country lass to be courted at local dances, flirted with during long walks with other young people or invited with relatives to visit. No doubt, her uncle would look askance at a barely landed gentleman such as Kit.

The idea was sobering, and Kit might have dwelled upon it, if the sound of another vehicle had not dragged him from his thoughts. Abruptly, he realized that the fog was becoming thicker, threatening to obscure approaching riders. Although he had traveled this section of roadway many times without concern, now the trees on either side seemed too close. Putting his hand on the pistol he had thrust into his bag, he urged Bay past the carriage to get a good look at whatever was coming.

At the sight of a horse and cart, Kit's tension eased, yet he remained alert, for just such a farm cart had been part of his undoing before the fire. Studying the driver and his load carefully, Kit saw nothing more threatening than a couple of old sows, but when it had gone by, he heard the echo of its noisy passage.

Too late, Kit realized that the sound was of something else. And by the time he looked behind him, the carriage had been stopped by riders who appeared out of the mist, kerchiefs obscuring their faces and guns in their hands.

Still, Kit might have prevailed with the aid of Miss Ingram's coachman and footman. But instead of presenting some kind of defence, the two cowered like frightened children, more frightened, in fact, than Miss Ingram, who was ordered to exit the carriage by one of the riders.

No wailing or sobbing or screaming ensued. Indeed, she stepped out with a composure that awed Kit, but made charging the riders impossible. He did not want her caught upon the ground among rearing horses.

"You stay in there," the taller of the two men ordered Miss Ingram's companion, who was more formidable than either of her male attendants. "We just want this one."

Kit tensed at the words that confirmed his worst fears. Highwaymen were mostly a thing of the past, and travelers were rarely robbed on today's busy roads. Although this was a quiet stretch that might be more prone to such thievery, why hadn't they taken Mrs Renshaw's jewelry or looked through the baggage?

More than likely, these two were responsible for the earlier accident, and they weren't intent upon questioning or searching, but kidnapping.

"Which one of those is yours?" the tall one asked, nodding toward the cases on top of the carriage. When Miss Ingram pointed to a valise, he told the footman to toss it down. Then he backed away, perhaps to avoid getting hit with the piece, an opportunity that the footman didn't have the good sense to act upon.

But Miss Ingram did. She glanced toward Kit, her gaze telling him everything before she dropped her head in seeming surrender. These men must know nothing of their victim, Kit thought, or they would have paid more attention to her, instead of training their pistols upon Kit and the men who cowered atop the carriage.

When Miss Ingram leaned down to pick up the baggage, Kit was ready. As she swung it round toward the tall man's mount, Kit kicked Bay forward. Reaching out an arm, he grabbed Miss Ingram and swung her up behind him as the tall man went down.

In the shouting and confusion that followed, Kit set off toward the woods on the opposite side of the road, hoping that the fog that had hidden his enemies would cloak their escape. Hearing a ball whizz past his ear, he ducked, pulling Miss Ingram down with him.

"Don't shoot her, you fool!"

The shout spurred Kit onward, with Miss Ingram clinging to his back and her valise flopping against them both. Kit nearly told her to drop it, but the way she hung on to it made him wonder whether there was something important inside that she didn't want taken.

Still, they were hampered in a way their pursuers were not, and Kit looked for some hiding place. Ahead, stones rose out of the mist that he soon recognized as an abandoned graveyard, its church looming beyond.

Kit did not hesitate. Heading toward the tall doors that were now worn and cracked, he leaned to the side, pushed one open and rode into the old building. Miss Ingram did not protest, but slid to the stone floor swiftly, and when Kit dismounted, he saw her slipping her valise under one of the old box pews, weathered, but still standing.

After leading Bay behind the fretwork at the rear of the small building, Kit stepped back to scan the dim interior. At first glance, the church still appeared empty, though anyone investigating thoroughly would come across the horse quickly enough.

But Kit had no intention of them getting that far.

He took up a spot at one of the narrow windows, his pistol in hand. The fog was growing thicker, which might work in their favor—or not, Kit mused as he squinted into the vapor. The heavy air blanketed the area, muffling sounds as he listened for movement outside, but all he heard was Miss Ingram's breathing, loud in the stillness.

Turning toward her, Kit braced himself for a delayed reaction to what she had just been through. But she did not swoon. Instead, her delicate brows lowered over caramel eyes that stared at him intently, her voice a whisper as she spoke a question.

"Where the deuce did you learn that?"

"What?" For a moment, Kit had no idea what she was talking about, then he shrugged. "My sister and I once saw some trick riding at a fair, and we practised until we could master some of what we'd seen. That was a long time ago, of course."

"Yet you managed to snatch up a grown woman, with baggage, and toss me up behind you with one arm."

"Well, not every woman would have the where-withal to follow my lead," Kit said, his lips curving in appreciation. In fact, most females would have fainted dead away at the sight of the masked men, instead of attacking one of them with her luggage. But Kit had the feeling that Miss Ingram had more than a few tricks of her own up her sleeve.

The crack of a twig outside drew Kit's attention back to the window as one of the riders came into view. The villain made a good target and Kit was tempted to shoot him through one of the broken panes. Better yet, he'd like to take the man down and beat some answers out of him, but he couldn't leave Miss Ingram alone and unprotected. And a shot would draw the other rider. But his choices were limited, and Kit lifted his hand as the man turn toward the church.

"Hey, you, get away from there!"

Kit jerked at the shout, which came from another direction, and as he peered through the mist, he saw a grizzled old man step out from behind one of the tilting gravestones. Kit was tempted to shout out a warning to the old man until he saw the fellow was armed with a rifle and appeared prepared to use it.

"This is a burial ground, not parklands! Off with you now, or I'll put a bullet in you," the old man shouted.

The rider paused, as though undecided, then kicked his horse and disappeared into the trees. When the sound of his passage faded away, Kit felt a measure of relief—until he heard the soft footfalls of the old man, heading toward the church. Perhaps the fellow was only securing the entrance, Kit thought, but he sank as low in the shadows as he could.

The creak of the door was ominous in the stillness, and Kit raised his pistol as the figure shuffled in. Dressed in worn and dirty clothes, his hair an untamed halo around his head, the old man had a wild look that made him appear not only dangerous, but possibly mad. No wonder the rider had been chased off.

Although Kit hoped the old man was making only a desultory check of the church, he turned unerringly toward the window where Kit and Miss Ingram crouched. Leaning close, Kit was ready to dive in front of her, should the fellow lift his rifle. But he only squinted and cleared his throat.

"Mr Marchant, is that you?"

# *Chapter Three*

Since Kit could not remember seeing the old man before, he remained wary until the fellow lowered his rifle and grinned, revealing some missing teeth.

"I'm John Sixpenny, sir," he said. "I look after the chapel. It's been on Oakfield land as long as I can remember. So I guess it's yours now."

"John Sixpenny, I could not be more happy to make your acquaintance," Kit said, rising to his feet. He didn't know if the old man survived on donations or some other source of income, but he planned to provide a hefty bonus for this day's work.

"I've got a little place over there," Sixpenny said, with a jerk of his head. "I'd be honored if you'd come have a bite to eat or a bit to drink."

Kit nodded in thanks. A visit would gain them some time away from the riders who were searching for them. And another man, especially one armed with a rifle, was all to the good. Still, he glanced toward Miss Ingram, but she was already retrieving her valise, and he hurried to lead Bay out of the church.

At the sight of the horse, the old man frowned, so Kit slipped him a coin for any damage to the floor. Following behind Sixpenny, they moved as quietly as possible along a barely discernible path, Kit carrying Miss Ingram's baggage, while she clung tightly to her reticule.

They had not gone far when they came across a small structure overgrown with vines and plants. The crumbling remains of other buildings could be seen, but the forest had reclaimed whatever settlement that had once been here, except for the church and the home John Sixpenny had made for himself.

The house was an odd one, its stone base having been built up with timber and thatch. At some point, a lean-to for animals had been added onto one side, but it was empty now, and Kit tied Bay there, away from prying eyes. The inside of the home was odd, as well. For despite his wild appearance, Sixpenny kept it neater than a pin, and the fire burning in the hearth was welcome.

There were several simple wooden chairs, but Miss Ingram took a stance at the small window, as though to keep watch. She did not appear to trust their host, and her reticence made Kit refuse food and drink as politely as possible. Although he did not suspect Sixpenny of planning any mischief, his own bout with doctored cider made him leery of any offerings, no matter how innocent.

"Well, then, sir, is there anything else I can do for you?" Sixpenny asked, his blue eyes shrewd as he glanced up from poking at the fire. "I can't help but notice that you were hiding in my church, just when I chased a ruffian away from my graveyard."

"Our carriage was attacked," Kit said.

"The villains. A man isn't safe in his own home any more, let alone on the roads," the old man said, muttering a low string of imprecations. "Do you want to stay here?"

The question was one Kit had been mulling over himself. Sixpenny's home was well hidden, but if the riders decided to search the area carefully, they would stumble across it, and Kit didn't like the idea of being cornered—or putting the old man in danger.

The most expedient course would be to go back to the carriage, but one or more of their pursuers might be waiting there or watching for them. These riders were no ordinary footpads, who would scatter at the first sign of other travelers. They had not been fooled by the switched conveyances, and Kit could not count on the cowardly coachman to do anything, even wait for their return.

There was a third choice, and Kit looked toward Miss Ingram, wondering whether she would agree. John Sixpenny's introduction had reminded him that they weren't that far from Oakfield. Heading across open country, they could reach the manor without returning to the road. But they would have to ride together on Bay.

As if reading his thoughts, Miss Ingram glanced his way, and her calm gaze assured him that she could do whatever he asked. So while Kit thanked the old man, he refused the offer of sanctuary.

"I think we'd better keep moving," he said, though he did not mention their destination. And Miss Ingram's nearly imperceptible nod of approval told him he had made the right decision—for now.

Raven liked to claim he had trained her well, but nothing had prepared Hero for her current situation: riding behind Christopher Marchant, her arms wrapped around his torso. Given his startling effect upon her, it did not seem to be a wise position to be in. But she had refused to dangle sideways and insisted upon riding astride, her cloak tucked around her legs. And if Mr Marchant was shocked, he did not show it. In fact, the man seemed undisturbed by anything, from gun-wielding robbers to wild-eyed hermits.

His capability was appealing, and Hero had to fight the urge to lay her head upon his strong back and lean upon him, in more ways than one. She could feel his warmth even through their cloaks, and for someone who was perpetually cold, it was like cozying up to an oven, only better.

Yet she could just as easily be burned.

Despite her scattered wits, Hero realized that Mr Marchant was not what he seemed. At first glance, he appeared to be a simple rural resident whose every thought was visible upon his face, but he had surprised her too many times for her to believe that. And Hero did not like surprises. They were too dangerous.

Just who was this man? The shabby gentry did not own enough land to include an abandoned churchyard. Nor did they have the skills to snatch a women off her feet with one arm while riding on the back of a horse. Nor did they hide beneath their simple clothes and relaxed demeanor a body that was hard with muscle.

Her suspicions aroused, Hero wondered whether Mr Marchant was spiriting her away for his own purposes. But pressed so close to him, she could not muster any panic. For protection, she had her pistol, though she did not know whether she would be able to fire at him. And what else was she to do? Hero could only follow instincts honed through years of doing Raven's bidding.

Was that what he had planned? Surely, even Raven could not have anticipated her reaction to the attractive Mr Marchant. And yet, it was just the sort of thing he would find amusing, toying with her or testing her, safe in the knowledge that nothing could come of it.

"I'm going to ride right up to the house," Mr Marchant said. His low voice dragged Hero from her thoughts and sent shivers dancing up her spine. "So we can get you inside as quickly as possible."

"And then?"

"I'll have someone go for the carriage, but you should be safe at Oakfield. I'll send word to your uncle and hire some extra men to make sure we get you home as soon as can be arranged."

He turned his head toward her, and the nearness of his face made Hero's heart hammer. His skin was not pasty and pale like the antiquarians she usually met, but a deeper hue that bespoke time spent out of doors. His lashes were long and thick, his hair as dark as his eyes, and Hero wanted to reach up and push a stray lock from his forehead.

Instead, she shook her head. "What we need to do is find what they're after. The book."

Mr Marchant groaned. "Not that again! What of your coach, your footman, your *chaperone*?"

"I think we both know that we can't go back there, and they provided little in the way of protection," Hero said. "We're better off by ourselves."

Mr Marchant slanted her a dark look of speculation. "We can't travel, just the two of us, unrelated and unmarried."

"If you refuse to help me, I will have to go alone."

"You're not going anywhere alone," Mr Marchant said with sudden ferocity, and Hero had to suppress a shiver.

"I assure you that I won't accuse you of compromising me," Hero offered.

"I'm not worried about myself!"

"Well, there is no need to worry about me," Hero insisted. "I am a nobody with nothing to ruin."

"Except your good name and your future," Mr Marchant said. "Your uncle would hardly approve."

"Raven couldn't care less about my reputation," Hero said. And neither her name or her future were of any consequence. To anyone.

"But you're his niece," Mr Marchant protested.

"Of sorts," Hero said, though she did not elaborate. What was between her and Augustus Raven stayed between them. "He's more concerned with his collections than people, which is why we should go to Cheswick."

Mr Marchant sent her another speculative glance. "Let me make sure that I understand you correctly. On the basis of a fragment of an old letter that might never have even been sent, you want to go searching for a book that could have been lost, destroyed or hidden beyond reach more than a century ago?"

"Exactly."

Kit sat facing his guest, unsure what to make of her as he watched her pick at her supper. She didn't look addled and had proposed her mad scheme without batting an eyelash. But how else could he explain such a proposal?

And yet, Kit had been tempted to agree, to bow to an urge to take action against the unseen foe, rather than kick his heels at Oakfield as he had been, brooding and impotent. But recent events had made him vow to become more responsible, not less so. And chasing after a snippet of torn paper with Augustus Raven's niece was not exactly sensible behavior, especially after the ride to Oakfield had left him feeling a bit too close to the young woman for comfort.

Kit reached for his glass of wine, flush with the memory of Miss Ingram leaning close, her slender form pressed against his back, her thighs bumping against his own, and her throaty voice whispering in his ear.

He had ridden double with Sydony many a time in their younger days, but that, he had discovered, was not the same. During the quick trip to the abandoned church, they had been in too much danger for him to think about it, but on the longer jaunt to Oakfield, the difference became very apparent. And it was one more reason not to travel unaccompanied with Miss Ingram, her assurances notwithstanding.

Of course, in the eyes of society, the damage was already done. They had been alone together for some time, enough to ruin any proper female. In fact, most young women would be having hysterics or fainting dead away at the very thought, yet Miss Ingram, as always, remained composed. Kit shot a glance at her, but her color wasn't even high. Throughout the meal, she had said little, affirming what he already knew: Miss Ingram played her cards very close to her chest.

Kit frowned thoughtfully. He'd never been the suspicious type; that was Sydony's job. But after all his sister's wild theories had proven true, he'd begun to view the world differently. Instead of accepting everything at face value, he questioned what lurked beneath the surface. And as he looked across the table at his guest, he felt a twinge of doubt.

Hero Ingram could either be the most composed woman he'd ever met, or she could have some other reason for not turning a hair when her carriage was attacked. Perhaps she'd been unafraid because there was nothing to fear. Were the riders her uncle's men, intent upon forcing his hand? But there was no denying the ball that had whizzed past his shoulder, Kit thought, shaking his head.

Another possibility, even more insidious, kept nagging at his thoughts. After all, what did he really know of the woman before him? Was she even who she claimed to be? Some of her comments had been so jarring as to make him wonder about her relationship with Augustus Raven.

The letter she presented to Kit could have been written by anyone. Those who accompanied her had been odd, at best, and seemed to have disappeared, along with the carriage. Although he'd sent Hob's young helper Jack out to the road, the boy had found no sign of it.

Hob hadn't returned, either, and Kit frowned at the darkness outside the windows. It had been just such a night as this when everyone in the household had been picked off. One by one, they had been lured away or drugged until no one was left except Sydony. Kit looked down at the mutton he had been eating and felt the sudden loss of his appetite.

A sound from the doorway made him glance up warily, but it was only Jack, half-hidden in the shadows, an expression of urgency upon his face.

"Excuse me," Kit said, rising to his feet. He did not wait for Miss Ingram's acknowledgment, but hurried to where the boy stood, drawing him farther into the other room for a whispered conference.

"What is it? Has Hob returned?"

His eyes wide, Jack shook his head. "No, sir, but when I was making the rounds, I saw a party coming toward Oakfield."

"A party?" Kit echoed. His normally inactive imagination conjured up his worst nightmare, a cloaked group of so-called Druids intent upon a virgin sacrifice. Only this time, Miss Ingram would take his sister's place.

"What kind of party?" he demanded.

"It's the parish constable and a couple of his cronies, sir, and they're nearly here," Jack said, obviously agitated.

Kit felt some of the tension in his body ease. It was about time the local authorities, who had been noticeably absent before, stepped in to help. But something about the look on Jack's face made him pause. "What's wrong?"

The boy's eyes grew even bigger, if that was possible. "They're claiming to have a warrant straight from the magistrate for your arrest—on charges of kidnapping a lady!"

The idea was so outrageous, Kit might have laughed, but coming as it did upon the heels of their earlier peril, he was not amused. If he were taken away, Miss Ingram would have no protection at all as, one by one, those around her disappeared. *Just like Sydony.*

After giving Jack some hurried instructions, Kit turned toward the open doorway and called softly to his guest, "Miss Ingram, I'm afraid there's been a change of plans."

Although he had recently eyed her composure with dismay, now Kit was grateful for it. She evinced no alarm, but rose to her feet and moved toward him quickly, her golden brows lifted slightly in question.

"I've been told that the authorities are approaching with the intent of arresting me on a charge of kidnapping, presumably you. Now, we can either try to sort it out with the locals, who view Oakfield and anyone who resides here as in league with the devil. Or we can depart before their arrival."

Miss Ingram took the news with her usual aplomb. "By all means, let us avoid any confrontations, especially since they might have been engineered to destroy our alliance," she said. "Just let me get my things."

"You'll find a pack to use in my sister's room to the left at the top of the stairs, and feel free to take anything in there," Kit called after her. His own bag remained with Bay, so he took a moment to alert Mrs Osgood to the situation.

That stolid personage was more horrified than Miss Ingram, but agreed to tell any callers that no one had returned since setting out with the carriage earlier in the day. Exhorting the maid to clear all evidence of a meal from the dining hall, she went into the kitchen, returning to slip a package into Kit's hand before aiding the flustered maid.

Heading toward the stairs to hurry his guest, Kit had to look twice at the figure on the landing before realizing it was Miss Ingram. A vastly different Miss Ingram.

Instead of her cloak, she wore a heavy greatcoat that was a fitting garment for traveling, but not often worn by women. And beneath the hem, Kit could see a pair of scuffed boots, not dainty slippers, while her lovely locks were pulled tight and tucked up under a boy's cap that cast a shadow across her features. At first glance, she would seem a youth. Had she even dirtied her face?

Acknowledging Kit with a nod, she moved down the steps toward him. "It will throw off any who search for a missing woman—or the man alleged to have kidnapped her," she explained.

Yet she didn't meet his eye, which was understandable. Most men would have recoiled in shock, but Kit could only admire her cleverness, while trying not to imagine just what she wore beneath the coat.

"Let's try to avoid the servants," he said. "It's better if no one else knows of your new appearance." With that in mind, he led her to the parlor, where they slipped out the tall doors into the darkness outside.

The fog still lingered, casting a disorienting veil over the landscape, and the burned garden was rough going, with clumps of stubble looming up to trip the wariest of walkers. But Kit told himself that whatever hindered them would work even more upon their enemies, though he doubted any locals would willingly be out at this hour searching the grounds of Oakfield, a property steeped in legend and dread.

Kit set a good pace, and Miss Ingram kept up without her skirts to encumber her. She didn't harry him with questions, but silently followed his lead until they reached the barn that was being used as a temporary stable.

Jack had their mounts ready, and Kit set the boy to keep watch while he helped Miss Ingram onto Sydony's horse. Having not seen her disguise, Jack could not report it to anyone, should he be questioned after their departure.

Kit had no time to ponder the whys and whos of their predicament. Right now, his only concern was to put more distance between them and the party Jack had heard approaching the house, so he urged Bay into the night as quietly as possible. He had a lantern, but he was loathe to use it, at least until they were away from the barn. Oakfield's eerie history would keep the locals at bay, but any others might not be so easily frightened.

When he and Syd had first arrived at their new home, Kit hadn't seen a pressing need to map the countryside. But after the fire, he had ridden out daily until he knew these lands like the back of his hand, and that knowledge served him well as he found the small path that led toward the arable fields.

By the time he reached an abandoned tenant cottage, Kit was eager for a respite. They could not ride indefinitely in such darkness, and although the Druids had once used this building, no one had been near it since the fire. Kit and Hob had made sure of that.

Dismounting, Kit led the horses into a small barn. After tethering them, he turned to help Miss Ingram, only to freeze as his hands brushed against a solid human form. His normally even heartbeat skipped in its rhythm as he wondered whether to reach for his pistol or slam the figure against the wall.

"It's me." The familiar sound of Miss Ingram's throaty voice made him loose a sigh. She had dismounted without his aid, and there was no one else in the barn with them. No Druids, no authorities, no bibliomaniacs. Realizing that his gloved fingers still pressed against her, Kit dropped his hand away, but a noise outside made him stiffen.

They both remained still while an owl hooted and then fell silent. But as the sound faded away, Kit became aware of a more immediate and more personal danger. He was alone with Miss Ingram, standing only inches from her, in the dark. The lack of light seemed to heighten his senses, and Kit caught a whiff of her scent, delicate and intoxicating.

"We can spend the night here and ride out again at dawn," he whispered, expecting her to move. But she remained where she was, and in the ensuing quiet, Kit thought he heard her breath catch. Did she feel it, too?

Just as Kit was tempted to take the single step that would bring them together, a snort from Bay broke them apart. It probably was as succinct a comment as any on his folly, a rebuke for behavior that would hardly be welcome at the best of times, let alone now, when they were in jeopardy. And Kit took the message to heart: *Remember that you are a gentleman.*

With that in mind, Kit peered outside before leading Miss Ingram to the cottage, where they were met by the smell of dust and disuse. But Kit knew the place was sturdy and would keep out the worst of the night chill. There was a lantern by the door, and he lit it, turning the wick low, though the windows were tightly shuttered.

"I'll tend to the horses," he said, trying to ignore the sight of Miss Ingram's greatcoat falling open to reveal her slim legs, clad in breeches. "Will you be all right?" It was a foolish question, and, of course, Miss Ingram nodded.

Still, Kit did not dally. Returning with their packs and some wood, he shut the door behind him, only to find that his companion had already started a fire. For a long moment, he simply stood still, transfixed by her costume, which boldly delineated her long legs, while hiding her breasts under a boy's coat. It was a paradox that kicked Kit to life.

Thankfully, Miss Ingram showed no signs of succumbing to a similar passion. "I found some cut logs and thought we'd need the fire for warmth," she said. "Unless you think we'll be seen."

Kit shook his head as he put down the baggage. "I doubt the locals will search for us at this hour, and no one else should know of this place." In truth, he was grateful to be out of the darkness, with its inherent temptations, especially now that he suspected he had conjured their earlier intimacy out of whole cloth.

Jack had given him a blanket from the barn, and Kit spread it in front of the fire for Miss Ingram. With a gesture toward it, he took his own place, seated on the floor, his back against the door. The hard wood and the cold floor did much to help him gather himself—and his thoughts. Since they were safe for the time being, Kit took the opportunity to consider the events that had led him here.

And when next he gazed at his companion, he looked beyond the enticing form to the person inside. Up until an hour ago, Kit had thought Miss Ingram an independent and daring female in the mold of his sister. But during the course of the evening, she had proven herself to be far more unusual than Syd. Obviously, Miss Ingram was no ordinary young lady. But what, exactly, was she?

"So why does Augustus Raven's niece carry boy's garments with her while traveling?" Kit asked without preamble.

If Miss Ingram was startled by the question, she didn't show it. She glanced toward him, but her face was in shadow, making it difficult for Kit to gauge her expression. "I like to be prepared for anything."

"And just what sort of 'anything' were you expecting?"

She shrugged. "It's not what I was expecting—it's the unexpected that concerns me, Mr Marchant."

"And that includes having to masquerade as a male?"

She nodded, but told him nothing, as usual. And, as if the conversation were over, she spread her hands toward the hearth and turned her back to him.

But Kit was not prepared to be dismissed this time. "I'm a simple man," he said. "A gentleman farmer who wants nothing more than a quiet life in the country. Yet over the past months, I've been treated to my fill of deception and threats from everyone from cloaked intruders to my oldest friend."

She swung round then, perhaps shaken by the raw tone to his voice, but he was not adept at dissembling. And his gut twisted at the thought that this woman might be a thief or some kind of Captain Sharp, out to hoax him for reasons he could not fathom. Although she might deny it, Kit had to put the question to her.

"So you'll understand if I won't be played for a fool, Miss Ingram," Kit said. He paused to fix her with a probing gaze. "Are you even who you say you are?"

The light was behind her, so Kit could not see her eyes. Still, she did not look away, and he felt a measure of relief. She did not launch into any outraged protests or weeping admissions, but simply nodded. Then she cocked her head to the side, as though studying him.

"But if you doubt me, why are you here?" she asked.

Kit could have given her a number of different answers, but in the end, he chose the simplest one.

"Because, Miss Ingram, I am a gentleman."

# *Chapter Four*

**W**rapping herself in her heavy coat, Hero lay down upon the blanket Mr Marchant had so graciously put in front of the fire. Perhaps he knew she was always cold, she thought, before rejecting such a notion. The real reason for his behavior was more straightforward and required no personal knowledge of her.

*It was the act of a gentleman.*

The word was a common one, used to describe nearly all males except the poor, servants and those with money, but no lineage. And yet, Hero wondered if she'd ever met a gentleman in the strictest sense of the word—one who was decent, kind, thoughtful… *I'm a simple man*, he'd said. But Christopher Marchant was anything but.

Her back to the flames, Hero looked from under lowered lashes to where he was seated against the door. Presumably he had taken that position so that any attempt at entry would waken him, if he nodded off. But he couldn't be comfortable, arms across his chest, long legs stretched out before him. Although not normally bothered by such things, Hero found herself wondering about draughts, the hard surface of the door, the awkward position.

*She could invite him to join her here by the fire.*

The wild thought was born of drowsy warmth and set Hero's heart to pounding with both anticipation and alarm. Fully awake now, she knew she could not relax into a false sense of security just because her companion treated her far better than anyone else ever had. Manners made for a fine show, but what did she really know of Christopher Marchant?

Although the urge to accept this near stranger as a protector was strong, Hero knew better than to rely on anyone except herself. And hadn't he already proven many times that he was not what he seemed? That might include being the gentleman he claimed.

Roused to alertness, Hero was determined to keep one eye open through the night. She was a poor sleeper, at best, and vowed not let down her guard when alone with this man, no matter how tempting it might be.

Yet the heat of the fire relaxed her, making her lids heavy, and soon Hero had closed them. The tension in her body eased, reminding her of her ride earlier in the day, when she had held on to Mr Marchant's warm and solid form. Even as she tried to banish the memory, Hero's thoughts returned to the moments when she had rested her head against his strong back, leaning upon him.

And she slept.

A cock crowed in the distance, and Hero awoke with a start. She heard a thud and opened her eyes to see Mr Marchant jerk away from the door, rubbing the back of his head. The sight of him made her pulse quicken and not just because she had slept the night away alone with a man she barely knew.

It was the length of his fingers threading through the strands of silky dark hair that held her interest, the tilt of his head, the full line of his mouth as he frowned, and the way his brows lowered in annoyance. If Hero's heart hadn't been pounding so painfully, she would have smiled at his reaction. Simple. Natural. *Endearing.*

As if aware of her study, he suddenly looked at her from under impossibly long lashes, pinning her with one of his probing gazes. And all that Hero felt for him—and more—was reflected right back at her. Startled, Hero sucked in a deep breath as she realized that she was sprawled before the fire, her cap long gone, her hair falling in thick tendrils from where she had secured it.

In short, she was in deshabille, warm and languid and witless from sleep, and she hurried to rectify the situation. She would not expect her boy's costume to incite passion in any man, let alone one who looked like Mr Marchant, but she had seen something in his eyes that made her both wary and exhilarated. Glancing away, she rose to her feet as she pulled her coat close.

"It's light," she muttered. "We'd better go."

Turning her back to him, Hero heard his grunt of assent as he stood, yet the hairs on her neck tingled at his very presence. She waited, tense, until she heard him step outside. Then, and only then, did she release the breath she had been holding and reach for her cap.

She straightened and saw, to her dismay, that her hand was trembling. What next? Would she start stuttering? Hero cursed this man's ability to discompose her, senses running riot, wits scattered when she needed them most.

Kneeling before the hearth, Hero doused the lingering embers there, and shivered. Better to be cold, she thought, than so warm that she couldn't think properly. By the time she had finished, Mr Marchant had returned, and Hero turned to face him with a chillier greeting on her lips.

He didn't seem to notice, and they made a quick meal of bread and cheese from the packet he had got from his housekeeper. Then he went out to ready the horses while Hero tried to remove all evidence of their presence. After sweeping away their tracks on the floor, she stood at the doorway, giving the place one last look.

Still laden with dust, it was nothing more than a small farmhouse, but the single room was cozier than her bedchamber at Raven Hill. Hero's gaze lingered before the hearth, where she had slept so effortlessly for the first time in long memory. A surge of unfamiliar feelings kept her where she stood until a draught rattled the shutters. The noise finally spurred her to step outside and shut the door behind her.

The early morning light was filtered by the mist, which seemed ever present. Although the atmosphere would have suited Raven's sensibilities, Hero was more concerned with making her way as rapidly as possible. In this fog, Mr Marchant could lead her anywhere, and it would be difficult to keep her bearings.

"We'll stay off the main roads as long as possible," he said, as he helped her mount. "Then head east."

"To Cheswick."

"To Raven Hill," Mr Marchant said.

"Cheswick is closer," Hero pointed out. He groaned, and Hero suppressed a smile, for he made the sound whenever she pressed him. She was beginning to find his groans even more endearing than his grins. *And all the more dangerous.*

Hero could not afford to be distracted, and she forced herself to pay more attention to her surroundings than her companion. But there was little to notice. And the routes Mr Marchant took were hardly more than paths, where she saw no signs of life, only barren moors.

The fog did not unnerve her, for Hero was not the fanciful sort. One did not stay long at Raven Hill and give in to whimsy—not if one wanted to retain one's sanity. Still, when they traveled into a dell, the haze settled around them, making their movements echo strangely. And Hero began to wonder if what she heard was their own progress or something else, perhaps even the sound of pursuers.

Then suddenly, something loomed out of the mist, a tall silhouette, dark and ominous. Hero stifled a gasp and grasped the pistol in her coat, while Mr Marchant continued on his way in front of her. Suspicion roiled through her, chilling her to the bone and closing her throat. Yet, as she faced it the shape took form, mocking her fears.

How amused Raven would have been to see her start at a rock, but it was large and unnaturally shaped, making Hero wonder at its placement here in the middle of nowhere. Urging her mount forward, she called to Mr Marchant, "What is that, a road marker?"

"A standing stone," he said. "I've discovered that there are many of them in the area. Sometimes they are alone, like that one, or they can be grouped in circles, rows and by cairns. All are thought to be the work of the Druids who once lived here. Maybe that's why Mallory built his home in this land, with its references to sacred oaks and waters."

Hero glanced toward him, but could see little of his expression. She hadn't known what to make of his earlier remarks about Druids and had long since dismissed them. The resumption of the subject, here and now, did little to cheer her.

"And you think that they want his book back?" Hero asked.

"The ones who left these stones are long gone, their true histories forgotten," he said. "And most who call themselves Druids now gather for social or philanthropic purposes. But there were some others who embraced a more violent view of their forebears."

Hero did not find his explanation comforting, especially when he lapsed into a brooding silence that brooked no further questions. And as she followed blindly, she couldn't help the thought that returned to mind. *He could lead her anywhere.* And for any purpose.

She was not a timid creature, but the possibility of being caught alone on foggy moors with a powerful man obsessed with Druids was something even Hero found unsettling. She remembered his mention of death and debauchery based on the Mallory, and she shivered.

Yet she kept following, for what else could she do? And even uneasy as she was, Hero realized that the whole situation felt like something Raven would orchestrate. Although he had never written a Gothic novel, he enjoyed living like a character in one, with all the attendant terrors and dramas.

Had he arranged for the seemingly gallant Mr Marchant to accompany her? Or worse, had he arranged for a mad Mr Marchant to abduct her? Her companion's admission of a warrant for his arrest took on new meaning when considered under such circumstances. Was Mr Marchant the gentleman he claimed to be, or something else entirely?

Hero had made a life hunting and fetching and bargaining for Raven and ignoring all else, but now she felt her purpose faltering. Just what was she getting herself into?

The sun was setting when they rode into the courtyard of the Long Man. The inn was a simple one set in the middle of Longdown, a community large enough that their arrival would not be marked. Or at least that's what Kit hoped when he looked for a place to stop for the night.

Inside the common room was busy, and Kit's request for a room for himself and his brother drew little attention. He was not dressed in the sort of finery that would demand special service; nor was he the kind who might be refused admittance. His coin was good, and the horses would be tended to.

"Will you eat, sir?" the burly landlord inquired.

"Yes, but can you have it sent to the room? My brother is bone weary, and I'm for rest myself."

The landlord looked like he might make Kit pay for a private parlour, but then he nodded, perhaps fearful of losing the business entirely, for Kit's "brother" was slumped in the shadows near the door, as though waiting to see whether they would remain. With the meal settled, Kit motioned for Miss Ingram to join him, and the landlord led them to the staircase.

The room was decent enough, clean and neat, with a narrow window and a large bed not far from the fireplace, where logs were set. "I'll have that lit for you, sirs," the landlord said before disappearing back into the hall.

Kit nodded absently as he glanced around. He could have got two rooms, but he was loathe to leave Miss Ingram alone and unprotected, even if she was dressed as a boy. His own desire to stay in her company had nothing to do with his decision. Or at least that's what Kit told himself as he eyed the single bed.

While no one would think it odd for a couple of brothers to bed down together, Kit would have to look elsewhere for his berth. Unfortunately, the only chair was stiff and straight-backed, so Kit looked to the expanse of hard floor and told himself it was no worse than where he had slept the night before.

Miss Ingram was already drawing the curtains, and Kit reached for the candle, lest they be plunged into blackness until the chambermaid came to light the fire. It was one thing to share a room with Miss

Ingram, another to be alone with her in complete darkness, as he had learned last evening.

But a low word from her stayed Kit's hand. He lifted his head in surprise to see her silently motioning him toward the window, where something had drawn her attention. He stepped behind her, looking over her shoulder into the courtyard below. The Long Man was not a posting stop, so the cobbled area was relatively quiet, making it easy to spy the two men leaning against one wall in the deepening shadows.

Kit felt the tension in Miss Ingram's body and had to stop himself from drawing her back against him in comfort. "I don't see how anyone could have tracked us here," he assured her. "They would have had to follow us from the cottage, and we saw no signs of that."

"They could have been waiting on the road."

"For how long? And which roads?"

"Any road that leads to London," Miss Ingram said. She turned her head slightly. "If we go to Cheswick instead, perhaps we can lose them."

Kit stifled a groan at the familiar refrain, but he was not surprised to hear it. Someone as determined as Miss Ingram did not give up easily. And hadn't she told him earlier that she would go by herself, if necessary? The memory of that threat, coupled with her impassive features and the presence of the two men below, however innocent they might be, made Kit distinctly uneasy.

He might have been blind before, heedless of the signs of approaching trouble, but he was more observant now, and his observations told him that Miss Ingram might very well slip from the room the minute his back was turned, going from danger into danger. Alone.

And that's when the truth hit him. It didn't matter whether her chase was a foolish one, leading nowhere, and it didn't matter what his own feelings about the possible existence of a Mallory might be. It didn't even matter whether Miss Ingram was being completely honest with him. The only thing that mattered was keeping her safe. And since he could not force her to go home, the only way to protect her was to go with her.

Kit admitted there were other, less admirable reasons to remain in Miss Ingram's company, his own selfish desires among them. But first and foremost in his mind was the task he had undertaken when her coach had broken down on its way to Oakfield. He'd failed his sister, but he wasn't going to fail this woman.

"All right, we'll go to Cheswick," he said. If Miss Ingram was startled by his sudden capitulation, Kit did not see it, for his attention was fixed on the men below. Perhaps it wouldn't hurt to see what they were up to, he thought. But as he watched, the taller fellow pushed away from the wall, revealing not the nondescript clothing of their attackers, but livery. And very fine livery, at that.

Kit was glad he had not gone down to confront them since he was already plagued by one arrest warrant. "These two may be similar in height, but that's not the way our pursuers were dressed."

Miss Ingram turned her head, as if to argue, but a knock came at the door, and she moved quickly away. She slid into a shadowed corner, as though expecting the two men to burst in. Kit knew that was highly unlikely, but reached for his pistol nonetheless just as the door opened to admit a harried-looking chambermaid.

After handing them a tray of food, she lit the fire and was on her way, leaving them to their supper. Kit let Miss Ingram have the chair and pushed the bed stairs between them, so that she could place her plate on the top step while he sat on the floor and used the bottom.

The room was dark but for the fire, and for a while they ate in silence, broken only by the crack of the logs. Kit told himself that the only difference between this night and the last was that their room was smaller and better appointed. Yet somehow this evening seemed more intimate. Perhaps it was the earlier hour or the fact that they were sharing a meal.

Last night Kit had leaned against a door, staring at a dark shape that was hardly recognizable. But tonight, the firelight danced across Miss Ingram's face, highlighting the line of her cheek, the curve of her lips. Her skin glowed golden, and Kit wished she would take off that wretched cap, so he could see her hair…

"What?"

It wasn't until she spoke that Kit realized he was staring, and he looked down at his plate. He was tempted to tell her that she need not wear the cap in here, with only the two of them to see, but perhaps that wasn't such a good idea.

"Nothing," Kit muttered. He needed to gain more control over his thoughts, especially since his companion appeared completely unmoved by their nearness, the firelight and the night outside. Yet when she reached for her wine, Kit could have sworn her hand was shaking. *Perhaps Miss Ingram was not unmoved, after all.*

"How can you be sure those weren't our two men?" she asked.

Kit barked out a low laugh. Now he was assured that Miss Ingram was not as entranced as he by their intimate supper. She was all business, a reminder that he would do well to heed. "Because they wore the livery of the Duke of Montford," he said.

"So?"

"So, I doubt that the duke's men are out searching for a book on Druid lore," he said, spearing a forkful of beef.

"And why not?" she countered. "The Prince Regent himself is a great collector, as is the Duke of Devonshire. The book madness strikes any and all, regardless of station. No less an authority than Reverend Thomas Dibin claims that it lasts year-round and through all of human existence."

"Perhaps," Kit acknowledged, "but I can't see a nobleman hiring thugs or arranging a kidnapping."

"Even to acquire such a rare book?"

"Even to acquire such a rare book," Kit said. He suspected that greed did not drive their pursuers, but something darker and twisted.

"I don't know. I've heard tales that you would not countenance," Miss Ingram said. "Stories of thievery and forgery, of collectors who have bought back their own books after having sold them or given them away, of despondent souls who killed themselves over lost libraries. One antiquarian actually bought a property that had been owned by the astrologer John Dee in the hopes that valuable books might be buried there."

Kit would have laughed at that example, if it hadn't hit too close to home—his home. Although the Mallory hadn't been buried at Oakfield, that hadn't stopped people from digging up the grounds for it.

"The most avid formed their own society, the Roxburghe Club, after the Duke of Roxburghe's collection went up for sale. And you must have heard of Richard Heber, who is filling several homes with books to the very ceilings, purportedly over a hundred thousand and counting."

"And I thought my father was devoted to them," Kit said with a shake of his head.

Miss Ingram paused to study him anew. "I'm surprised you did not catch his mania," she said, as though she suspected Kit of hiding his expertise.

"I never shared my father's singular fascination with study. I loved him, and I'm very grateful for his tutoring and his gentle wisdom, but he seemed to prefer the inside of his books to the world itself. And that wasn't for me—or Syd," he said with a grin.

"Syd?"

"My sister Sydony."

"An unusual name."

"She's an unusual woman," Kit said. He slanted her a glance. "Actually, you remind me a lot of her."

Miss Ingram ducked her head. "And your mother? Was she fond of books?"

Kit drew a deep breath. "She died when I was young."

"I'm sorry," she said. "Perhaps that is why your father sought to escape into his work."

The romantic suggestion coming from the pragmatic Miss Ingram made Kit look at her in surprise. But as always, her face, bent over her plate, revealed nothing.

"Perhaps," Kit said. He barely remembered his mother, so he could not recall if his father had behaved differently, and yet he'd always felt the loss. It might well be that Miss Ingram was right, and his father, always a scholar, had simply retreated further into his pages.

"What of your parents?" Kit asked. "Are they collectors?"

"They, too, are dead," Miss Ingram said briskly. Putting down her fork, she set aside her plate.

"I'm sorry," Kit said. "Have you been long without them?"

"Long enough," she said. "Now, before we head to Cheswick tomorrow, let's go over a few things."

The sudden change of subject took Kit by surprise. Had the conversation become too personal, or was Miss Ingram loath to reveal anything of herself?

"As you probably know, libraries are often arranged according to the owner's specifications," she said, and from her tone, Kit realized that the earlier intimacy would not return.

"A collector may group his prizes together by subject, date of publication, date of acquisition, or any other method that strikes his fancy or the fancy of whoever handles the purchase and cataloging of the books," she said.

"Well, that's helpful," Kit noted drily.

Miss Ingram's mouth quirked at that, and Kit realized just how rarely she smiled. Here in the glow of the firelight, even that gentle curve of her lips was delightful and alluring—and all too fleeting. What had made her so serious, and how could he coax more smiles from her when their situation was not exactly humorous?

"One famous collector housed his volumes in presses decorated with Roman personages, so there would be no way of knowing where to find something without looking through his 'emperor system'," she said. "And Samuel Pepys shelved according to size."

Her descriptions only confirmed Kit's opinion that their search was futile. But he knew that she would not be satisfied until she realized the truth: that they weren't going to find a copy of the Mallory. If he didn't know how dangerous the book was, he might even wish for her to obtain it, if only as reward for her dogged persistence.

"So how do you expect to find anything, let alone a volume that's been missing for a century?" he asked.

"I'll see when we get there."

Kit did not bother to ask how they were going to gain access to the Earl of Cheswick's library. Perhaps tomorrow, Miss Ingram would see for herself that her quest was impossible. And then…like the gentleman that he was, Kit would have to deliver her safely into the hands of her uncle. Unharmed. And untouched.

Kit might rue his earlier claim, but it was not something he could deny. Although honor was not much discussed in the Marchant home, his father had made his expectations clear, and his children did their utmost to live up to them. It had not required much effort on Kit's part. He had never been tempted by the dissipations that once had threatened Barto's future, and his most difficult challenge had been holding the Marchants together after the death of their parent.

But now, alone in a shadowed bedroom with a woman like no other, Kit began to sweat. Somehow, he didn't believe that this was the sort of test his father could ever have imagined.

Bringing Bay to a halt at the edge of the hill, Kit looked down at the house that lay nestled below. The afternoon sun lent a golden glow to the front of the neat stone structure and glittered off three stories of windows. Cheswick wasn't one of the grandest homes in the land, but it was grand enough to make Kit think twice about breaking into it.

"Well, here we are," he said, turning to his companion. "What do you suggest we do?"

Kit had expected that Miss Ingram might veer from her course when confronted with the sight of the ancestral home of the Earls of Cheswick. But she evinced no doubt or confusion, simply eyeing the estate with her usual calm deliberation.

Then, glancing around her, she frowned. "First, we need to find a place where I can change."

Kit swallowed a grunt of surprise. He could understand her wish to get out of boy's clothing, but how? He only hoped that she did not intend to march into Cheswick, demanding the use of a dressing room.

Thankfully, she did not. Nor did she attempt to use

any of the numerous outbuildings. "Too many servants. Too many eyes," she told him, turning away from the house. Instead, she rode into a copse of trees and dismounted.

Kit followed, dismounting, as well, though he was unsure of her intention until she shook out the blanket and flung it over some branches. The next thing he knew, her hat and coat were perched upon a limb, too.

Kit found himself staring at the sight of her head and shoulders visible above the makeshift curtain. Then he blew out a breath and promptly turned around. He had slept a few feet from her the past two nights, but he was not prepared to watch while she removed her clothing with only a thin piece of material standing between them.

His back to her, Kit could not see what was happening, yet he could hear well enough. And he tried not to picture what else was being removed. Her shirt? The breeches? Did she wear a shift beneath? She had to be cold, and the inevitable reaction of certain parts of her anatomy had certain parts of Kit's anatomy reacting, as well.

Drawing in a harsh breath, Kit concentrated on keeping a lookout, rather than taking a look behind. Just because the two fellows they saw at the Long Man were liveried servants in the employ of a duke, did not mean he could lapse into inattention. And the thought of anyone coming upon Miss Ingram in a state of undress kept him alert.

"I'm ready."

Although Kit was surprised to hear Miss Ingram speak so soon, he swung round only to gape in wonder.

Surely no female had ever dressed herself so quickly—or transformed herself so completely.

The boy with the cap was gone, replaced by a prim young woman, her gloved hands clasped in front of her, her eyes downcast. Having acquired a taste for the sight of those long legs clad in breeches, Kit was prepared for disappointment. But a glimpse of a revealing bodice, visible below the ties of her cloak, banished all such concerns. In fact, he could have spent some time savoring the view, but Hero was already turning away from the trees.

Abruptly, Kit was reminded of their whereabouts, and he realized that they still faced the problem of gaining access to Cheswick, no matter what Miss Ingram's guise. He shot her a speculative glance. "Now what?" And he didn't know whether to be encouraged or disappointed when she answered without hesitation.

"We take the tour."

# *Chapter Five*

As Hero had hoped, Cheswick's housekeeper was authorized to give tours of the great house, and who could refuse Mr Marchant and his sister, two genteel tourists visiting the countryside?

Although Mr Marchant accompanied her without protest, he said little, and Hero was forced to comment admiringly on the elegant furnishings and works of art, while keeping her eye out for books. Yet as they moved from one spacious room to another, she didn't see any. Had she made a misjudgment? Although she knew the current earl was no collector, she didn't think he had sold off the family's library. But if not here, where?

Hero tried to recall what she knew of the man, including his other properties. Perhaps Cheswick was too new and had never housed the Mallory. When had the family gained the earldom, and where had they lived before? Hero wondered frantically. If the volume was not here, she would have to look elsewhere, for whether Raven had orchestrated this little jaunt or not, he would expect her to return with the prize in hand.

Despite her growing unease, Hero kept up a constant stream of chatter for the benefit of the housekeeper. But she must have given something away, for Mr Marchant shot her a speculative glance. Even as she ignored it, Hero felt suspicion roil through her again. Did he know something she did not? Is that why he hadn't wanted to come here?

Just when Hero was trying to work out what she might do next, Mrs Spratling stopped before a closed door, opened it and ushered them through, with a curt explanation. "His lordship doesn't often use this room, so it is usually kept shut, but it's a fine library."

Indeed it was. All four walls were lined with shelves, and all of those shelves were lined with books. Yet the room was open and airy, as was all of Cheswick, a relatively new house with none of the quirks of Raven Hill. Breathing in the scents of bindings, paper and beeswax, Hero felt her tension ease. She could have spent weeks browsing, but she knew they didn't have that sort of time.

Catching Mr Marchant's eye, she inclined her head toward the opposite wall, so that they might each search a section. As he had since their first acquaintance, Mr Marchant seemed to understand her direction without any speech passing between them. And when he casually strolled away, Hero turned to face the shelves. She paused, her hands behind her back, as though gazing in wonder at their contents. However, she was more interested in discovering their order, and she had to bite back a cry of dismay at what was soon evident.

The books in Cheswick's library were carefully arranged, but not by a system that would do Hero any good. As she stared at the great blocks of hues, Hero cursed the earl or his decorator or whoever had decided it would be stylish to order the library according to the color of the covers.

Since Hero had no idea what the Mallory looked like, her only option was to seek out older volumes. However, a book's condition depended upon a number of variables besides its age. If secreted safely away for a number of those years, it would bear few marks of usage, but if tossed in the cellar or worse, it could be damaged beyond repair.

Hero's heart sank as she eyed the shelves. While this collection was not vast, there were far too many books to search quickly. And the housekeeper already was making noises about returning to her work.

"Oh, but the books are all so pretty," Hero said. She turned to smile at the woman, then walked to where Mr Marchant was pondering the editions along the opposite wall.

"See how cleverly those are grouped," she said aloud. But her whispered message was far different. "We need more time."

"And how do you propose we arrange that?" Mr Marchant asked.

"Bribe the housekeeper?" It was no secret that most of the staff of these large homes were underpaid and overworked, but this one didn't have the slack-jawed look of desperation. Still, it was worth an effort.

Turning away from Mr Marchant, Hero walked the perimeter of the room, checking the rows for a volume that appeared old or pushed behind another. And all the while, she chattered away about her love of novels with the hope of distracting the servant.

Since Mr Marchant continued his inspection in silence, Hero could only deduce that he was unwilling to offer money to the woman or that he was waiting for the right moment. But it soon became clear that they could delay no longer.

With a loud harrumph, Mrs Spratling planted her formidable form directly in front of Mr Marchant. "I'm afraid I must insist that we move on."

"Oh, please don't say so," Hero said, with an expression of dismay. "Couldn't we just look around a bit longer? Christopher, give this wonderful woman a little something to let us linger. This is the most beautiful library we've seen yet."

But Mrs Spratling would have none of it. "His lordship doesn't allow for lingering," she said, her lips pursed. "He's having a ball tonight, and his party will be arriving soon."

"A ball!" Hero clapped her hands with feigned delight. "Did you hear that, Christopher?"

Behind the housekeeper's back, Mr Marchant shot her a pained look, which she promptly ignored.

"What kind of ball is it?"

"A masquerade," Mrs Spratling said, unbending a bit. "His lordship does love the theatricals and such."

"Oh, I can only imagine what sort of things they wear," Hero said. She donned her most ingratiating expression as she turned to the housekeeper. "I suppose you have a hand in arranging them all."

Mrs Spratling shook her head, but she smiled, obviously flattered. "His lordship does keep costumes on hand for those who aren't prepared, but I just have to lay them out, keep them all in good condition. It's the ball itself that I—"

Hero cut her off. "Oh, please, you must let us see! Just a peek," Hero wheedled. "I'll bet you have your favorites."

"Well, I..." Mrs Spratling smiled. "I do have a couple that I recommend, only if the ladies or gentlemen ask for my assistance, of course."

"Oh, you must show us, just for a moment, and they'll we'll be off, straight out the door," Hero said. She squealed with glee when Mrs Spratling nodded her agreement and hurried to the woman's side. Thankfully, Mr Marchant had the sense not to say anything, and as soon as the housekeeper marched ahead, Hero fell back, grabbing his arm to pull him close.

"We're going to the ball," she whispered.

When he turned to her with a dubious expression and a protest upon his lips, she shook her head to silence him. "You distract her while I get some costumes for us."

And before he could argue, Hero moved toward Mrs Spratling, more flattery upon her lips. It had been her experience that most people loved to show off what meant the most to them. Obviously, the housekeeper was proud of the grand home in her charge, but she also had a soft spot for fripperies, the creative bent of her master and her own opinion, all of which Hero used to gain entrance to the dressing room, where the masquerades were kept.

Mrs Spratling swung open the door, and Hero stepped inside just as a loud thump echoed behind them. Hero did not pause, but hurried forward, scanning the room for what she could slip inside her cloak. Unfortunately, most of the garments appeared to be housed in matching wardrobes, and she did not know how much time she had. Mr Marchant was quickwitted, but the housekeeper would not be diverted for long.

A domino with an odd mask that could be folded lay upon the arm of an Egyptian couch, perhaps in need of mending, but it would serve her purpose. Rolling it as quickly and tightly as possible, Hero tucked it inside her cloak. On a nearby table was a set of brightly colored garments. Hero snatched up the top items, then spread another on the couch in place of the domino, just as she heard Mrs Spratling's loud step behind her.

"Look at these," Hero said. "Did you make them yourself?"

But Mrs Spratling's mood had been ruined by Mr Marchant's stumble and subsequent complaints about the slickness of the floors.

"Certainly not. His lordship employs seamstresses for such tasks," she said. Hands on her hips, she surveyed the room with the look of a general inspecting his troops. Hero inched in front of the couch, hoping that the missing domino would not be marked. She held her breath, heart pounding, until Mr Marchant provided another distraction.

"Are the costumes in here?" he asked loudly, limping to one of the wardrobes.

"Don't touch that," the housekeeper said. Barreling past Mr Marchant, she opened the doors to display a variety of hanging items, as well as numerous masques and headdresses.

"There. As you can see, his lordship likes to keep a good supply on hand, especially for those he favors," she said with a sweep of a beefy hand. Obviously, she no longer intended to show them any contents of the wardrobes, Mr Marchant having fallen out of her graces literally. "Now, I have work to do, so you must be off."

Hero nodded, but waited for the woman to lead the way before moving from her position. Mrs Spratling's small eyes narrowed as she glanced behind her, as if looking for something. And Hero held her breath.

"I thought we were going," Mr Marchant said, coming to the rescue again. "I dare say I think I might need your help, ma'am, for I can hardly walk. If you could just let me take your arm until we reach one of the carpets. Sister, if you would assist me, as well?"

Hero would have smiled at Mr Marchant's posturing, if her heart hadn't been pounding so fiercely. Pulling her cloak close around her, she loosed a low sigh of relief at escaping the dressing room. She had maintained her composure in worse situations, with no one to count on except herself. But she wasn't sure that she could have managed this time, and she suspected that Mr Marchant had saved her from discovery.

As she took his arm, Hero was hard pressed to maintain her charade, for his effect on her was anything but brotherly. Fighting off the urge to press herself closer, she reminded herself that Mr Marchant was not what he seemed.

Nothing appeared to disturb him, not highwaymen, nor arresting authorities, nor difficult travels or accommodations. *Not even a sudden need for posing and deception.* On the contrary, he appeared to take everything in his stride, perhaps even thriving on their adventures.

Glancing surreptitiously in his direction, Hero noted that the dark circles under his eyes were gone. Had the grief and anger she had once seen been real, or had it all been a pose? And was Mr Marchant simply an actor playing a part?

As Sydony often said, there was very little that rattled Kit, but skulking around the Earl of Cheswick's property was one of them. After practically being thrown out of the home by the housekeeper, Kit was anxious to make their escape. But Miss Ingram insisted upon looking over the outbuildings and admiring the grounds, though nothing was blooming this late in the year.

"Haven't you seen enough, *sister*?" Kit asked, when a stable boy eyed them quizzically. He'd begun to wonder if she was like Lady Caroline Lamb, who was rumored to dress as a man, courting danger and pushing the boundaries of society. But Miss Ingram claimed she was checking out all available structures for later use.

"*Later* when?" Kit asked. "And *use* by whom?"

She only shook her head, smiled at the stable boy, and continued on her way. When, at last, she had seen her fill, Kit coaxed her back to the horses, eager to leave before the earl and his party arrived—or Miss Ingram's theft was discovered.

After they exited the graveled drive that led to Cheswick, Kit breathed a sigh of relief, for no shouts rose from behind them, and there were no signs of pursuing footmen. "Don't we have enough people chasing us without you stealing from the Earl of Cheswick?" he asked, slanting her a glance.

"How else were we going to get into the ball?"

Kit groaned.

"We need more time to find the book."

As if posing as brother and sister, conning Cheswick's housekeeper and outright theft weren't enough, Miss Ingram wanted to return? Kit shook his head. Her facility for deception made him leery, for a woman who fooled everyone else might be fooling him, too. If she were playing some sort of game, it could have deadly consequences that she didn't anticipate. And it made Kit's task even more difficult, for how could he protect Miss Ingram from herself?

Once Hero was back in her disguise, it was easier to get a room without dealing with maids—or separating. As difficult as it was to spend the night with her, Kit was not about to leave her alone. And he insisted they take time to eat a meal.

But as soon as the sun set, they headed back to Cheswick. The terrain was familiar now, and they tethered their horses in a stand of trees well enough away to avoid the footmen and grooms and arriving guests. Under the cover of darkness, they hurried closer to the house, Miss Ingram steering him toward a small shed.

Apparently, this is what she had meant by later use,

for she opened the door and slipped inside, motioning for Kit to follow. He swallowed a protest, for this trespass probably would be the least of his worries before the night was over. Still, Kit balked when he saw the shadowy shapes of a large table and various gardening implements.

"A potting shed?" he muttered. Were they going to take a turn at impersonating the earl's outdoor staff, as well?

"I was hoping there would be more room," Miss Ingram said, moving over so that he could join her inside.

"For what?" Kit asked. Stepping into the dark and dusty interior, he was assailed by the smell of soil and manure. His eyes were still adjusting to the lack of light when Miss Ingram shut the door, plunging them into pitch blackness.

"For dressing," she said. "We can change in here and walk to the house."

Kit blinked blindly. *"What?"*

"Here's your costume." She pushed something into his gut, and Kit grunted. Although he grabbed the bundle, he was still reeling from the idea that they should change clothes here. In the dark. Alone. Together.

"I should wait outside," Kit said, clearing his suddenly dry throat. "It's too cramped in here."

"Nonsense," Miss Ingram said briskly. "And we can't have someone seeing you lounging about."

Her apparent indifference was annoying, but if she didn't see anything untoward, then why should he? Kit vowed to pretend she was his sister and get on with it. *The quicker the better.*

Kit's disgruntlement only grew when he shook out

what she had given him and realized it was not a domino, the traditional hooded cloak worn with a half-mask that was the simplest of costumes.

"What the devil did you get me?" he asked, wishing now that he had taken a look in the light. Back at the inn. *By himself.*

"It's a Harlequin," she said. "And it was the only thing at hand. There were a pile of them, matching shirts and trousers, and I took the top set."

"I can't put this on," Kit said. Just from fingering the material, he could tell it would not fit over his clothes. And he had no intention of stripping down to his drawers in the cold shed, with or without Miss Ingram's company.

"Fine," she muttered. "You can have the domino, and I'll wear the Harlequin."

"No, you won't," Kit said. The thought of Miss Ingram traipsing around in nothing but the masque was even more repugnant than donning the outfit himself. At least in her current incarnation, her breeches were loose, and she was covered in layers of shirt and vest and coat. Harlequins, as a rule, were notoriously snug, making them a favorite of preening dandies who wished to show off their figures.

"Why don't you let me have the domino, and you can simply wear your boy's clothing?" Kit asked. "Women often masquerade as men, and vice versa, at these things."

"I don't want to be marked in my usual disguise."

"So you're wearing a costume over a costume?"

Kit felt a punch in his stomach as she shoved the domino at him. "Here, I'll trade you," she said.

"No." Kit held the Harlequin out of reach, though he enjoyed the touch of her hand, groping blindly against him. If it weren't so cold and their situation so peculiar, he would have leaned into it and…

"Then hurry," she whispered. "We need as much time in the library as possible."

With a groan, Kit turned around. They had traded their heavy traveling coats for cloaks, but he struggled with his coat and did not dare ask for Miss Ingram's help.

In polite company, men were rarely seen in their shirtsleeves. Did Miss Ingram even realize what she was asking of him? Kit was beginning to wonder if she'd been raised by wolves or in some foreign tribe that did not adhere to the dictates of society.

Folding his coat as best he could, Kit tried to pull the tunic over his shirt, but it was too small, requiring him to strip down to his skin. But he was already warmer than when he'd entered the building. And the more he took off, the hotter he grew.

Kit tried to concentrate on undressing, but it was difficult when he caught a whiff of feminine scent and heard his companion rustling beside him, much too close for comfort. In response, he inched away from her, lest she come in contact with an unexpected expanse of his flesh. But there was too little room, and he banged against something that was hanging on a hook. It tottered precariously, rattling in the silence.

"Shh!" Miss Ingram whispered, and before Kit knew it, her hands were on him, steadying him. It was far worse than the accidental brush he had feared, for her gloveless fingers were splayed full upon his bare chest.

"Wh-wh-what are you doing?" she asked, sounding decidedly unlike herself.

"I'm trying to put on a tunic that was made for someone half my size," Kit whispered. It wasn't as though he was taking off his clothes for any other reason. And if he were, he wouldn't be doing it here in the Earl of Cheswick's potting shed.

"I should have taken the Harlequin," she said. "I'm smaller than you are."

"Yes, but, no," Kit muttered, as he tried not to imagine Miss Ingram stripping down to her skin. And in the ensuing silence, he simply stood where he was, unwilling to move from beneath her caress. The air in the confined space seemed to crackle with the tension between them, and Kit was tempted to cover her hands with his own.

Since neither one of them seemed to be breathing, the silence was broken only by the distant sounds of arrivals and their servants until Kit heard something else. Was it a rat, scuttling around them, or was someone outside? The reminder of just where they were chilled him like a dose of cold water. Miss Ingram, too, was startled into action, for he felt the loss of her hands as she broke away. They both stood motionless, listening, but the scraping stopped.

Still, it was an impetus to be about their business, instead of dawdling dangerously. There was too much at stake, not the least of which was Miss Ingram's tattered reputation should they be discovered in a compromising position.

Tugging the tunic over his head, Kit leaned down to remove his trousers, then pulled on the bottom half of the Harlequin costume. But he could not rush, for fear of tearing the material, which was tighter than anything he had ever worn. Straightening, Kit inhaled deeply, just to make sure he could breath, then tried to adjust the snug areas of the material as discreetly as possible.

"Perhaps we should be husband and wife."

Kit froze.

"It might make a better story should we get caught *in flagrante delicto*," Miss Ingram said. "A brother and sister wouldn't be sneaking off to the library for an assignation."

Of course, she was talking about their masquerade; Kit had never considered any other possibility. And she was probably right. If the library were empty, then it would not be unusual for a couple to meet there, though they were more likely to be married to others. Still, a certain degree of intimacy would be implied.

"It's Kit," he said, abruptly.

"What?"

"No one calls me Christopher."

"Oh. Kit." She must have turned toward him because Kit could have sworn he felt the warmth of her breath when she spoke his name.

"Hero," she whispered. "My name is Hero."

"Out of the play?"

Kit could hear her shrug, though she did not reply. "You remind me more of Beatrice," he said, referring to the feisty heroine of Shakespeare's *Much Ado About Nothing*.

Of course, calling each other by their first names was inappropriate, but so was changing their clothes here in the dark together. *And so was planning to sneak into the Earl of Cheswick's masquerade ball.*

"Let's go," she said, as if reading his thoughts. Groping around in the dark, Kit found a dry bucket and stuffed his clothes in it. Hopefully, they would be there when they returned. Reminded of what he currently wore instead, Kit wrapped his cloak around himself.

Inching forward, Kit nudged the door open a crack and peered out. The scuttling sound began at once, and he froze where he stood, half-expecting an assailant to loom out of the darkness. But when he saw a squirrel dart up a nearby tree, and he loosed his pent-up breath and slipped from the shed, his companion not far behind.

By the time he shut the door, Miss Ingram—Hero—was already headed toward the house, and Kit hurried to follow. They skirted the stables, with its light and activity, yet Kit remained alert, lest someone notice them wandering the grounds. But no one marked their presence, and they reached the tall doors that opened onto the lawn, where the party would spill out in warmer weather.

Despite the cold, they could claim they were snatching a few moments alone in the moonlight, away from the colorful figures that could be seen moving about the glowing interior. Still, they chose the doors farthest from the assembly and made their entrance as discreetly as possible to avoid notice.

Inside, the vast room they had viewed earlier in the day sparkled with light and activity, and Kit blinked against the sudden change. People in outrageous costumes were milling upon, clutching glasses of punch and gossiping, while dancers took up much of the floor, moving to the music of an orchestra.

"A little chilly out there, isn't it?" a low voice asked. The man, dressed as a house, leaned toward Hero, dark eyes leering through the window that opened across his face. "I've got a fire going in here."

Ignoring him, they slipped past a witch, a monk and a man wearing a toga to disappear into the crowd.

"We should separate and meet in the library," Hero whispered, but Kit shook his head. Although he'd not been to many masquerades, he had just been reminded that some people were emboldened by their disguises. And this was no simple country gathering with its innocent pleasures. Kit knew from Barto that the higher ranks of society often displayed the lowest levels of morality.

"Go on," Hero urged.

"No," Kit said, even as she darted behind a tall character with a towering turban. He turned to go after her, but a hand on his arm stayed him.

"Do I know you?" a Columbine asked. She was dressed in extremely low-cut servant garb and might have been looking for her Harlequin. But Kit was not it.

"No," he answered, trying to get by her.

"But perhaps I'd like to," she purred, her fingers tightening on his arm. The woman's face was completely masked, which meant the bosoms bursting forth from her tight bodice were probably those of a female past her most alluring age.

Still, Kit would not insult her. He took her gloved hand from his arm and kissed the fingers. "Perhaps another time, fair Columbine," he said, and he moved past a shepherdess and her sheep before the woman could grab him again.

Having made his escape, Kit realized that Hero had disappeared from his immediate view. And his search for her quickly became frustrating. There were plenty of black dominoes, but as he scanned the crowd for a slight figure dressed in boots, he saw none with her lurid mask, at least none turned his way.

"Well, hello, there." A six-foot nun with a baritone sidled up to him.

"Pardon me," Kit said, making his exit before the fellow could become more familiar. Pushing past a bewildered-looking pair of Quakers, he realized that the longer he lingered, the more unwelcome attention he was drawing to himself. And still he could not find Hero.

There was nothing for it but to go to the library—and hope that she was there.

## Chapter Six

Hero moved easily through the rooms, drawing no notice on her way to the library. As Mrs Spratling had claimed, it was not in use, but a fire burned in the grate, casting a warm glow upon the tall shelves. Shutting the door behind her, Hero lit a candle and set it upon a drum table, so as better to see the titles.

When she heard the door open and close in stealthy fashion, she saw no reason to turn and greet Mr Marchant. *Kit.* They had only recently parted after being closeted together far too long, and Hero shivered at the memory of his skin beneath her fingers. Smooth and so very warm...

She heard his quiet footsteps as he neared her, and her heart began hammering at his approach. What was he about? He should be searching his own shelves, not looking over her shoulder. Yet that's just what he was doing. In fact, he was leaning against her, his breath hot against her cheek—and reeking of wine.

With a start, Hero turned around to face, not Kit

Marchant, but a stranger dressed in green, a great plume dangling from his cap. He was reaching for her, and Hero evaded his touch by stomping down hard upon his foot.

"Ow!" the man muttered. He seemed no more than a drunken guest, but Hero moved away quickly. Had he seen through her disguise, or was he indiscriminate in his tastes? Hero did not know, but she did not care to find out.

"I beg your pardon. I did not think anyone was here," Hero said in her deepest voice. She glanced toward the closed door and wondered where Kit was even as she cursed herself for relying upon him. Didn't she know better? She had become careless and witless and must face the consequences of her own inattention.

That meant dealing with this interloper so she could get back to searching. Hero glanced at the door, but she didn't want to leave the room, for fear she would not be able to return. Looking back at the man, she attempted to gauge the threat. He wasn't tall, but he was sturdily built. Just how drunk was he?

"Here now, Master Scarlet," he drawled. "What kind of greeting is that?"

He must have been referring to her bloodred mask, or perhaps he thought her someone else, for he was dressed as a fellow of the greenwood. "You must be mistaken," Hero said. "I know you not, sir."

"Well, let us remedy that, by God," he said, lurching forward. An elegant rosewood couch stood between them, but it provided little protection. Hero did not intend to participate in some French farce, but neither did she care to resort to her pistol. The success of her venture depended upon secrecy, and she did not want to cause any outcry.

Hero edged around the couch, but her companion was not deterred. In fact, he seemed to enjoy the game, grinning behind his half-mask and feathered cap. The green hose he wore beneath his short tunic left little to the imagination, and Hero was alarmed by what she saw.

"You are confusing me with another, sir," Hero said, backing toward the door. "I am not Will Scarlet. Now be off with you before I crack a cudgel upon your skull."

Hero heard the door open behind her and felt her heart constrict. If someone was blocking her escape, she was well and truly trapped. But instead of welcoming the newcomer, her companion warned them away.

"We are occupied here," he shouted.

"We are not!" Hero called out. Turning her head slightly, she glanced toward the entrance and felt a mixture of relief and joy at the sight of Kit Marchant.

As usual, he was completely unruffled by the scene before him. "Excuse me, but this is my assignation, Sir Robin, arranged earlier this evening," he said.

For a moment, Hero thought the interloper would argue. Kit must have, too, because he stepped forward, sweeping his cape out of the way, as though prepared to draw a sword, even though Hero knew he didn't have one.

What he did have was an extremely close-fitting costume, and Hero drew in a sharp breath at the sight. The shiny material with its garish red, yellow and blue diamonds seemed to hug every well-formed inch of Kit's body, revealing each sleek muscle, especially in the area of his groin, where a strategically positioned piece of red cloth called attention to that part of his anatomy.

Hero felt an answering rush of color flood her cheeks. Although she knew little of such things, her assailant's hose appeared ill filled by comparison. Indeed, as if echoing her thoughts, the man erupted in a loud harrumph and staggered toward the door.

"Well, I can see why you are wearing that, my friend," he said with a nod. "And I concede to my better."

When Robin Hood had quit the room, Kit turned toward her once more. "At least some good has come of this damned constricting costume," he said.

Then he looked down at himself for the first time, and despite herself, Hero found her gaze following his own. For a heart-stopping instant, her wits fled, and all she knew was the hot swell of what she could only guess was desire.

"Is it my imagination or is there a star on my—?" Kit began to ask, but he must have heard Hero's choked sound of dismay because he didn't finish. Instead, he lifted his head to slant her a glance, and in his dark eyes Hero saw a glint of seductive promise that robbed her of breath.

That look alone was far more dangerous than anything in Sir Robin's arsenal, and Hero had to struggle to keep a tenuous hold on her rioting senses. She tried to remember where she was, what she must do and, most of all, who she was, as her fingers clung, trembling, to the back of the couch.

A loud thump and raucous laughter from outside the room saved her from herself, for it seemed to call Kit to attention. Striding across the thick carpet, he easily lifted a heavy chair and put it in front of the door, so that they would have some privacy and warning, at least, of interruption.

Flushing, Hero ignored the giddy thrill that seemed to produce and turned her back upon the compelling figure of Kit Marchant. But he was not so easily put from her mind, and even as she scanned the shelves, searching for the Mallory, Hero was aware of his presence, both a comfort and a danger far more perilous than a host of drunken masqueraders.

Kit kept an eye on the hands of the ormolu clock, for he did not know how long the ball would continue. Usually, such events dragged through to the wee hours, but he had no wish to be found here after the other guests had left or sought their beds.

Already, he was weary of an activity that seemed pointless. And the sooner he got out of his costume, the better; he was beginning to feel as though blood was being cut off from necessary parts, parts that he might some day want in working condition…

Kit pushed aside that thought and all that came with it to concentrate on getting Hero out of Cheswick safely.

"The Mallory at Oakfield had been slipped between another cover to conceal it, which is why it remained hidden all those years," he said, hoping to put an end to the search.

As usual, Hero was undeterred. "We have no evidence that Martin Cheswick did the same."

*Perhaps because half the instructions he received were missing*, Kit thought, though he said no more. Even if the book was here, which he doubted, they would need to pull out each volume and examine it in order to find what they were seeking. And that sort of task was not going to be accomplished in one evening.

Still, Kit ran his fingers over the spines, looking for anything unusual, while the clock ticked, the only sound besides the crackle of the fire. When it came, the noise of something else was startling in the stillness, and Kit looked to the door, where the chair held fast despite being rattled.

Hero was already glancing his way, but she was crouched before another bookcase on the opposite side of the room. It was hardly the pose of two lovers, and Kit hurried toward the rosewood couch, motioning for her to join him.

Without hesitation, Kit pulled her down against the round pillow and leaned over her, all the while staring at the door. But after the initial rattling, it fell silent. In the quiet that followed, he waited, yet heard nothing else. Perhaps some other guests, seeking an assignation, had realized the library was occupied and moved on.

Kit loosed a low sigh at the respite and turned his head toward Hero. She had removed her mask, and had he seen his relief reflected on her features, he would have got to his feet and returned to the search. But in the candlelight, her beautiful face glowed, just as when he'd first seen her, like a beacon in the dark that he could not ignore.

Her hood was thrown back, revealing wisps of

golden hair that escaped their confinement to catch the light. Her usual cool expression was gone, her eyes heavy lidded, her lips parted and her cheeks flushed. Abruptly, Kit realized that he was bent over her, his chest nearly touching hers, his mouth only inches away from her own.

Without pausing to consider his actions, Kit lowered his head to brush his lips against hers, tasting, exploring and delighting in the soft curves. Beneath him, he heard Hero's low hum of surprised pleasure, and he smiled. For one long moment, they were in agreement, savoring their shared sense of discovery and the heat that flowed between them.

But even in his current state, Kit recognized a potential firestorm, and he pulled back slightly. Lifting his hand to Hero's throat, he stroked his thumb against the line of her jaw, teasing the corner of her mouth until it opened for him. Her eyes closed, his formidable companion looked oddly vulnerable, and Kit felt something expand within his chest. Leaning close, he kissed her again, more deeply, as if he could take her inside himself, hold her to him at last…

But this time, Kit heard no sigh of pleasure, only the jarring clang of the clock as it struck midnight. And like Cinderella of the old tales, Hero was transformed by the sound. Nothing turned into a pumpkin, but the warm and willing woman in his arms jerked upright, knocking her temple against his in her haste to escape his embrace. Rising in her wake, Kit rubbed his brow and wondered when his head had last suffered such repeated abuse.

"Are you all right?" he asked. But Hero was already

reaching for the books, her mask and domino in place, the telltale trembling of a hand the only sign of what had happened between them.

Kit was slower to recover, but it didn't take him long to realize the ramifications of his behavior. Rising to his feet, he returned to the search, cursing himself. He had been thrown together with Hero in more than one intimate situation, with just her coolness and his restraint standing between them. Yet when her coolness had wavered, his restraint had disappeared, and he had only himself to blame. Wasn't he supposed to be a gentleman?

"Now, isn't this interesting."

Kit swung round at the sound of speech. He looked at Hero, but she, too, had stiffened, and a quick glance at the door revealed that it held fast, the chair firmly lodged against it. Eyes narrowing, Kit scanned the room and was surprised to see a figure in a shadowed corner. Had it been there all along, unnoticed?

"You may bar the door of my own library against me, but I have more than one way to enter nearly every room in this house," the figure said, stepping forward. Behind him a section of decorative panel clicked shut, revealing the manner of his access.

Kit felt a moment's relief that the man had not been present earlier, but his appearance was still daunting, and his words had Kit thinking fast.

"My lord," Kit said, bowing slightly.

"You may call me your Grace, as I am good King Henry for this eve," the Earl of Cheswick said, with a regal nod. He was dressed in enormous purple robes trimmed in fur and wore a crown, presumably not of pure gold, upon his head, and surveyed them with a jaundiced eye.

"And who might you be?"

"I am but a simple Domino, your Grace," Hero said, in a deep voice. "And this is Harlequin."

The earl laughed as he moved farther into the light. "My dear young woman, I assure you that I can tell the difference between a youth and a maid," he said, waving about the sceptre he held in one hand as he paused to study them more closely. "Well, aren't you the loveliest couple."

"We're siblings."

"We're married."

Since Hero spoke at the same time Kit did, there was no recovering from their faux pas, especially considering the amused expression on the earl's face. At least he didn't call for some burly footmen to toss them out.

"How very interesting," he murmured. Moving closer, he lifted a quizzing glass and looked Kit up and down. When his gaze lingered on the red star that seemed designed to draw attention to a certain area, Kit frowned.

The earl dropped his glass with a sniff. "One wonders why a fellow who appears to be averse to attention would don such a masque."

"It's my fault," Hero said. "I chose it for him, not realizing it would be too small."

The earl turned his quizzing glass upon her. "A sad misjudgement for a *wife* to make," he said, and Kit groaned.

"You are right, my lord...er, your Grace," Hero

said. "We are married to others, and I persuaded him to meet me here for an assignation. I beg you to keep our secret."

But the earl wasn't having any of it, and he held up his hand as though to stop her speech. "You'll have to do better than that, child. And before you do, perhaps I should tell you that I do love my masquerades—so much so that I personally choose every costume that I provide for my guests. So you can imagine my surprise when I caught a glimpse of two of my favorites being worn by persons unknown to me."

The earl paused to eye Kit. "Not that I'm complaining, mind you. For I do like an intrigue."

Hero drew a deep breath, as if to tender a new explanation, but the earl waved her off. "I would like to hear what our manly Harlequin has to say. And don't try to hoax me with any talk of assignations, for that's hardly what you were doing when I came in."

It was time to lay their cards on the table, Kit decided, and he turned to face the earl without apology. "We were looking for a book," he admitted. He heard Hero's sound of distress, but he was not one to invent Banbury tales.

"A *book*?" the earl echoed.

"It was given to one of your ancestors, Martin Cheswick, for safekeeping," Hero said, in a not-so-subtle attempt to lay claim to the volume.

The earl dropped his quizzing glass with a look of annoyance. "Well, that's a sad disappointment. I had hoped for something a bit more interesting. A scandal broth, a bamboozle…a ménage à trois," he said, with a hopeful glance.

Kit shook his head.

Sighing, the earl waved a hand to encompass the room. "Well, you are welcome to it. I've no use for them, though they are pleasing to the eye. And really, what else can you fill the shelves with, except books?"

"I take it you aren't a collector?" Kit asked.

"Good heavens, no," the earl said, with a shudder. "Spare me from the dusty old mopes, although I do have an antiquarian costume that is rather amusing."

Obviously, the earl would have no idea what was or was not in his library, and while his offer was magnanimous, Kit didn't put much stock in it. Such a frippery fellow might be prone to whims and on to the next fancy before they could finish their search.

"Are they catalogued?" Hero asked, as though the same concern had crossed her mind.

"Lud, no!" the earl said. "I believe Father engaged a man to do that—Richard Poynter, was it? A waste of coin, if you ask me, and I have no intention of throwing good money after bad."

He looked around the room with a shrug. "I don't care what's here, as long as they look well. In fact, I think the architect had blank pages bound to his specifications in many cases. I certainly didn't want any of Father's old ones, horrid, musty, smelly things. That's why I sold them off."

"You sold your family's collection?" Hero asked.

"And why not?" the earl asked. "They meant nothing to me."

Kit could tell the earl was growing bored with the conversation, and he rushed to ask the most important question.

"Were the books sold at auction? Do you have a record of the buyers?"

"I don't need a record," the earl said. "I can tell you right now where they all went. We broke them up into four lots, very neat and tidy, and sold only to those among my acquaintances who like that sort of thing." He paused, as though proud of his own cleverness.

"The Greek went to Devonshire, for far too paltry a sum, I might add. The Latin I gave to Chauncey Jamison, a decent enough fellow I went to school with. Apparently, he's joined the antiquarian society and fancies himself some sort of scholar now," the earl said with a derisive laugh.

"And the rest?" Hero asked.

"The French went to Claude Guerrier, as he is known since his hasty exit from his own country, and the English to Marcus Featherstone."

"You sorted the books according to the language of the text?" Kit asked, trying to keep the surprise from his voice.

The earl gave a regal nod, obviously pleased with himself. "I couldn't be bothered with a protracted sale, so messy and time-consuming, dithering over every single volume."

"But I thought…" Hero began, only to pause, as if to reconsider her words. "That is, I had heard that one of the lots went to Augustus Raven."

"That queer fish? Certainly not," the earl said. "Why, the fellow has no taste. Have you seen that monstrosity of his, Raven Hill? Spare me from the Gothic lovers!" He shuddered.

"Thank you so much for your help…your Grace,"

Kit said hurriedly before Hero might betray her identity. "We have taken up far too much of your precious time when your guests are waiting."

"Yes, we should go," Hero said. Taking Kit's lead, she began backing toward the door.

"But you must stay! As king of all I survey, I command you. And a private audience with you, my mysterious Harlequin, is in order," the earl said, pointedly eyeing Kit. "Perhaps you'd like to get out of that tight costume. I own I fear for you. Constriction of the blood. We wouldn't want any…damage."

"Thank you, your Grace," Kit said. "But I'm afraid I can't leave my…sister."

"A pity," the earl said, putting his quizzing glass to his face once more to scrutinize his guests. Although Kit felt no sense of threat, he was aware of just how long they had been ensconced in the library as trespassers. And who knew what awaited them outside?

Hero was already at the door, and when she pulled the chair away from it, it burst open.

"My lord, are you all right?" A man stumbled over the threshold, a bit breathlessly. Kit couldn't tell if the fellow was a butler or simply masquerading as one, and he did not intend to linger long enough to find out.

"Of course I'm all right," the earl said, waving his scepter. "Behold my new subjects."

But Hero had already exited, and Kit was quick to follow. He hurried after her, hoping they could escape into the crowd before a hue and cry was raised against them. But no shouts erupted from behind, and they slowed their pace so as to draw no attention.

Yet they did not pause until they reached the tall

doors that led outside, and there only long enough to make sure they were not marked before they slipped into the night air. Kit blinked as his eyes adjusted to the darkness, a welcome cloak after the brightly lit, perfumed rooms. There was no one to note their movements on the lawn, and they veered away from the stables and any signs of activity.

Although the small shed seemed a veritable haven, Kit approached it carefully and nudged at the door, lest someone be waiting for them inside. But all was dark and silent, just as they had left it. Still, he did not intend to linger, and, once inside, he put his garments on over the Harlequin costume. He gave no thought to the closeness of his companion and didn't even care if his trousers were on backward, so eager was he to quit Cheswick.

Hero, who had only to remove her domino, was already finished and silent in the darkness, and Kit was struggling into his coat when he heard voices outside. He didn't need Hero's sudden grip upon his arm to stay his hand; he froze where he was, one sleeve on, the other off.

"They aren't here, I tell you."

It was not the man's voice, but his words, that chilled Kit, and he strained to listen.

"And how would you know when everyone's wearing costumes?" a second voice asked. The two must have been walking, for Kit heard the crunch of gravel growing closer, and he tensed. If men were searching the outbuildings for their unnamed quarry, he would be of little use, trussed halfway up in his coat.

"Because I talked to the servants, that's how, and there aren't any guests that aren't accounted for, with maids and valets all."

"What of those who aren't staying at the house?" the second voice asked. Were their steps slowing? Kit curled the fingers of his free hand into a fist.

"I've talked to every coachman here. You don't think they drove themselves, did you?" The tone was mocking, and Kit heard the other man curse as the footsteps resumed.

"Maybe," the other man said. "I wouldn't put anything past them. Didn't they ride—?"

Although Kit held his breath, he could not make out what else the fellow said, and he dared not lean toward the side of the shed, lest he blindly knock into something, calling attention to their presence. He waited, poised for trouble, but eventually, both the voices and the footsteps faded as the two men passed out of earshot.

When Hero finally loosed his arm, Kit tugged on the rest of his coat and stepped to the door, easing it open slightly. In the surrounding night, all was silent, and he saw no sign of a presence nearby.

"There! Look toward the stables," Hero whispered beside him.

Kit glanced in that direction and saw two men approaching the structure, but others milled about as well, coachmen, stable hands and the like. There was no telling if the two men Hero noticed were the same they had heard talking. But Kit could see why she had pointed them out.

Even in the pale lantern light, there was no mistaking the fact that the men wore livery, and Kit recognized the now familiar insignia of the Duke of Montford.

# Chapter Eighteen

## Chapter Seven

The exhilaration Kit had felt after their escape from the library was short-lived, deflated by the odd conversation they had overheard and Hero's concern over it. She hadn't even wanted to return to the inn, but Kit convinced her that they needed to get their things and rest the horses.

It was too late to set out upon the road to London and too cold to sleep in the open. And despite her insistence otherwise, Kit did not want Hero falling from her mount along some dark road. A fire, some food and some rest were what they both needed.

The hour was such that Kit was fairly certain they had not been followed back to their small lodgings. He had even been forced to wake a sleepy boy in the inn yard to tend the horses. And a quick exploration of the area revealed no one lingering suspiciously in the courtyard or beyond.

Even the common room was quiet, with only a few travelers or locals drinking ale before seeking their beds. Yet once ensconced in their room, Hero took up a stance at the window, as though she intended to keep watch all night.

"We don't know that those men were after us," Kit said.

She turned, her face in shadow. "Then who is?"

Although Kit wasn't sure himself, he doubted the Duke of Montford was responsible. Yet Hero seemed so convinced, he slanted her a speculative glance.

"You think I know?" she asked, as though taken aback.

Kit shrugged. Although he hadn't accused her of anything, even the most oblivious dolt would have wondered about his companion, who had proven herself adept at all manners of deception.

"You think this is all part of some elaborate scheme of *mine*?" she asked him sharply.

But Kit was not cowed by her anger, if that's what it was. "Let's put it this way—if you know anything that would be helpful, now's the time to tell me."

"I could ask the same of you," she said.

Kit bit back a laugh. "You don't trust me?"

"Should I?"

Kit snorted. "Then I'd say we are at an impasse." Yet suddenly, it didn't feel like one. In fact, their parrying had only seemed to heighten the tension between them, and Kit was struck with a want so powerful he didn't know whether he could contain it. He stood still, unwilling to move, lest he march across the room, take her in his arms and continue where he had left off in the library.

As if Hero could see his intent, she drew in a sharp

breath and turned to look out the window. When she spoke again, it was over her shoulder, her tone so distant that she appeared to put more than her back between them. "You cannot deny that the duke's men were there, just as they were at the first inn where we stayed," she said.

This time her coolness prevailed, and Kit was grateful for it, even though all of his senses screamed a protest. Running a hand through his hair, he ignored the clamoring of his body and tried to engage his brain.

"We cannot know that those two men we heard talking were discussing us," he said. "Or that they were the fellows dressed in the duke's livery. Or that those two were even the duke's men. They could have been wearing costumes."

"The earl's guests wouldn't be traipsing about the stables," Hero said. "And those were the same men we saw before. I recognized the livery."

"Perhaps," Kit conceded. "But the duke could be traveling, as we are, and attending the earl's ball."

"I don't believe in coincidences," Hero said.

Kit didn't, either, anymore, but he was not sure what to make of the sightings. "All right. Let's say those two are the ones pursuing us. Why would the Duke of Montford send a couple of thugs to kidnap you? Do you know him?"

"I know of him. He is a respected collector, so I can only assume he's infected with book madness and willing to do anything to get his prize." Turning her head, she eyed Kit directly. "Which makes it all the more imperative that we find the Mallory."

Kit shook his head at her stubborn certainty. It was

one thing to stop at Cheswick on their way to London, quite another to go elsewhere, continuing a lunatic search for something that might not even exist.

As if judging his mood, Hero continued. "I've found needles in haystacks before," she claimed.

Kit did not doubt her. "But this is different, unless you regularly tear around the country with a man who is no relation," he said, fixing her with an inquiring gaze.

"Of course not."

"Well, then, the longer we dally, the more hue and cry will be raised over your disappearance."

"Perhaps," Hero acknowledged, looking away. "Perhaps not."

"Your chaperone has gone missing, there's a warrant for my arrest, and you don't think your uncle will be concerned and alert the authorities?"

"He was not expecting me back for some time, so unless someone informs him of recent events, Raven will spare no thoughts for me," Hero said. "And even if he should become aware of the change in my circumstances, he would hardly raise a hue and cry. Raven's main concern always is the acquisition, and he will not question where I am or what I am doing until he is certain that I have not been successful."

Kit tried to absorb that bald statement and all it implied. He knew that not everyone shared his genteel upbringing. In a world where poor children were bought and sold and even royal progeny bartered away in marriage with no consideration of their wishes, Hero's situation was not that startling. And yet Kit was shocked and outraged. And if her uncle cared so little for her, where did that leave Kit?

Although he tried to mask his reaction, Hero must have seen it, for she returned her attention to the window. And when she spoke, she made it clear that the subject was closed. "What we must do is seek out the lot of English language books that went to Marcus Featherstone."

Kit groaned. "Do you even know the man?"

"I have heard of him, since he collects. He has a town house in London."

"But if all the English books were sold to him, then how did your uncle get the scrap of letter?"

Hero shrugged, but would not face him. "Perhaps Featherstone later parted with that volume or lost it in a game of chance. I understand he's an inveterate gambler."

Or, considering Kit's rapidly dropping opinion of Augustus Raven, there were other possibilities. A man who did not take care of his own niece might be unscrupulous in his dealings with others. Had he stolen the paper? Suddenly, the idea of continuing their quest didn't seem so insane. At least, Kit could continue to protect Hero from any who would do her harm—even her uncle.

"All right," Kit said. "Let's get some sleep so we can head to Featherstone's town house. But no more costumes, please."

Hero's lips curved slightly, whether in amusement or relief at his assent Kit wasn't sure. "I'm sorry about that," she said. "I'm not used to working with anyone."

Kit did not comment on her use of the word *working*, which only confirmed his earlier opinion of Augustus Raven. "Well, let's forge an alliance then."

Her delicate brows lowered, as though she was studying him with more than her usual care. "I can see how you would be of help to me, but what possible reason would you have for this alliance?"

Kit grinned. "I told you before. I'm a gentleman."

She did not seem well satisfied with that explanation, but Kit didn't know what else to tell her. Obviously, she thought he had his own reasons for staying with her, and he did, but they were not any he wanted to share at this point. And if he had not convinced her thus far of his honesty, he did not know how else to do so.

Instead, he turned his thoughts toward the morrow as he climbed into one of the two beds available, grateful for a soft berth after the last few nights. Trying not to listen to the sounds of Hero seeking her own rest, he focused on which roads would be best to take to London without alerting their enemies, whoever they might be.

The uncertainty was frustrating, and Kit felt as if he were groping blindly in the dark, unsure of what lay ahead or behind. Cut off from any source of information, he didn't know whether word had spread of the warrant for his arrest or if it had been quietly withdrawn, remaining a local matter. Despite what Hero said, had some hue and cry been raised about her disappearance? Kit had seen no broadsheets with his picture on them, but he did not fancy being carted off to prison by some sharp-eyed fellow on the lookout for felons.

But in order to get news, he would have to make contact with someone he trusted, a dangerous prospect at best. Still, Kit was tempted to appeal to his old

friend Barto, a nobleman with the wealth and resources to provide aid. Kit and Hero could rusticate
at Hawthorne Park while everything was sorted out.
But how could he convince Hero, who already distrusted him, to abandon the search that drove her?

And as much as Kit would like to call a meeting of
the knights of the round table of his youth, what would
he tell his old friend, especially of Hero? Both Barto
and Syd would have questions for him that he couldn't
answer. And even feeling the way he did, Kit wasn't
sure whether Hero was involved up to her pretty neck
in some deeper deception. Was that really the kind of
introduction he wanted to give to his sister and future
brother-in-law?

No matter what the truth was, Kit did not want
them to think ill of Hero. It was a petty reason, and so
he added to it the fact that Syd and Barto would be
deep in planning their wedding, and he did not want
to disturb a happy time that had been so long in coming.

So, if not Hawthorne Park, where? Kit had few relatives, and his friends were clustered around where
Barto lived. Frowning in the darkness, Kit knew they
couldn't return to Oakfield, but there was another stop
on the way to London that might yield up some answers.

"Hero?" Kit whispered, lest she already be asleep.

"What?" Her tone was one of caution, perhaps even
tinged with alarm. And who could blame her after what
had happened in the earl's library? Before, their
dealings had been all business, but now a certain aware-
ness seemed to have seeped into their every encounter.

Kit hurried to explain himself. "I'm thinking of stopping in Piketon."

*"What?"*

"That's where my coachman originally wanted to meet us."

"But I thought he was to leave the coach at Burrell?"

"He urged me to meet him at Piketon, where we could exchange carriages, but I didn't like the idea of dropping the ruse so soon. Not that it mattered," Kit added wryly. "But if something went awry with his plans or he returned to find chaos at Oakfield, he might go there, in the hopes of contacting us."

Kit paused to glance toward the other bed, but could see little in the darkness. "He's more than a simple coachman."

"Just as you are more than a gentleman farmer."

Hero's statement sounded like an accusation, and Kit snorted. "Hardly. Or I would have prevented my sister's abduction."

"What happened?" Hero asked softly.

During the ensuing silence, Kit heard a creak in the room next door, and lifted his head. But it was nothing, only an excuse for him to remain silent. For once, he was the one who did not want to conduct such a personal discussion, and yet somehow the words came spilling forth.

"It began, for us, with my father's death. He and our neighbor Viscount Hawthorne were killed in a carriage accident. We found out later that he had received a shipment of books from the household of my great-aunt, and among them was the Mallory."

Kit heard Hero's indrawn breath, but she said nothing, so he continued. "Father had no idea of its rarity or its significance, but he knew the viscount belonged to some latter-day Druid society. The group was nothing more than an excuse for wealthy landed gentleman to socialize, but at least one other, led by a man named Malet, was not so innocuous. Malet had been searching for the Mallory at Oakfield, driving my great-aunt mad with his efforts to find it and his midnight trips through the maze there. Of course, we knew nothing of that. She died before Father, and I then received the legacy of Oakfield."

Kit winced at the memory of his delight in the inheritance. "From the moment of our arrival, there were strange happenings, but I ignored Syd's concerns. Thankfully, Barto was not so blind, and it is due to him that Syd lives."

"I don't believe that you were that stubborn or heedless," Hero said.

"Oh, I finally believed her when Barto told us of his own suspicions," Kit said, taking no pride in the fact.

"And then?"

"Then Malet picked us off, one by one. He knew that none of the locals would remain at Oakfield on Samhain, and I did little to hold them there. He arranged for some tainted cider to knock out the rest of us. Barto found me along the road."

"If your friend Barto was so clever, why didn't he stop everyone from drinking the cider?"

Kit paused, for he had never really questioned Barto's whereabouts at the time. "He wasn't there."

"Perhaps he was simply luckier than you."

"Perhaps." But Kit couldn't see Barto downing the home-brewed drink even had he been at Oakfield. *Because he was smarter than that. More cautious. Less oblivious.* Kit felt his anger and frustration return.

"Or perhaps his own suspicions made him more wary, and you could hardly be privy to his information or thoughts," Hero said.

That was true, but still, Kit should have paid more attention to what was going on around him.

"So Barto saved your sister?"

"No. Yes," Kit said. "We both rode back to Oakfield, but Syd managed to set fire to the great oak in the centre of the maze, and it spread."

"She sounds like a resourceful woman—who saved herself," Hero said.

"But if I had just believed her from the beginning, she wouldn't have been there, scared to death by hooded Druids intending to murder her." Kit's regret threatened to choke him.

"What happened to them?"

"We assumed they were all killed in the fire, but now I'm not so sure." The admission was a harsh reminder that he needed to stay alert, to protect Hero from such madmen, perhaps even to redeem himself, at least in his own eyes.

"You're taking the blame that should be directed at those responsible," Hero said, absolving him in her usual brisk tone. "Your anger is festering, probably because you never faced the men who did this to your family."

She might well be right, but what good was that realization? Kit could hardly raise Malet from the dead.

"And you may never be able to face them," Hero said, as though reading his thoughts. "But you might make do with those who are chasing us."

Kit's lips curled at the thought of some measure of retribution. He would gladly dole it out if he could get his hands on them, especially since they might well be one and the same.

As they approached Piketon, Hero watched for anything unusual. Although the town was on the way to London, she didn't like veering from her goal, and she was leery of meeting up with anyone else. There were too many variables, too many chances for surprise.

But Hero could hardly refuse to stop unless she was prepared to quit Kit's company, which she was not yet ready to do. The roads presented too many threats to the solitary young man she appeared to be, and though she had many skills, she did not overestimate her abilities.

Nor could she fool herself, Hero admitted bitterly. For no matter how many pragmatic excuses she might give, truth be told, she remained with Kit Marchant because she could not bear to part with him. He had proven to be just as dangerous as she first expected, wielding a power over her that Raven never had possessed.

Hero flushed at the memory she had tried most to banish: the night in the dim library when Kit had leaned over her, pressing his mouth to hers. He had taken her unawares, but like someone under a spell, Hero had let him, overwhelmed by the unexpected sensations, her innate caution abandoned in the heat of the moment.

If that was his sole effect upon her, Hero might have been able to dismiss the incident as a sudden weakness of her gender. But Kit Marchant was insidious, luring her with his gentle touch, his warmth, his humor… *Everything about him.*

Nothing seemed to disconcert the man. He remained calm in every situation, keeping his head while he took appropriate action, all solid strength and reason. Indeed, he was so remarkable, that it was easy to see him as her rescuer, and not just from the storm. But Hero could not take shelter with him permanently.

Raven would not allow it, of course. But more importantly, she could not allow it. Her circumstances were such that she could never form an attachment to anyone, for the risks were too great. For everyone.

And when that knowledge threatened to overcome her, Hero told herself that Kit Marchant could not be what he claimed, that no one would help her unless they had their own motives for doing so. *Even a gentleman.*

And yet… She thought of the tale he had told her last night in the closeness of the room they had shared. For a moment in the dark she glimpsed what she had seen at Oakfield, a man who was holding in anger and grief. And despite her best intentions, Hero had been affected.

*No doubt, that was what he intended.* Hero frowned, uncertain, but unable to dismiss her suspicions. Perhaps someone else could accept Kit Marchant's help and his explanations for it without question. But she had been raised differently, as a pawn on Raven's chessboard. His machinations had so altered her outlook that, even now, she wondered what part he played in all of this.

Hero shook her head. All she could do was move toward the goal and hope that she was on the right path. Nothing else mattered, she reminded herself. And yet, when Kit turned his head toward her, her pulse leapt, her gaze settling upon his handsome face with an eagerness she could not deny.

"This is the place," he said, nodding toward a tall brick building ahead. A large sign proclaimed it the site of the Crowned Head, and belatedly, Hero scanned the area for anything suspicious. The inn was a large one, which meant that they could blend in with the crowd, but others could do so, as well.

Once inside the courtyard, they gave their horses over to a stable lad and walked among the bustle of grooms, postilions, coachmen and servants, all providing for the mail coaches and post chaises, horses and passengers.

Hero looked from the hurrying throng to Kit. "Where would he be?"

Kit shrugged in his usual casual manner, though Hero doubted he was as unconcerned as he appeared. "Let's just look around."

Although Hero felt a measure of safety in her disguise, she still kept a wary eye out, for Kit was recognizable and anyone with him would garner scrutiny. "Perhaps we should separate," she suggested, but he gave her a black look. Was he being protective or laying a trap? Hero slowed her steps, hanging back just enough to avoid any sudden entanglements.

They had nearly completed a circle of the perimeter when Kit paused. "He's here, all right, there by the door to the kitchens."

Hero glanced in that direction and saw a stocky fellow, his cap slung low, lounging against the brick wall.

"I'll keep my distance," Hero said. "I'd rather he not see me dressed as I am." At Kit's nod, she sauntered toward a farm cart that was rolling to a stop nearby. "I'll take care of this for you, sir," she said to the driver, ducking her head.

"Molly usually doesn't need tethering, lad. Just make sure no one steals my goods," the farmer said. Dropping to the ground, he unloaded a large crate of apples, passing by Kit on his way into the kitchens.

Standing silently at the horse's head, Hero kept her face turned away even as she inched closer to the man Kit had pointed out. Although loath to be recognized, she wanted to be privy to the conversation. And as long as the two didn't whisper, she was in a good position to listen.

"Are you all right?" the man called Hob asked.

"Yes, and you?"

From the corner of her eye, Hero could see the fellow nod. "I left the coach in Burrell. Didn't see a sign of the two men, sir, and began to think perhaps they were just a pair of thieves looking for something to steal." He paused. "Then I went back to Oakfield. It appears they raised the stakes."

"Are the authorities still looking to arrest me?"

"I don't know. When I found out about the warrant, I didn't stay around to be questioned. I sent word off to the viscount and decided to come here. I didn't know where else to catch up with you."

"Obviously, they were not fooled by the switch in vehicles."

"No, and they seem to mean business, sir. What of the young lady? Is she all right?"

"She's safe," Kit said.

"Really? And just where might that be?"

At the sound of the new voice, Hero did not turn, but kept her eyes resolutely fixed upon the ground.

"Here, now, put that away before someone gets hurt," Hob said.

Only then did Hero glance surreptitiously toward Kit. He and Hob were pinned against the wall, facing a third man whose back was to her. Obviously, he had some weapon, a pistol or a knife that kept them at his mercy, and Hero's heart hammered violently at the sight.

They had been threatened earlier, but that was before she had come to know Kit Marchant. In fact, the assault on the carriage seemed a lifetime ago, so far in the past that Hero could not believe she had once thought he played some part in it. Now, his life was in danger because of her, and Hero felt a horror that even the worst of Raven Hill's frights had never induced. For an instant, she could do nothing except stare, stricken numb.

"Tell me where the girl is and no one will get hurt," the man said, and his words finally roused Hero to action. Although she could not see his face, she heard the sneer in his voice, the falseness of his promise, and she knew that no one would come out of this unharmed by co-operating with him.

"And just in case you're hesitating, my friend is across the courtyard, ready to join us," he said. "He's still smarting from the tumble off his horse, so if I were you, I wouldn't annoy him."

Tugging on her cap, Hero glanced up and saw that a tall man, hat shadowing his face, was approaching. She had no time to draw her own weapon, and the horse and cart stood between her and Kit. So she gave Molly a smack, sending the animal charging toward the doorway.

Kit and Hob moved out of the way, but the other fellow, obviously counting on his cohort to watch his back, was taken unawares. Knocked aside, he was soon being pummeled by Kit, who exhibited the kind of boxing men paid to witness. Hero had only a startled moment to admire his skill before she maneuvered the horse and its load backward, putting them between the kitchen and the approaching man, who had broken into a run. A quick shove to the cart sent it careening into him.

"Here, now, what's going on?" The farmer, emerging from the kitchens, shouted in annoyance.

"He ran into your cart," Hero called.

The farmer might have been more forgiving if the fallen man had apologized. Instead, the villain lurched to his feet and shoved the approaching farmer out of the way, intent upon reaching his companion. Not taking well to such treatment, the farmer tackled the tall man and an brawl ensued.

By the time Hero reached Kit, he had his assailant shoved against the wall, trying to get some answers. But even as Kit pressed him, the fellow sank to the ground, unconscious. Seizing her opportunity, Hero darted forward and grabbed Kit's arm. He swung round, ready to strike her, before recognition flashed in his dark eyes. Then he shouted for Hob, but a stream of men and boys were pouring from the stables to watch the fight, and they had pushed the coachman into the doorway.

Hob waved them away even as he backed into the kitchens, unhurt, and Hero pulled at Kit, dragging him beneath the cart. Exiting on the other side, they dodged the growing throng and ran to where their horses waited, making good their escape.

# *Chapter Eight*

Hero did not know her way around Piketon, so she followed Kit as he took a circuitous route through the narrow roads and lanes. Perhaps he was sighting from the sun because it soon became apparent that they were heading north, not east. She could only guess the change in direction was to escape their pursuers, who would be watching the road to London when they recovered.

But for once, Hero did not care where Kit led her. She was simply glad that he was unhurt and astride his mount, his familiar form only feet away from her. Although she had learned long ago how to hide her fright, her hands were still shaking after what they had been through.

Before her fear had always been for herself—for her safety, for her sanity, for her ability to evade a situation or to complete a task. But when Kit was threatened, Hero had felt a panic such as she had never known. And it lingered, making her cold and queasy.

She kept her gaze on his wide shoulders, as if he might suddenly disappear from the saddle. *From her life.*

When Kit finally headed off the road toward a sluggish stream, Hero was grateful for the respite. She dismounted quickly, driven by an urgent need to touch her companion, as if the feel of his solid form might assure her of his safety. But she did not know how to approach him, and simply stood by, uncertain, while he watered the horses.

As she watched his graceful movements, Hero felt her throat thicken, as though clogged with some kind of violent emotion. But Kit's casual demeanor was not conducive to dramatic declarations. Nor was she accustomed to making them.

Hero took refuge in a less personal observation. "Y-you handle your fists very well for a gentleman farmer," she said. And he did. She had caught only glimpses, but she was certain that not every member of the landed gentry would be able to acquit himself so admirably in a fight.

"I know a bit of boxing. Just enough to protect myself from someone who doesn't," Kit said, in his usual modest fashion. Then he turned his head to flash her a grin. "You were right. I do feel better after thrashing one of them, though I wish I could have got some information from him first."

Hero might have been gratified by his statement, but she was too horrified by the sight of blood on his mouth. "You're hurt."

He lifted a hand to finger his lip gingerly. "That's to be expected, I suppose, but at least the fellow didn't nick me with the blade he was brandishing."

Hero felt the earth sway beneath her feet. Not only had Kit been in danger, but he had been injured. He was so capable that she had thought him invincible, and the realization that he was not filled her with alarm.

"Don't tell me the imperturbable Miss Ingram swoons at the sight of blood?" he teased.

Hero shook her head as she searched for a handkerchief. It wasn't the blood that made her uneasy, but the fact that it was Kit's blood. The knowledge that he could have been knifed or killed terrified her, making her throat tight. She had blithely traveled with this man, using him just as she would any convenience to meet her ends. And she had justified her actions with the assumption that he was using her, as well.

But suddenly that wasn't important anymore. What was important was Kit's well-being, Hero realized, as she dipped the handkerchief in the cold water and moved toward him. Stepping close, she lifted the cloth to dab at the drop of red, but she was so near that memories of his kisses rushed over her, threatening her tenuous composure.

Hero's trembling fingers slipped, her thumb brushed against his lower lip, and she thought she heard Kit groan. Had she hurt him? Abruptly, he had her wrist in a tight grip, and her gaze flew to his dark one. For a long moment she stood there, her pulse pounding under his touch, before he released her hand.

"Thank you for your quick actions," he said. "I'm glad you didn't leave."

Did he think her so heartless that she would abandon him to his attackers? Hero felt stricken.

"The men didn't know you were there, dressed as you were. So you would have been wise to go since it was you they were after," Kit said. "But as much as I wanted you to get away safely, I wondered how I'd ever find you again."

In the silence that followed his admission, Hero could hear her heart thundering. The husky tone of Kit's voice hinted at something that so closely echoed her own feelings that she was afraid to look into his eyes for fear he might see her thoughts. Yet she stood rooted to the spot, unable to move away, fighting the urge to touch him that had somehow turned into an urge to throw herself into his arms. And stay there.

Even in her current state, Hero knew that no good would come of that desire. Pursuing any sort of relationship was impossible because of what she was, where she had come from, and what her future might hold. That bitter reminder finally spurred her to turn away. All that she had left unsaid would have to remain so, for Kit's sake and for her own.

It was time to resume their journey, to return to her quest and the life that had no place in it for anyone like Kit Marchant. Mounting, Hero watched him do the same, the emotional interlude seemingly forgotten. But her hands shook as she took the reins, proof that she could not so easily put it from her mind.

Kit frowned when the rain began. They'd had unaccountably good weather for days, so it was to be expected. But that didn't make the cold pelting any more comfortable. Hero turned up the collar of her greatcoat and donned a wide-brimmed hat to replace her cap, yet Kit couldn't help worrying about her, and when they came upon a private home that had been converted into a country inn, he was more than ready to retire for the day in front of a blazing hearth.

Unfortunately, all inns were not created equal. Some had terrible food, abusive proprietors, poor servants or those who did little or stole or demanded coin for any service. Others had rooms that were dirty and bug-ridden or cold and damp, without even the meanest of comforts.

Kit should have recognized their fate when the private parlour where they ate boasted only a meagre fire, and their sumptuous meal consisted of hard pota-toes, undone mutton and even less palatable fare. As they sipped their watery wine, Kit tried not to imagine what would have been awaiting him at Oakfield— good, simple food and a hot bath. Thoughts of the latter made him sigh into his plate.

"What is it?" Hero asked, looking up.

Kit shook his head. She must be chilled to the bone, but had not complained at all, so how could he voice his grievances?

"Are you feeling all right? How is your lip?"

Was that concern that shadowed her face? Kit grinned at the thought and touched his mouth gingerly. "I'm all right."

And he was. Despite the discomforts, Kit realized that the dismals and moodiness that had plagued him after the fire were gone, banished perhaps by time or the pummeling he had given his assailant or Hero herself. But now that he felt a bit like his old self, Kit was ready for a little less excitement. And the home he had viewed so dimly just a week ago now seemed a veritable haven, where he could make a life for himself—if he had someone like Hero to join him there.

The thought brought Kit's attention back to his companion, and he frowned at the damp spots on her sleeves. "If you're finished, we should get you out of those wet clothes," he said. The words came out differently than he intended, and Kit pushed away from the table rather than face Hero's reaction. He walked to the small window, where daylight was fading into darkness, but the thrumming of the rain continued.

"I don't want you catching a chill," he explained, something seizing within him at the notion.

"I'm very hardy," Hero said in a wry tone.

Kit turned round to look at her. Certainly, she was taller than most women and seemingly capable of just about any task, but that didn't mean she could not be felled by the illnesses that struck everyone. "Perhaps we should think about taking a coach."

"Passengers on the stage have been known to die from exposure," Hero stated baldly.

"Those on the outside, yes, but I was thinking of hiring a coach, so we could be out of the weather."

"What of the horses?" she said. "And I don't like the idea of being dependent upon anyone else."

Kit frowned. Nothing except their own mounts would give them the ability to escape quickly when necessary, as well as to go about their business without anyone taking note of them or their whereabouts, an important consideration after what had happened at Piketon.

"All right, but if the weather gets too bad, we'll stop for a while," Kit said.

"The sooner we get to London, the sooner we can find the Mallory and foil our pursuers," Hero argued.

Kit felt a twinge of annoyance at her eagerness to end the journey, but he pushed it aside. Right now he had more pressing concerns, and there was something that neither one of them had mentioned.

"The men in Piketon weren't wearing livery," Kit said. Although he'd never believed there was a connection between their pursuers and the Duke of Montford's staff, still he had to admit that such men would be recognizable.

"Maybe they took off their livery, the better to avoid notice."

Kit snorted, unconvinced.

"Or maybe the men in livery are waiting outside."

Kit would have laughed if she hadn't been so serious. Indeed, her calm expression was so alarming that he posed the question even though he knew he would receive no answer.

"Just how many people do you think are chasing us?"

Hero breathed in the moldy odor of the small room and sighed. Although they had asked for two beds, there was only one, and the paltry fire in the small grate produced little warmth. Circumstances had forced her into worse places, but not often. Yet what else could they do unless they were willing to travel by night in the rain?

While Kit went out to call for a chambermaid, Hero

took his advice and quickly changed her breeches and socks. She had no other coat, so hung it up as best she could, though the room's dampness boded ill for anything drying during the night, especially two great-coats and a variety of lesser garments.

She had just finished dressing when Kit returned with a belligerent girl who obviously did not intend to be of much help. She carried a poker with which she stirred the fire, but she did not add any wood until Kit promised her good coin. And even then, the room did not heat.

It was a gloomy night, and Hero might have been excused for being sunk in the dismals. But instead, she felt as though something hard inside of her had crumbled, freeing her from its grip. And even the grim accommodations could not dispel the odd sense of lightness in her chest.

They were alive and well and together for now, and perhaps that was enough, Hero thought. Glancing surreptitiously at her companion, she studied his mouth, where his beautiful lower lip was cracked. Fighting back the urge to touch it, she contented herself with helping him off with his coat.

"Did you change your clothes?" he asked, and his protective manner warmed Hero far more than the wretched blaze. No one had ever cared for her welfare, and no matter what the reason behind his concern, she delighted in it.

At her nod, he began rummaging through his own pack. "Better get into bed then. It's got to be warmer in than out, and I don't want you catching a chill."

Hero didn't pause to wonder just why he cared, but

enjoyed the proof that he did and crawled under the covers, trying not to think about the general cleanliness of the place. What she wouldn't give for a bath. Instead of curling up to sleep as she usually did, she turned over, peeking out at Kit, who was sitting on the lone spindle chair and pulling off his boots.

Hero knew she should look away, but after what had happened in Piketon, she found it difficult to let the man out of her sight. And her view of him in his shirtsleeves, his wide shoulders straining, was arresting. As she watched, he set his boots aside and then stripped off his socks, and there was something about the sight of his bare feet that made her heart trip.

When he covered them with a dry pair of socks, Hero wondered if he would change his breeches, as well. And although she flushed at the thought, she didn't look away when he stood and turned his back to her. He peeled away the buckskin to reveal a brief white garment that clung to his behind and thighs hard with muscle before donning another pair.

They had been sleeping in their clothes, but Hero wondered what he wore when alone. A nightshirt? Nothing at all? Hero stifled a bubble of hysterical laughter at questions that only a week ago would have been unthinkable.

Kit must have heard something because he paused in his circuit of the room, perhaps looking for the driest bit of floor. "What?" he asked.

Without pausing to consider the reckless thought that came to mind, Hero moved over and threw back the blankets. "Here," she said. "As you pointed out, it's the only warm place."

For once, the easygoing Kit appeared startled. "No, I'll be fine in front of the fire."

Hero shook her head. "It's the only sensible solution."

Kit looked right at her, that dark and dangerous glint in his eyes. "I don't think sharing a bed is a good idea."

Hero shivered at his low tone, husky with promise, and she knew she was on treacherous ground. She had no business encouraging any closeness between them, but neither did she want him to lie freezing upon the filthy floor.

"Huddling together might be the only way we both fend off illness," Hero said. "And I don't see a problem because, as you so often point out, you are a gentleman."

Kit's mouth twisted at the reminder, and he put a hand to his split lip, with a grimace. "Even a gentleman has his limits."

Hero shivered again at the stark admission. Although they were both fully clothed, something in Kit's gaze hinted at a different arrangement, should he join her. And her heart thundered in response. For one wild moment, Hero wanted nothing more than to give this man her all, to deny him nothing.

And then? All actions had consequences, and it was the knowledge of what they might be that kept Hero from succumbing to the temptation Kit Marchant presented. Swallowing a groan, she pulled the covers over her head and turned to face the wall, her lightened spirits abruptly dimmed.

But then Hero felt the bed dip and a sudden warmth

by her feet. Peeking out once more, she saw that Kit had taken up a position at the other end. He was sitting up against the bedstead, his long legs stretched toward her, and the last blanket tossed over them both.

"You can't be comfortable," Hero protested.

"I'm all right," he said. Hero would have argued further, but the comfort of his closeness and heat made her shut her eyes.

"Tell me more about this uncle of yours," he said, his voice low in the darkness. "Why does he have you fetch books for him? Is that how he adds to his collection?"

"He never leaves Raven Hill," Hero said. *Like a spider at the middle of his web, he sends his minions out to do his bidding.* "He looks at the auction catalogues and knows booksellers, but he usually won't pay what they are asking. He prefers contacts who look through the various booths and backstreet sales and report what is available."

"Why doesn't he just have them buy it?"

"He doesn't trust anyone."

"But he trusts you?

Hero would have shrugged, had she not been tucked against Kit's solid form. "To a point," she muttered. She often arranged buys, especially whenever Raven thought her wiles and attractiveness might sway a client. And he always said she was smarter than anyone else, though it was hardly a compliment. *Cleverness and cunning will out every time, my girl,* he often said.

But he had many other resources. "He sometimes sends my, uh, cousin, Erasmus Douthwaite Raven,"

Hero said. But Raven claimed Erasmus was too stupid and too greedy to be depended upon not to take his own portion out of the dealings. Which didn't sit well with Erasmus.

"He was for the law, but he would rather be a gentleman of leisure, like Raven. Unfortunately, he doesn't have the necessary funds."

"And where did Raven come by his fortune? What are his connections?"

"I don't know," Hero said. "He probably inherited most of it, for he bought Raven Hill many years ago. Perhaps he sold other property in order to do so. He does have a man of business, so he might well have other investments."

"But he spends it all on books."

"He has done a lot of work on Raven Hill over the years," Hero said. *So-called improvements that suited Raven's fancy.* "That continues, but his main interest now is books and other acquisitions. He's a member of the antiquarians."

However, he hadn't joined in order to write papers or see lectures, but to show off that which he owned and try to obtain that which he sought. Collecting was Raven's mania. Sometimes Hero thought he considered her part of his collection, a pretty decoration no more valuable than the least of his possessions.

At the reminder, Hero frowned and feigned a yawn in order to put an end to the discussion. But she could not return to her earlier ease, and sleep was long in coming. The conversation had cast a pall over her mood, as though Raven, like his namesake, was spreading black wings over her, even here, and reaching out to steal her from her cozy nest.

The next morning, Hero woke to the sound of rain pelting against window panes. Snuggling deeper into her bed, she became aware that she was not at Raven Hill, for she had slept long and well. And she was more comfortable than she ever had been in her life.

The reason for that condition soon became apparent, for when Hero opened her eyes, she saw that she was clinging to a large lump of blankets. Since it was solid and gave off an enormous amount of heat, she realized that Kit must be in there somewhere.

Heart thudding, she glanced around to view the room crookedly. Sometime during the night she must have migrated to the other end of the bed in search of Kit's warmth. Although he was still on top of most of the bedding, it was a tangle, and Hero struggled to extricate herself. For in the bright light of day, the dangers of sharing a bed were far more glaring than in the seductive darkness.

Thoughts of what might have happened—and the dire consequences—robbed Hero of her breath, and she pulled at the material trapping her, only to hear the distinctive sound of it ripping. In an instant, she was staring into dark eyes, alert above her, and for a moment she felt the full weight of Kit's hard body.

"What the devil?" he murmured.

Hero did not care to make her explanations while lying beneath warm, muscular male, and she slid out as best she could, trying not to think about the way he looked, the way he smelled, the way he *felt* against her.

Stumbling to her feet, Hero clasped her arms about her, as though to ward off the man's potent allure.

"I—I think I tore your shirt," she said.

Having discovered no outside threat to either of them, Kit leaned back against the pillow, a lazy smile on his handsome features. "Did I miss something?"

"No!" Realizing that she was reacting far too strongly, Hero tried to compose herself. Where was her cap? She grabbed at her hair, pulling it up tightly once more.

"Look at how late it is. We've slept away half the morning," Hero said, only to choke on the words. "We'll have time to make up."

A grunt signaled that Kit was finally stirring from the bed, though Hero studiously avoided looking in that direction. She busied herself putting on her boots, donning the guise of a boy when she felt less like one every day.

"It's wasn't my shirt that tore, just a bit of pillow-case," Kit said, and Hero sighed in relief. She did not want to waste time trying to find someone to mend it in this awful place, while her own sewing skills were definitely lacking.

She just wanted to leave, to escape the confines of the room, although she knew that the danger did not lie here, but would be traveling with her, ever present, ever tempting… Still, she turned to hurry Kit along, only to find him standing unmoving, a thoughtful expression on his face.

"What?" Hero asked. For once, she couldn't divine his mood. In fact, the man who usually was so relaxed appeared tense and awkward, and Hero braced herself for the worst.

"I have a proposal for you," he said.

Hero drew in a sharp breath at the bald statement and what it might mean. Was Kit finally going to admit to some ulterior motive? Did he want to split the profits from the book when they found it? If so, Raven would never agree, and she could not return to Raven Hill empty-handed.

"What is it?" Hero asked, despite the panic that threatened.

"A proposal," Kit said, as if the word explained itself. He cleared his throat. "Of marriage."

Hero felt the world spin again, and this time, she was so startled that she reached out to the wall in order to right herself. Surely, she had not heard Kit correctly?

"Wh-what?"

Kit smiled. "That's not exactly the reaction I was hoping for," he said. "I know I should be talking to your uncle, but these aren't the usual circumstances, and knowing you, I assume you'd want a more straightforward approach."

But that was just it. *He didn't know her.* So why was he asking her to marry him? The answer came to Hero all too quickly. *It was the act of a gentleman.*

"Is this because of last night, because we shared a bed?" she demanded. But before he could answer, she remembered what else had occurred during the evening. Had she revealed too much of herself—and Raven—in drowsy conversation? "I don't want your pity, thank you," she said turning away.

"I'm not offering you pity," Kit protested.

Although Hero didn't believe him, the reasons for

his proposal mattered little. She could not marry him—or anyone—and she answered automatically. "Thank you for doing me the honor, but I must decline."

"May I ask why?"

Kit's voice was curiously flat, and Hero wanted to explain, but how could she? Perhaps she had caught a chill after all, for she felt the same queasiness that she had yesterday, along with a sudden thickening of her throat that made speech difficult.

In the end, she simply shook her head. Although another male might have stormed off, indignant or angry, Kit was no ordinary man, and perhaps his proposal was not typical, either. As though unaffected by her denial, he nodded curtly and turned to put on his coat.

Hero told herself the offer had been a sham, an act of pity or some ruse to obtain the Mallory. Yet the very notion of wedding Kit Marchant made her chest hurt and her eyes sting. She hurried through the doorway past him, so that he could not see her weakness.

Fighting back a sniffle, Hero realized that she truly was ill, but it was not a chill that afflicted her. She was heartsick. It was an ailment that she never expected to have, but she never could have anticipated Kit Marchant and his power over her, a power that rivaled Raven's.

# Chapter Nine

The foul weather didn't let up, so they rode through a drizzle most of the day. Kit kept trying to veer east, but it seemed that the roads curved, turning back on themselves, and by the time the day was fading, their route had become a muddy track that seemed to lead nowhere.

The proliferation of inns in the past decade had done much to eliminate the time-honored tradition of seeking shelter at private homes, but when Kit glimpsed a light in the distance, he did not hesitate, for soon they wouldn't be able to see their way at all.

The prospect of a night spent in the open put his own disgruntlement in perspective. But he could still not shake the mood that had settled over him after this morning's ill-fated conversation. Obviously, he had learned nothing from Syd and Barto's idiotic behavior, for he'd made a mess of things that equaled their own.

He had spoken too soon. If he'd had time to consider his words, Kit would have handled the situation differently. But when he woke up in bed with a woman, a gentleman tried to make things right.

Although nothing untoward had happened, any reasonable person would view their entire association as untoward, improper…scandalous. Kit's motives were good, but this morning even he realized that things had gone too far and he must do the honorable thing.

Of course, it was not as though he hadn't toyed with the idea ever since first setting eyes upon Hero Ingram, so his heart was in perfect agreement with his head. And the rest of him wasn't averse, either.

But he had spoken too soon, tipping his hand when he should have bided his time, especially considering how little he had learned about the mysterious woman. There was a reason for her refusal, Kit was certain of it, unless he was entirely wrong in his perceptions, which was possible considering what had happened at Oakfield.

Kit shook his head, only to dash his face with cold water from the brim of his hat. He was chilled to the bone, so he could only imagine how Hero must feel, and he spurred Bay forward, past farm fields, low stone fences and a barn. Finally, the light revealed itself to be a rambling farmhouse, with windows glowing and wafts of smoke trailing from its chimneys.

Dismounting, they followed slippery flagstones to the worn door, and Kit knocked loudly to be heard above the rain. A sturdy, genial-looking fellow answered, and Kit doffed his hat, explaining that he and his brother were hopelessly lost.

He had barely finished speaking when a stout female appeared, wiping her hands on her apron. "Oh, let the poor gentlemen in. They'll be drowned out in that, I'll warrant, if not frozen to death."

With a nod, the genial fellow motioned for them to enter, and Kit stepped inside, trying not to drip on the wooden floor inside the entrance.

"Tad, see to their horses," the woman said, and a scrawny lad ran past them like a blur. Two more hastened to follow, but the woman put out an arm. "Did I say Luke and Bill?" she asked the two boys, who were smaller than the blur. They shook their heads. "Then off with you!" But the youngsters, obviously curious about the arrivals, hung back, eyes wide.

"You've got out of the way, that's for certain. We don't see many travelers here," the woman said. "I'm Min Smallpeace, by the way, and this is Bert."

"Christopher Marchant," Kit said. "And my brother Sid."

"Sid," Bert said, with a nod. But Min only gave Hero a sharp glance and continued on. "As it happens, our nephew Clyde is away."

"Off trying to woo a young lady," Bert said, with a chuckle.

"So his room is empty, for the time being."

"Perhaps forever," Bert said.

"Nonsense. I told him he could bring Sal back here," Min argued. "You two get out of those wet clothes, and I'll see what I can find for you to wear. Where's Cassie?"

"Here, ma'am." A young woman appeared, probably some sort of hired girl, and gaped at them, unable to hide her interest in the strangers.

"See what you can find for these two to eat, some of the pork pie and potatoes and apple tart for starters."

"Oh, we can't impose on you," Kit said.

"Nonsense! We can't save you from drowning just to let you starve."

And before Kit knew it, they were in a cozy room under the eaves, with a fresh fire burning in the hearth and a pile of clean, dry clothes in hand.

"Let me have all that you've got with you. I'll wash everything tonight and string it up in the kitchen," Min said, reaching for Kit's pack. For a moment, Kit thought the woman was going to rifle through their things, which might prove awkward.

"We'll bring them out to you," Hero said, stepping in front of the stolid female.

Without pausing, Min turned away, heading toward a low cupboard. "See that you do, and I'll have the boys bring up some hot water." Pulling out a small tub, she eyed Kit up and down. "Not big enough for the likes of you, young man, but perhaps you can squeeze in with your knees up to your chin."

Kit laughed with delight. "Ma'am, if you were not already married, I'd have to propose to you right now, for surely you are the most wonderful of all women," he said, sweeping into a low bow.

"Oh, get on with you," Min said, waving him away with a smile. Her cheeks flushed, she bustled out, shutting the door behind her.

Kit sighed with pleasure in anticipation of a thorough wash, though Hero appeared less enthused. Perhaps she was concerned about his presence, Kit thought, his chill body surging with heat at the notion. But he had no intention of lingering. There was a limit to his control and sharing a bath definitely went beyond it.

Kit slanted a speculative glance at her, for she was rooting through her pack, her back to him, curiously silent. And when she did speak, she tossed the words over her shoulder with a carelessness belied by the tone of her voice. "You've been busy with the proposals today, haven't you?"

"And twice denied," Kit said. "I must be a poor bargain."

For a moment, he thought she might say more, but she shook her head, as though confused by his nonsense. But she needed more nonsense in her life, and Kit would be happy to provide it. *If she let him.*

"Anyone who offers to feed me, clothe me, give me a clean bed *and* provide a bath deserves my devotion," Kit said.

"I don't trust her," Hero said, turning to face him. "And I'm certainly not giving her all of my male clothes."

Kit snorted, rolling his eyes heavenward at her suspicions. "Oh, yes, you are," he said, stepping toward her purposefully. "Even if I have to remove them myself."

Fortunately—or unfortunately—it did not come to that. When the water arrived, carried by a troop of boys of varying sizes, Kit insisted that Hero take advantage of it, while he waited outside the narrow door. When she appeared, she was dressed in someone's cast-offs, complete with a clean cap, and carried her own clothes in her arms.

Ducking inside, Kit made sure that she had left nothing behind, then stripped down to his skin and poked one arm out the door to hand over his wet things, as well.

Although the small tub provided the basic of necessities, Kit vowed then and there to install a bathing room at Oakfield, smaller and less grand than the one they had seen at Cheswick, but a room devoted to bathing nonetheless.

Tossing the dirty water out the window, he could see little but blackness outside, where night had fallen and a steady rain continued. His garments were worn and ill fitting, but dry, and Kit heaved a sigh of relief at the turn in their fortunes.

The neat farmhouse with its hospitable occupants loosed the tension that had gripped him for most of the day, and he was reminded of his childhood home. This place, with its tilted floors and narrow hallways, might not be as well-appointed, but it was comfortable and welcoming.

As if in confirmation of his thoughts, Kit found a couple of boys waiting for him outside the room under the eaves, and they led him down the narrow stairs to the kitchen. When he did not immediately see Hero, Kit felt a momentary panic. Had she been right to suspect even these simple people lodged in the middle of nowhere? But before he could act, Min pushed him into a hard chair and nodded toward the line where Hero was helping Cassie hang up their wash.

"Your brother is quite handy in the home, isn't he?" Min asked.

Kit could only nod. He might have given some explanation for Sid's helpfulness, but then Min set a steaming plate in front of him, and all else left his head as he relished a hot meal that put any inn's offerings to shame.

"Your husband is a lucky man," Kit said between mouthfuls.

"Oh, go on with you," said Min.

Hero lay in bed, staring at the window where a subtle glow gave evidence to a new day, but the sound of raindrops continued. From the direction of the hearth, she could hear Kit's soft breathing, as she had throughout the night, and she felt a sudden pressure behind her eyes.

If she had not slept as well as the night before, Hero blamed her strange surroundings. Inns, with their impersonal accommodations, whether shabby or elegant, were a known commodity, while this place and the quiet farm life it represented was as foreign to her as an Indian dwelling.

Even though the cozy space was warm and dry, the bed as clean as Hero was herself, she had tossed and turned all night. But she suspected it had more to do with what was missing than anything else. Lying there in the half-light, she had to admit that no number of blankets could produce the heat generated by Kit Marchant, who had chosen to bed down upon the floor.

It was the only sensible decision, and yet Hero decried it. Even now she was tempted to join him on the floor, just to be beside him, a mad impulse that set Hero's heart to pounding at the possibility that what she most feared was finally happening. Was she losing her heart or her mind?

A knock on the door made her start, and she reached for the pistol tucked beneath her pillow, but no one tried to enter the room.

"Breakfast is on," the woman of the house called. "Come while it's hot or go without."

Weapon at the ready, Hero watched the door for a long moment before her attention was drawn to the man in front of the hearth. The sound had woken him, and he rolled over, looking delightfully disheveled. His dark hair hung over his eyes, and Hero felt her throat thicken. The worn shirt he wore only made him look more appealing, more manly, more *real. Or was it all part of her fantasy?*

"Ah, breakfast on the farm," he said, his voice deep from sleep. "Who could want more than that?"

Hero shook her head, though she had many more wants, all of them impossible and most of them generated by the man who rose to his feet with such casual grace. Wildly, she wondered whether he could hear her heart pounding at the sight of him; but he seemed oblivious.

"Hurry, I don't want to miss a bite," he said, flicking a dark lock back from his face. "That tart last night was better than anything we've had on the road."

Food didn't interest her at all, but Hero knew she could not remain in bed. Slipping out from the covers, she did the best she could with her hair, thankful for the cap that covered it. If questioned as to why she wore one in the house, she would claim that a scalp problem required constant covering and hope that fears of contracting it would silence the family.

Kit was out the door before she had her boots on, and Hero hurried to keep up with him, following as he veered toward the sound of voices. There, they found the whole family seated at a long table in a dining room, and Hero paused on the threshold to stare at the sight of children eating with adults. Min and Bert or one of the older boys were helping the little ones, but the six youngsters seemed to talk in unison and wiggle as though unable to keep still.

Kit did not hesitate, but stepped forward, while Hero lingered, uncertain. In her dealings with Raven or his antiquarian acquaintances, she had never faced anything like this.

"Here, come sit by me, sir!"

"No, me!"

It took Hero a moment to realize the boys were shouting at her. She looked around for Kit, but he was sandwiched between two of the older ones.

"Settle down, now, lads," Bert said. "Sid can find his seat without any help from you."

Sid? Again, it seemed like a good minute passed before Hero realized they were referring to her, and she hastened to the nearest spot, tucked between two of the smaller fellows.

But her heart was hammering, for when was the last time she had forgotten her role? Although she had never masqueraded as a youth for long, she had always been able to keep her mind on her task. *Always.* Without such concentration, she was liable to make a mistake, a dangerous liability.

Focusing her attention, Hero resolved to eat as quickly as possible in order to soon make her escape from the Smallpeace household and its sharp-eyed matriarch. But the boys kept trying to serve her helpings, and she had to stop them from slopping food all over the table. The one on her right, Max, even dropped a piece of toast in the milk she had been given.

Although Hero tried to follow the adult conversation, there was too much going on around her, too many voices raised in high spirits. She heard something about clothes not being entirely dry and the rain continuing. Was Kit agreeing to remain here?

"We really need to reach our destination, brother," Hero said, dodging a bit of food that flew from Ty's mouth while he talked beside her.

"Nonsense! You'll not get far in this weather. Better to rest yourselves for a day," Min said, and Hero shot her a suspicious glance. She did not trust these seemingly innocent people, though she could not figure out what possible connection they could have to the Mallory.

"Sir? Sir? *Sir!*" Hero gasped as the boy on her left, Danny, tugged on her shirt sleeve. Unlike Kit, she had been given an old waistcoat that hid her breasts, though not as well as her usual costume. But she did not need anyone pulling on her clothes and revealing her secret.

Detaching his grip, she leaned toward the boy's dark head. "What?"

"If you stay, you can meet Harold and George."

For an instant, Hero imagined liveried assailants hiding in the barn, waiting until she and Kit had been lulled into a false sense of security. "Who are Harold and George?"

The boy mumbled an answer, his mouth full of food, and she was forced to duck her head closer to his own.

"They're my kittens."

Hero's face was only inches from the boy's, and instead of viewing him as a strange, vaguely threatening creature, she realized he looked more like an angel, his eyes shining brightly as he spoke. "Kittens," Hero echoed.

"Yes, they're lovely," he said. "You'll love them, too." He reached up to touch her cheek as if in reassurance, and Hero felt the now familiar pressure at the back of her eyes. And for the first time, it had nothing to do with Christopher Marchant.

Maybe she *was* going mad. And yet, the sensation was not frightening. In fact, she lifted a hand to awkwardly pat the boy's head. And when she glanced up, she found Kit watching her so avidly that she blinked.

He raised a finger to point to his cheek. "Um, you've got a bit of jam…"

Embarrassed, Hero swiped at her face with her napkin, removing a splotch of red.

"You'll do well when you have children of your own," Min said approvingly, but Hero jerked in alarm. That could never happen. *Must never happen.*

To cover her reaction, Hero finally resumed eating her breakfast, which tasted as good as Kit had predicted. And after the meal was finished, the youngest dragged her into the main room of the house, which was cluttered with a variety of clothes and toys and implements, none of them collectible, but all more important to these people than anything Raven possessed.

Again, Hero was reminded of her duty, and she realized that she needed to talk to Kit about leaving. But he had promised to play with the children, and they were leaping around him as though he were the Pied Piper, shouting so happily that she could not be heard above the dim.

While they played some kind of game involving marbles, Hero took the opportunity to watch her companion, noting his loose-limbed grace, the wide shoulders that filled out the simple shirt, and the crinkles at the corners of his eyes that proved how often he smiled. His laughter rang out repeatedly, as did that of the boys, until Hero felt as though she had stumbled into a fairy story, where all was warmth and ease.

She knew that the lot of the farm family was not as appealing as it seemed, dependent as they were upon weather and hard work. But there were no harsh words spoken in this house, no machinations, no deceptions, no vying for power. What was treasured was character and goodness and willingness to complete chores, not some trinket whose value was set by greedy old men counting their coins.

Strangers, instead of being judged upon their business acumen, were welcomed and dragged out to the barn to meet Harold and George. Part of a seemingly enormous population of felines, the two were Danny's favorites, an orange tabby and a calico that were smaller than most of the others.

Danny instructed her carefully on how to pick them up. "You mustn't hurt them," he said. "But if you are nice to them, they'll be nice to you."

Such wisdom from such a little fellow, Hero thought, and advice that she should heed more often. Despite Raven's claims otherwise, not everyone was out for their own gain. And Hero recognized that Kit just might be one of those who acted out of charity, not selfishness. Perhaps it was time to let her suspicions go and accept him for what he was, a gentleman.

Lost in thought, Hero was surprised when Danny pressed one of the kittens to her face. The soft fur tickled her skin, as did the gentle purring, and she felt her heart lurch in her chest. Although there were cats on the property, Raven did not believe in pets, so Hero had never befriended them. And, no doubt, he would prevent her from doing so.

That realization left Hero feeling pensive as they returned to the house. Once inside, Danny asked her what she would like to see now, and Hero automatically asked if the family owned any books. The boy excitedly led her to an area in the kitchen where there was a comfortable chair and a small cupboard that held a variety of titles.

"Because of the heat and smoke and moisture, this isn't the best place to keep them," Hero warned.

"Oh, we don't keep them, we read them," Danny explained, which made Hero smile. *As well they should*, she thought.

Crouching before the cupboard, she had just begun to look through the volumes when Kit came to join her. He leaned close to whisper in her ear. "Tell me you aren't going to steal any rare editions from these people."

Startled by his words, Hero jerked her head up, nearly knocking into him. Surely he did not think so little of her? But his mouth was twisted into a wry grin, and she shook her head. Would she ever grow accustomed to his teasing?

It was after he had turned away and Hero was left holding one of the Smallpeaces' older volumes in her hand that the idea came to her. She nearly flinched at the audacity of the notion, but refused to dismiss it outright. After all, she knew how much Raven was willing to pay for the Mallory, so she could guess just how much the edition was worth.

The question was whether she could use the book as a bargaining chip—and gain something for herself for the first time in her life.

While the boys raced outside, Kit stood in the doorway of the stone farmhouse, lingering in order to slip Min a payment for her hospitality. Although she waved him away at first, he persisted, for no inn would have provided such good care.

More importantly, the doubts that had nagged at him since his first glimpse of Hero Ingram had faded away in the midst of the farm family's friendly embrace. Hero might have behaved awkwardly at first, but Kit watched her now as she reached down to hug the youngest, and he could envision his own dark-haired boy in her arms.

"Tell me you'll be marrying the lass."

The words that so mirrored his thoughts made Kit suck in a sharp breath. He turned to see Min's shrewd gaze upon him, leaving him no opportunity to dissemble.

"Of course," he answered simply.

"When?" Min demanded.

"She's a bit reluctant," Kit said, though that was an understatement. Sometimes, he felt like one of those fellows who tamed wild horses, using lots of patience and a gentle hand in order to coax a ride from the most wary. But Kit's recent experiences had taught him that the important things in life were worth the effort.

"What? Why?" Min asked. "Surely you're a prize to please even the most discerning."

Kit studied the unusual creature before him, dressed as a youth and knee-deep in little boys. Although she was out of her usual habitat here, Kit had never seen her behave more naturally. "I don't know," he muttered. "But I'm going to find out."

Hero picked at the meat pie they had sneaked into their room, hoping to eat in silence. Lately, Kit had been asking her all sorts of probing questions about her childhood, her interests, what music she liked, and what books she'd read. But with the exception of the last, she had little enough to share.

Tonight, presumably their last before reaching their destination, Hero longed to just enjoy the company that she would not be keeping much longer. But, as had become his habit, Kit turned to her with a curious glance.

"Have you ever been to Almack's?"

Hero nearly choked on her dry forkful at the question. The thought of Raven making an appearance at the exclusive assembly rooms was laughable. As was the idea of him sending her there. Unless she could complete a book transaction in some secluded alcove, while the *ton* danced around her, there would be no reason for Hero to venture into that world.

"No," she answered, without elaborating. "Have you?"

Kit shook his head. "I understand that you have to be invited to attend, and I've only been to London a few times."

The thought of Kit among all the marriageable young ladies gave Hero a pang, but she pictured him looking dashing in his finest clothes and dancing with the skill he evidenced in everything else. "Since your sister is marrying a viscount, she should be able to gain you admittance."

Kit laughed. "I can't quite picture Syd there, following their strict social rules. And she would have no need to go," he said. "I thought the main purpose of the dancing there was for young ladies to make a good match. Isn't that why it's called the Marriage Mart?"

"I wouldn't know."

"And why should you? You've no need of their services," Kit said. "A beautiful, clever young woman like you could have your pick of suitors. They probably trail after you eating out of your hand, though perhaps not when you are dressed like this."

"No," Hero said, smiling at his lifted brows. No one in society would approve of her disguise or her duties. But then, she didn't aspire to such company.

"No, what?" Kit asked, not to be diverted from his probing.

"No, I don't have any suitors," Hero said. "Where would I make such conquests?" She hesitated to admit that Kit was the first eligible young man she had really met.

"You've never been to balls, dances, country house visits?" Kit asked, his expression dumbfounded.

Obviously, the gentleman farmer had an unrealistic view of her position. Even in the wealthiest of households, poor relations served as retainers, companions, nursemaids or other drudges. At least her occupation was a more interesting one, and in dealing with antiquarians, Hero had met far more unfortunate females—wives, sisters and aunts relegated to unpaid service.

But Hero had no interest in discussing the plight of women. Suffice to say that Kit was wrong in his assessment of Raven as the sort of person who attended such activities or hosted them. "Raven doesn't believe in purposeless socializing," she explained. "He has no interest in others unless he can acquire something from them."

"So he only lets you out to do his bidding?" Kit asked, giving her a sharp look.

Perhaps she had said too much. "You make it sound like I'm a prisoner," Hero protested, her tone light.

"Are you?" Kit's usual careless demeanor was gone, and he suddenly looked dark and dangerous.

Hero's heart pounded, for she had no wish to entangle this man any further in her problems. Raven's reach was long, his resources many, and she did not want his machinations to extend to Kit Marchant.

"I am grateful for the home Raven's given me," Hero said. Rising to her feet, she signaled an end to the conversation.

Kit looked as though he would like to say more, but, as usual, he respected her wishes, and Hero knew a measure of relief for that. But her uneasiness lingered, and suddenly, she hoped that Raven had no idea where she was or who she was with; a hope, like so many others, that was probably in vain.

# *Chapter Ten*

⦿⦿⦿⦿⦿

Once they reached London, they were able to find Marcus Featherstone's home without much trouble, blending into the bustle of town, crowded with conveyances and horses and people hurrying about their business.

"This is it," Kit said, inclining his head toward a tall brick facade in one of the less fashionable squares.

His words seemed sadly prophetic, for this *was* it, perhaps the end of their search and of so much else, Hero realized. Swallowing hard against the sudden thickness in her throat, she knew she must focus on the task at hand, for she would need all her wits about her if she were to carry out her plan.

And that plan meant she was loath to contact Raven, as she once might have, for information about Marcus Featherstone. But without Raven's supply of facts, secrets and rumours that might be used to her advantage, Hero would be going in blind. So she remained leaning against the wrought-iron railings, hesitant to take the next step, for she suspected that Featherstone was not as careless as Cheswick.

"Once we speak to him, word will get out we are looking for something," Hero said to Kit. "And then we'll not only have the duke's men, but every collector in the city in pursuit."

Kit appeared dubious, for he was not convinced of the power of book madness, but he said nothing. And with a frown, Hero finally pushed away from the fence and headed toward the steps to seek out the owner of the Mallory.

A rather worn-looking butler answered their knock, only to inform them that Mr Featherstone was not at home.

"But we've come from Cheswick," Hero said, inching inside before the door could be closed against them. "The earl himself sent us upon an errand."

The butler looked them up and down and shook his head. "You may come in, if you insist, but he is not here."

Featherstone didn't appear to be all that was missing, Hero noted as she looked around. The foyer was empty of furniture, paintings and other decoration, and a glance through doorways into other rooms revealed little else. Was Featherstone moving? Hero felt a stab of panic.

"Is there a man of business we can speak to?" Kit asked.

"All creditors should present a detailed account," the butler said. "If you have one, I can take it."

"We aren't creditors," Hero protested. "We're here on an important errand, referred by Cheswick himself."

The world-weary butler did not appear impressed.

"It concerns a book from the earl's collection," Kit said. "If you would show us into the library—"

The butler shook his head. "The library is empty, sir."

"Empty? But what happened to all the books?"

"I couldn't say, sir."

Hero had an inkling. *Creditors.* Perhaps the collection had been sold to pay them off, she thought with a sinking feeling. But she drew herself up and donned her most businesslike expression. "Then it is even more vital that we speak to Mr Featherstone at once, for the offer I have for this edition could go a good deal toward paying off any debts he may have incurred recently."

The butler appeared skeptical, but shrugged. Perhaps he had gone without his own wages for some time and was long past caring. "You might look for him at the Three Aces," the fellow said.

"The Three Aces?"

The butler pursed his lips. "I believe it is a gaming establishment located on St James's Street."

"Thank you," Hero said. "We will seek him out there."

"No, we won't," Kit whispered as they made their exit. "It must be a gambling hell," he added, once outside. "A wretched establishment designed to part the green or desperate from their money. More often than not, the poor devils can't even win fairly, and if they do, hired thugs are on hand to dispute it."

When they reached the railings, Hero halted. "You are probably right, and normally I wouldn't choose to visit. But this could be our only chance to talk to Featherstone."

"We can wait here until he comes back," Kit suggested.

"*If* he comes back," Hero said, turning to face Kit. "We could kick our heels here indefinitely while Featherstone disappears to the Continent or elsewhere, fleeing one step ahead of his creditors."

"But you can't just walk into such a place and talk to him," Kit said with more vehemence than usual. "These sorts of dens frown on idle chatter."

"Then we'll have to join in the play, if that's the only way to speak to Featherstone."

Kit looked pained. "And what are you going to use for a stake? Those with empty pockets aren't welcome."

"I have some money from Raven to use for expenses, if necessary, in order to procure the Mallory."

Kit frowned. "Fine. I'll go," he said. "We'll find somewhere safe for you to wait since genteel young ladies don't frequent St James's, and I'll talk to Featherstone."

Hero was touched, as always, by his protectiveness. The fact that he still saw her as a genteel young lady after all they had been through said more about Kit than herself. But she shook her head. They were too close, and this was too important for her to take any chances.

For a moment, Hero thought Kit might argue, but he groaned, a sure sign of his capitulation, and she took comfort in the knowledge that he would be with her a little bit longer.

"It could be worse, you know," she said as they headed for St James's.

"What could be worse than marching into a gambling hell with you dressed like that?" Kit asked.

She flashed him a smile, eager to prove that he wasn't the only one with a sense of humor. "At least it isn't a brothel."

Kit stood in front of the Three Aces, eyeing the facade with a jaundiced eye. Although not as elegant as some of the other establishments, such as Crockford's, it gave an appearance of gentility, which probably was why it drew the likes of Marcus Featherstone.

The two massive "gentlemen" at the door looked them up and down with such disrespect that Kit moved closer to Hero, wary that her disguise had been penetrated. It was one thing for her to ride upon the roads dressed as she was, quite another to travel about the city, where all manner of villains were ready to prey upon women and young men alike.

"Are you members?" one of the giants asked, and Kit choked back a snort. Surely, they weren't required to join in order to lose their fortunes at the shady tables inside?

"Marcus Featherstone wanted us to meet him here," Hero said.

"We don't allow creditors to bother our patrons," the other fellow said, studying them through narrowed eyes.

"We're here to recoup our losses...or perhaps not," Kit said, adopting a bored tone.

"He must have a private game going on upstairs," the one fellow said to the other as he ushered them inside.

The interior of the Three Aces was spacious, boasting several salons with high ceilings, chandeliers and mirrors that reflected the scene. Men crowded around the green baize tables of hazard, faro and the decidedly illegal E.O., while servers provided tea or stronger brews. The more serious players wore odd coats or leather protectors upon their sleeves and bizarrely decorated hats in order to conceal their eyes from the light and their thoughts from each other.

When a loud bang erupted from above, Kit wondered what kind of "private games" were to be had there. Some of these places were supposed to be run by famous abbesses, who dealt not only in cards, but in female flesh. The thought that he might have brought Hero into a brothel after all made him wince, and he was all the more eager to complete their business.

"Do you have any idea what Featherstone looks like?" Kit whispered.

"No, but didn't the man say he might be having a private game upstairs?" she asked, glancing in the direction of the curved staircase.

Kit shook his head. "Oh, no, you're not going up there."

But Hero was already moving away from him, toward a drunk stumbling down the steps. "Is Marcus Featherstone up there?" she asked.

"Just blew his head off," the man said. Then he proceeded to cast up his accounts.

Pulling Hero out of the way, Kit wondered if the fellow's words were some kind of gaming cant. A servant came to clean up the mess, but most of the players were too sunk in their own dissipation to even notice the disturbance. The turn of a card, the roll of the dice or the spin of the wheel held them enthralled. Surely, this really was a madness, Kit thought as he surveyed the room.

When he glanced back at Hero, she was again moving toward the stairs, where a couple of white-faced fellows were stumbling down. Whatever the Three Aces was serving up there, it must be strong. Or perhaps the party had been imbibing all night, for when questioned by Hero, they simple shook their heads, hurrying for the exit.

Catching up with her, Kit managed to catch her arm before she could bolt upward. And he was grateful for his hold upon her, for the next two men who appeared were not foxed, but sharp-eyed, shifty-looking fellows. At the sound of Hero's query, they headed straight toward her, frowning and intent.

"I don't think that's him," she managed to say before Kit dragged her away. By the time they reached the exit, Featherstone's name had traveled from one end of the club to the other, voices rising above the usual din of conversation and gambling. And the men who were following them had stepped up their pace.

The burly fellows at the entrance had abandoned their post, perhaps called to more important duties, so Kit and Hero threw open the doors and began to run, trying to disappear into the throng on the street.

"You there, stop!"

The shout that rang out only fueled Kit's steps, and he cursed his height, which made him easier to spot. Ducking, he sought a cart that he and Hero could jump on in order to make their escape. But before he found a likely candidate, Hero surged ahead to where a couple of young men stood with Dandy Horses, or whatever such apparatuses were being called. Knocking one of the fellows aside, Hero climbed on the thing and took off.

Kit could do little else but follow her lead, pushing aside the youth who protested the loss of his fellow's contraption, only to watch himself fall victim. "Excuse me, but I need to borrow this for just a moment," Kit said, as he hopped into the saddle and pushed off as hard as he could. The wheels sent him careening away from his pursuers, and soon he had left both them and the owner of the machine behind.

Kit had seen such things the last time he was in London and knew that young men liked to race them along the thoroughfares, adding to the congestion and crashing into anything and everything. But viewing the contraptions and propelling one were two entirely different things. Without reins, there was no way to change directions, and the two wheels did not respond to nudges, as did a living, breathing animal.

Keeping his balance as best he could, Kit tried to remain upright and propel himself forward, but eventually, he hit a bump in the road and tilted sideways. Although he managed to stop himself by using one leg, he ended up on his side on the ground, his body bruised and battered. Rising to his feet, Kit counted himself lucky not to have caused worse damage.

Kit had been too busy hanging on for dear life to notice what was going on about him, but now he looked frantically for Hero. Although he saw no sign of her, the other Dandy Horse was propped against a shopfront up ahead. Kit put his own beside it, for retrieval by the owner, and looked inside the small shop, but Hero was not there. Stepping outside again, he scanned the crowd to no avail, his worst fears realized at last.

She was gone.

Kit hurried to the inn, afraid of what he might—or might not—find there. Just in case their meeting with Featherstone could not be conducted at once, they had taken a room on the outskirts of the city. It was genteel enough to pass as long-term accommodations for visitors, but out of the way in order to avoid any acquaintances. *Although it didn't sound like Hero had many.*

Kit amended that thought. Hero didn't have the experiences of a typical young woman in society, so she could not count upon such friends for help. But such friends probably would be of little help anyway, especially if she made an afternoon call while wearing boy's clothing.

But Hero might well have contacts throughout town, collectors, book dealers and even seamier sorts that might serve her better. Kit only hoped she was somewhere safe and hadn't been snatched off the streets. No matter how capable she seemed, she was still a woman alone in a dangerous city, harried by at least two villains.

Kit went up the stairs of the inn as fast as he could without drawing attention to himself. Upon reaching the door, caution made him knock softly before opening it. But there was no answer to his summons, and the room, when he entered, was empty.

Cursing under his breath, Kit walked the length and breadth of the space, as though Hero might be hidden behind the curtains or beneath the bed. Unable to face the emptiness, he left as quickly as he had come, hurrying out to check the common room and the courtyard for signs of her low-slung cap. But soon it became evident that Hero was not skulking anywhere around the inn under any guise, male or female.

Kit considered returning to the area where he'd last seen her, but he guessed she hadn't stayed around there any longer than he had. He could go looking for her at Raven Hill, but she appeared extremely wary of returning home, and Kit had no desire to explain to Augustus Raven how he had allowed her to go missing.

The inn was the only meeting place that they had agreed upon, and there was little sense in heading back out to comb the city. Finally, Kit was forced to accept that he had only one choice.

So he sat down to wait.

Hero didn't pause to look behind her. When her velocipede crashed into the rear of a moving cart, she dropped it to the ground and clambered into the load of hay in front of her. Hoping someone would retrieve the abandoned apparatus, she burrowed deep and leaned against the rear panel. It was only after she'd finally caught her breath that she realized Kit had not joined her.

Frantically pushing aside some of the hay that cushioned her, Hero peeked through a crack in the wood, but she could not see him. Even the buildings looked different, and she realized the cart must have turned, its different route taking her farther away from Kit.

A sharp stab of panic nearly sent her leaping from her berth, but the wariness that had served her well in the past kept Hero from moving. If she left her hiding place, there was no guarantee that she would locate Kit, who might have traveled past her in the traffic or fallen behind. But there was a very real danger that she might be found by those who had chased them from the Three Aces.

She could not go back.

With a map of the city in her pocket, Hero could take a sedan chair or some other conveyance back to the inn. But she needed to get her bearings, and the next time the cart slowed, Hero climbed out, slipping into the shadow of the nearest building.

Her first thought was to hurry to the inn, if only to make certain Kit was all right. The fear that he wasn't created a knot in her chest to match the one in her throat. But she needed information, and returning to their room would do little to aid her cause, especially when time was of the essence.

For the first time in years beyond count, Hero felt hope, a fluttering, glimmering glimpse of something beyond the walls of Raven Hill. It was that hope, and the plan it depended upon, that gave her strength of purpose. Hailing a passing boy, she gave him a coin to find out what had happened at the Three Aces in St James's, promising him another coin upon his return.

The sun would be setting soon, so Hero urged him to hurry. And just in case he should be waylaid, she glanced across the street for a place to wait and watch for his return. As fate would have it, there stood a bookshop, William Strong's, and Hero headed toward it.

These days the retail book trade was centred in Picadilly, Pall Mall and St James's, with new shops springing up to cater to the customers living in the most fashionable new sections of London. But Hero rarely did business in such public places, so she did not know them all.

Still, the moment she entered, she was assailed by the familiar smells of ink and paper and leather bindings, as though being welcomed home. Inhaling deeply, Hero wandered the premises, looking over the newest publications, as well as the many reprints of older titles, while glancing periodically out of the bow windows for the boy.

William Strong's had nothing for the serious collector, unless such offerings were kept behind the counter, and Hero resisted the temptation to ask. The less contact she had with others while in her current guise, the better. Such thoughts set her nerves on edge, and at the sound of a door opening, Hero flinched. Since she heard no corresponding tinkle of the bell, she glanced up warily.

The front of the shop was still and quiet, so she looked over her shoulder. Behind the long counter, a door had opened, perhaps leading to a storage area or select stock. The latter was probably likely because the man who exited clutched a wrapped parcel to his breast. He was short, with dark, stringy hair and shifty eyes, and Hero was struck by the sensation she had seen him before.

Quickly, she turned her head and hunched over a book to avoid notice. Was he one of Raven's minions, or just a fellow buyer she had glimpsed during some past encounter? Either way, he should not recognize her, dressed in her boy's costume.

Yet, somehow Hero felt his gaze upon her. Refusing to look up, she ducked her head and tugged on her cap, pulling it down over her face. Hardly daring to breath, she waited for the sound of footsteps to go past her, but they did not, and suddenly she was nearly knocked down by a hard jolt.

"Excuse me…sir." The man's voice sounded odd, and Hero did not respond, but crouched to retrieve the volume she had been holding, her eyes focused on a pair of worn boots.

"How clumsy of me," the fellow said. "I hope you are not hurt."

Shaking her head, Hero cursed herself for stepping into the shop. She should have known better, for the book world was an insular one where most serious players knew each other by name, by reputation, and perhaps even by face.

When the man finally shuffled away, Hero still kept her head low, refusing to lift it until she heard the tinkle of the bell over the door. Only then did she surreptitiously peek around the cover of the volume she held to her face. She was in time to see the back of the shifty-eyed man's coat as he stepped outside, confirming her suspicions that he was the one who had run into her. But was the action deliberate?

Putting aside the book, Hero walked to the bow windows, but the man had already disappeared into the street. Had theirs been a random encounter, or was he even now hurrying to alert Raven to her presence in town? Hero knew only that she could not afford to linger here where she had been marked.

Slipping from the shop, she glanced up and down the street, taking special note of any shadowy corners where shifty eyes might be watching. Although she did not see him, she saw the boy she had paid approaching their meeting place. Again, Hero scanned the area for any signs that he might be accompanied or followed, then hurried across the roadway to meet him.

"Sorry I'm late, sir, but I'm not used to finding out the news, just handing it out. I'd sold all my gazettes when you saw me. But now, I'm thinking I might just become a reporter someday."

"Maybe," Hero answered, too nervous to smile at the boy's bravado. "What did you find out?"

"It was a shooting," he said. "A gentleman killed himself right in one of the gambling places, not one of the fancier establishments, mind you, but still, the kind where they aren't used to that sort of thing. It's called the Three Aces. He'd lost his fortune, they said."

Hero felt a stab of panic. "Killed himself? Are you sure he's dead?"

"Saw him for myself, sir," the boy said. "Or what was left of him as they carried him out. I guess his brains are splattered all over the salon where he did it. And on some of the patrons, too, I'll warrant."

Hero felt sick. Perhaps men, even boys such as this one, could handle such frank talk, but her stomach churned and bile filled her throat.

"You all right, sir?" the boy asked.

Hero nodded, trying to fight off the nausea that threatened, along with the emotions that Raven claimed she didn't possess. He was wrong, of course. She simply had learned to keep her feelings to herself, and now she used that skill to dismiss visions of Marcus Featherstone, a young man in the prime of life, reduced to debris on the mirrors of the Three Aces. She had never met him, but he was a lover of books, a collector, someone's friend, someone's relative, and Hero felt the loss.

Fighting against the thickness in her throat, Hero managed to catch her breath only when her own loss became glaringly apparent. Without Featherstone, how was she to follow the trail of the Mallory? Her sorrow over his death twisted into despair, as all the hopes and plans she had so recently devised were dashed.

Was she doomed to resume her old life, hunting and fetching at Raven's beck and call, prey to his increasingly bizarre whims? Hero's heart thudded at the thought of returning to that world of darkness and gloom, greed and deception. Helpless. *Hopeless.* After her brief escape, it would only be that much harder to endure.

As would Raven's displeasure at her failure.

Perhaps Kit was right about the Mallory. It certainly

had a history of bringing misfortune to all those who owned it—from the murdered author through to poor Featherstone, dead by his own hand. In that case, Raven would be a fitting owner for the calamitous volume, Hero thought, though she instantly regretted it. Despite all, she did not wish Raven ill, just that she might be free of him.

If only there was a way to satisfy him without actually proffering the book, but how? If the Mallory had been among Featherstone's possessions, it would eventually make an appearance. Unless, if Kit was correct, and there was no copy to be found, then…

Suddenly, Hero thought of Thomas Laytham, a respected bookseller and collector whom Raven dismissed with contempt. Although Laytham hadn't a hint of scandal to his name, Raven didn't trust him or the hundred-year-old pamphlets that he was famous for procuring for his wealthy clients.

"He's a clever one, I'll give him that," Raven had told her. "And as long as he does me no ill, I'll keep my suspicions to myself. But it takes one to recognize one, my dear, and I think someday the truth will come out when it comes to the revered Mr Laytham."

The idea that came to Hero now was so audacious, her breath caught. Surely nothing could come of her wild notion, yet the urge to pursue it was so strong that she could not easily dismiss it.

"Are you all right, sir?"

Absorbed in her own thoughts, Hero had nearly forgotten the boy standing before her until he spoke. "Yes," Hero answered, handing him the coin she had promised.

"Will there be anything else, sir?"

Glancing at the waning day, Hero was filled with a sudden urgency. "Yes, you may fetch me a hackney coach."

While Hero watched the boy set off with a nod, she realized she wouldn't have time to return to the inn. But perhaps that was just as well, for she suspected that Kit would not approve over her plan. *It was not the act of a gentleman.*

But Kit could not understand what this opportunity meant to her. He'd never been desperate, for even stripped of his property, he had opportunities. He could join the military, take up a trade, cast himself in with friends or relatives. Hero could do none of that. Still, she did not want him to think poorly of her—or see her for what she was: what Raven had made her.

In an instant, Hero decided to pursue this scheme alone, though her pulse pounded at the thought. Raven's presence in her life had been omnipresent and stifling, but the realization that she had no one, not a chaperone or footman or companion of any sort at her side, was more alarming than freeing.

The wisest course would be to send a message to Mr Laytham, but Hero could not risk anyone learning of her interest. Nor did she have the time to wait for an appointment. If the shifty-eyed patron at William Strong's recognized her and reported her presence to Raven, it wouldn't be long before his minions were out looking for her.

Her heart hammering, Hero hesitated, but the stakes were too high to give in to personal fears. When the hackney coach arrived, she straightened her spine, stood tall, and gave the driver the address of Thomas Laytham, Bookseller.

# *Chapter Eleven*

Mr Laytham was not in the habit of working behind the counter in his shop, so Hero spoke to one of the men in his employ. Since her clothing hardly marked her as the sort of wealthy client with whom Laytham normally dealt, she had to convey that it was a matter of urgency and importance, involving one of the hundred-year-old pamphlets he so prized.

The ploy worked. Hero was immediately shown into an office where Laytham conducted his more mundane business. He was an older man, his middle grown thick, with a shock of white hair and the air of a scholar about him. At the sight of his solemn demeanor, Hero felt her resolve weakening and took a deep breath.

"And what is so important, pray tell, Mr…?" Laytham looked askance at her obvious youth and ill-fitting clothes.

"Sidney Marchant," Hero answered automatically. "Thank you for seeing me, sir."

By all appearances, Mr Laytham was just what he professed to be, a gentleman, a collector and a purveyor of books, and yet Raven was rarely wrong in his assessment of people. And despite Laytham's studied air of annoyance as he looked down his nose at her, Hero thought she detected a bead of sweat upon his brow. Either way, there was only one way to play this.

"I'm here for a favor, actually," Hero said in her most businesslike manner. "I'm looking for a book by Ambrose Mallory."

Laytham grunted in surprise. "Aren't we all?"

Hero smiled. Leaning forward, she steepled her hands in front of her. "Yes, but all I need is a facsimile."

Did the man twitch? Hero saw a flash of something in his eyes before the white brows lifted, and she was grateful for the years of experience that kept her own face impassive.

"I don't know what you mean," he said.

"It's a prank," Hero said, falling back against the elegant cushion of her chair. "Nothing that will be sold, of course, but it must be able to pass initial scrutiny."

Laytham's brows fairly leaped off his face, which was growing ruddy in color. "You are asking me to…find you an edition of a book that is not authentic? A…hoax?"

Hero nodded. "It shouldn't be difficult." Indeed, she could do it herself, if she had access to an antiquarian library, except for printing the title page and the cover. After all, no one knew the contents except for some dead Druids. "Since there are no reliable sources as to the contents, any old occult text would do."

Laytham's skin turned beet-red. "And why on earth should I agree to this preposterous request?"

Hero met his angry stare without wavering. "I think you know why."

Laytham held her gaze for a long moment before looking away. "If you mean to tell me that you have chosen Laytham's for its ability to acquire the unusual and meet its customers' expectations, I will not disagree. However, what you are asking for is hardly within our purview."

Hero said nothing, while Laytham fiddled with his watch fob, then grunted, as though coming to a decision. "If it is to be used only for amusement, I suppose I could ask one of my contacts within the book business to prepare something for you." He paused to eye her directly. "No money would change hands, of course."

"Of course," Hero said, though she had not foreseen this development. She had been prepared to use some of Raven's funds in order to deceive him, an irony that was not lost upon her. But obviously, Laytham was more concerned with whom she might be working for, and it was not Raven or any other collector who had him worried. Someone in authority or a wealthy patron could well have put her up to this game in order to catch Laytham at it.

"I'll need the volume as soon as possible," Hero added.

Laytham winced, but nodded. "And where shall I have the parcel delivered?"

"I'll come to pick it up," Hero said, unwilling to give out an address, even that of the inn. "Tomorrow."

"That's absurd," Laytham sputtered. "It might take weeks—or months—to find an appropriate text."

*I don't have months or weeks or perhaps even days*, Hero wanted to scream. But she schooled her features to reveal none of her panic. "The day after."

"The ink will hardly have time to dry upon the page!" Laytham protested.

"Then let it smear," Hero said. "I'm sure you don't want long, drawn-out dealings in this matter."

Gaping at her, Laytham shook his head in honest reaction. Then he rose to his feet and ushered her from the room, displaying only the barest civility, his relief at her departure obvious.

Once outside the bookshop, Hero felt her knees shake, and she leaned against a nearby fence in order to right herself. She was playing a dangerous game—one that could cost her everything, for she shuddered to think of what would happen if Raven found her out. But when fright threatened to overcome her, Hero told herself that she would use what Laytham provided only if absolutely necessary.

Meanwhile, she could still try to track down Featherstone's books. With that in mind, Hero went over all that had led her to this point, considering any pieces of the puzzle that she might have missed. But she came up with nothing, except the oddity of Raven having the scrap of paper that referred to the Mallory, but not the book itself.

Perhaps Raven alone knew the answer to that mystery. And yet…there might be another who could help. Straightening with new determination, Hero pushed away from the fence and began looking for another hackney coach. By now it was full dark, and she had no intention of walking the streets of London alone, even in boy's garb. Besides the various men who had trailed her since Oakfield, she wanted to escape anyone who might have followed her out of Laytham's.

For Hero was not so witless as to savor her triumph over the bookseller. A lifetime of wariness told her that despite the seeming ease of her transaction, she might have made a powerful enemy—to add to those already in pursuit.

Kit was pacing. It was something Barto might have done while Kit watched askance, sprawled in comfort, with no real worries of his own. But now he understood the need for movement, the urge to do something to alleviate the fear that pressed down on him like a weight. *Fear for Hero.*

Looking back, Kit wished that he had not left St James's, but had combed the area for her. He had thought the Dandy Horse proof of her escape, but anyone could have retrieved it and propped it there for its owner—even the two men from the Three Aces.

The thought of Hero being manhandled by those thugs and discovering that they had a young woman, not a boy, in their clutches was enough to make Kit's blood run cold. They were after money, he told himself, not anything else, yet that sort could easily turn from bad to worse.

And here he was, useless and helpless, just as he'd

been at Oakfield. Swearing under his breath, Kit swung a fist in the air, nearly punching a hole in the wall. At the thud of a knock, he looked at his own hand, as though it was responsible. Then he turned toward the door, where a chambermaid probably waited to light the fire.

But when he thrust open the worn wood, Hero stood before him, and without conscious thought, Kit snatched her up in his arms, hugging her to him with bone-crushing zeal. He might have kissed her, too, if not for the sound of a throat loudly clearing itself down the hall. A glance revealed a large man with expansive mustaches eyeing them with disfavor.

"It's been a long time, brother!" Kit cried, before dragging Hero inside.

And then he did kiss her.

Slamming the door shut, he pushed her up against the smooth surface and lowered his head, taking her mouth for the first time since those brief moments in the library at Cheswick. And this was no tentative exploration, but a white-hot possession, an exultation that she was here and unharmed.

When his lips touched hers, Kit felt her startlement, yet she was soon clinging to him, returning his greeting in kind. Her arms wrapped around his neck, and her body, dressed in boy's clothes, strained against his own. He kissed her until they were both breathless, his blood running loud and fast in his ears, and still he did not stop. The cold room, bereft of light and fire, dropped away, leaving only heat and scent and sensation.

The darkness had always been his downfall where

Hero was concerned, for it was easier to ignore the promptings of his conscience when nothing existed except the two of them. Running a hand up the back of her neck, he knocked aside her cap and loosed her hair, wrapping his fingers in the smooth silkiness, just as he tried to wrap himself around every bit of her.

In fact, he might have tried to take her to the bed, stumbling across the unfamiliar floor to grope for its soft surface, if not for the knock that soon sounded. Kit was of a mind to ignore it, but he felt Hero stiffen in his arms, and then her palm came up to cover his mouth, a silent warning not to forget their situation.

Kit stepped back, prepared to tackle anyone who would gain entry, all his unspent passion now changed to fury. But it was only the chambermaid, coming to light the fire. Mumbling uneasily, she cast an odd glance at the darkened room seemingly occupied by two men, for Hero stood behind Kit, her hair and cap restored.

If only Kit could regain his senses so easily. As soon as the maid left, he turned on Hero. "Where the devil have you been?" He lifted a hand to run through his hair. "I nearly went mad with worry!"

"I was trying to find out what happened to Featherstone."

"Featherstone!" Kit wanted to throttle her. "Don't tell me you went back to the hell."

She shook her head. "I paid a boy to nose around and report back."

Kit felt a tumult of anger and relief. "You should have come directly here," he said, even though he knew remonstrance was useless. Hero would always follow her own course, risking her life over what seemed senseless to him. With the taste of her still on his lips, Kit wondered whether she would ever be content to sit back, out of harm's way, with no dealings to make, no mystery to unravel, no treasures to search out.

The thought sent his mood deflating like one of Montgolfier's balloons, all his emotions spent. Perhaps the answer he'd been seeking had been before him all along, a realization that left him stunned and gaping, while Hero prattled on about Featherstone.

"What?" Kit asked, his voice strained, as he tried to marshal his wits.

"They're saying Featherstone shot himself, supposedly despondent over losing his fortune."

"I imagine his fellows think ill of him for dirtying up their table," Kit muttered. He had not known Featherstone, but lost fortunes and even deaths were little regarded in a world where gaming was encouraged without thought for the consequences.

"Probably," Hero admitted. She wore an expression Kit had come to know too well, and he stifled a groan.

"What?" he asked.

"I'm sure the boy faithfully reported what people were saying, but what if Featherstone didn't shoot himself?" Hero asked. "Perhaps those men who started chasing us killed him over the Mallory."

"In a roomful of gamesters?" Kit asked. "I doubt it."

"We don't know who else was in there."

"I'm guessing the fellow who cast up his accounts at our feet," Kit said drily.

Hero frowned. "But if Featherstone shot himself, why were those two men chasing us?"

"We have a sign over our heads asking two men, not one or three, mind you, to chase us at all times?"

Hero was not amused, and Kit sighed. Sometimes, her logic was more convoluted than sensible, for he could not imagine how two thugs from a gambling hell could be connected to an old book that probably did not exist.

Kit shrugged. "They heard us asking about Featherstone and thought we might be friends or relatives from whom they could squeeze the money he owed them."

"What?"

"Some of these cent-per-centers are quite capable of ungentlemanly actions," Kit explained. "Murder would do them little good, but seeing their hopes of repayment dashed, they might look to their victim's heir. Some hells provide their own unscrupulous lenders in order to better fleece their clients."

Hero appeared unconvinced. "Why would such fellows give chase?"

"To get a name, an address, a payment, a promise. If Featherstone has nothing, they have little chance of recouping their losses, but they might press his acquaintances to make good his name. The entire world doesn't revolve around your quest," Kit said, more sharply than he intended.

"No, but sometimes I think the entire world revolves around Raven," Hero muttered.

"So now what?" Kit asked, before realizing that his words could be interpreted in many different ways.

Hero sat down in the room's only chair, and Kit realized just how tired she must be. He had been so consumed with his own fears and frustrations that he had forgotten that Hero, despite her often stoic bearing, was not invincible. She leaned forward wearily to stare into the fire.

"Obviously, Featherstone cannot tell us the fate of his books," she said. "And we could spend weeks trying to hunt them down, interviewing his servants, his friends, his family."

Was she giving up? The suspicion startled Kit, but her features soon took on the cast he well recognized.

"But I was thinking that there's someone else who might be able to verify where those lots went, someone we might approach first." She glanced up, her gaze intent. "Only the people who arrange the sales can really account for the whereabouts of the volumes under their care."

"You think Featherstone had someone in charge of his collection?" Kit asked, dubious.

"No," Hero said, waving a hand in dismissal. She eyed him intently. "I'm talking about Richard Poynter."

"The man who handled Cheswick's library?"

Hero nodded.

"Do you know where to find him?"

"The world of books is an insular one. And more often than not, the only place one leaves it for is the grave." Leaning over to tug off one of her boots, Hero rubbed the sole of her foot. "These days Mr Poynter works with the London Institution."

Kit shook his head at her determination. There was no stopping her, ever, which meant if she really wanted something, she would surely go after it with the same single-mindedness she exhibited in her search for the Mallory. The thought was a discouraging one.

"Here, let me do that," Kit said. Kneeling before her, he brushed away her protests and unrolled her sock. Her foot was pale and smooth, delicately formed, and cold to the touch. He rubbed it briskly with both hands, then began to gently knead.

"Y-you prove your skills yet again," Hero said softly. She cleared her throat. "For a gentleman farmer you handled the velocipede very well."

"I assume that you didn't see my ignominious dismount," Kit said. "And where did you learn to ride such a beast?"

"One of the antiquarians," she said with a faint smile. "A member of the society gave one to Raven, who had no use for it, of course."

"And you quickly mastered the technique."

"I don't think there is much technique involved," Hero said.

She groaned at his touch, and Kit had to remind himself that the massage he was giving her was therapeutic, not erotic. Removing her second boot, he set to work on the other foot. "Though I imagine one would have an even more difficult time trying to ride side saddle."

Hero made a low sound of amusement that turned into another groan. "I don't care to know how you acquired this skill, gentleman farmer," she said. "But is there nothing you can't do?"

*Yes*, Kit thought. *I can't seem to capture the one thing I want.* But he didn't voice his thoughts aloud.

Hero leaned back her head and sighed. "Kit…"

"Hmm?"

"You'll remember that you are a…gentleman."

"Yes," Kit assured her, despite his ministrations.

He'd forgotten that for a while, earlier this evening. But it was a momentary lapse in judgement, a mistake that he would not make again.

It felt good to take off the breeches.

Although there was a certain freedom to be had in wearing boy's clothing, Hero was happy to don her feminine garb. And Kit's surprised delight in her transformation only added to her contentment. For a moment, Hero felt nearly normal—until she had to sneak out of their room, which was supposed to be occupied by two brothers from rural environs.

Once they were outside, Hero relaxed into her role and Kit gave her his arm. "To what do I owe the pleasure of your company, miss?" he asked.

Hero tucked her gloved hand over his sleeve, and she was surprised to feel her cheeks grow pink at the gallant gesture. Although they had spent a lot of time together, little of it was in her current guise, and even less engaged in the typical pursuits of a young man and a young woman.

"And where shall we go today, to see the sights of London?" Kit asked, inclining his head toward her.

Hero laughed, though she suspected he might be serious. She was reminded again that her quest was not his, and she was grateful for his continued company. "I live on the outskirts of town, so I am no visitor."

"Well, then, perhaps you would show me the city?"

Hero shook her head, but could not stop her smile. She was glad to see the return of the careless charmer that was Kit. Last night, he had been moody and sulky, unusual behavior for which she felt accountable. Hero didn't know much about what went on between men and women, but she knew that they should not have kissed as they had.

Warmth flooded Hero's cheeks at the memory, a wild, wonderful interlude in which she had thrown caution to the wind, along with most of her wits. But she could not afford to do so again. And walking about the streets of town, where anyone might mark her steps, would not be wise. As she had discovered, Raven's contacts were everywhere.

"I'll be happy to show you the Institution, which is in the house that once belonged to Sir William Clayton," Hero said, focusing upon her goal. "And it is to Richard Poynter that you owe the return of Miss Ingram, for I hope to trade upon my connection to Raven."

The gamble was a risky one, of course, for Raven would soon hear of it and know of her presence in town. *If he didn't know already*, Hero thought, the memory of the shifty-eyed fellow from William Strong's shop still fresh in her mind. But with Featherstone dead, Hero was counting on Richard Poynter's help, and he was far more likely to meet with Miss Ingram than Sid Marchant.

Suddenly, Hero slanted a glance at her companion. "But how shall we introduce you? We can hardly pass you off as my brother."

"Perhaps I could be your cousin, Erasmus."

Hero laughed aloud at the thought of the handsome, dashing and kind Kit impersonating the stooped, balding and grasping Erasmus. She could only hope that Mr Poynter had never met Erasmus before—and that Erasmus would never discover the charade. If she obtained the Mallory, it would matter little, for Raven would handle his nephew, and then…

Hero drew in a sharp breath. *If she obtained the Mallory.* But she refused to consider the possibility that she would not, and she marched up to the Institution, just as though Richard Poynter was expecting her to call.

He wasn't, but they were shown into the small salon, where Hero began to hope that he would see them. She perched nervously on the edge of a cabriolet armchair, while Kit roamed the room, looking at the books that were scattered about.

Hero idly wondered if they had traded places, for she should be the one searching out some rare title in the hopes of bartering it from its owner. And then she wondered at the changes in herself, for not that long ago she would have suspected her gentleman farmer of searching among the volumes for his own gain.

But Kit was no bibliomaniac, and when he spoke, it was not to marvel at some obscure edition, but to quote from it. In the original Greek. Hero glanced up at him in surprise. "You *are* a scholar."

Kit laughed. "Hardly. I just had a good teacher."

"But you are still a reader?"

"Of course, though I've pretty much abandoned the ancient texts that so consumed my father. I'm more interested in the new fields of science, especially agriculture these days," he said, flashing her a grin.

"That doesn't make you any less of a scholar," Hero said, the need to defend him nearly sending her to her feet. Admiration for him swelled, then turned into something else so strong that it nearly frightened her. But she was never one to shrink in fear, and she would not do so now.

"You are a gentleman and a scholar," Hero said, her voice cracking with the force of her emotion.

Kit must have noticed, for he shot her a speculative glance, but Hero was saved from any questions by the arrival of an elderly man. Slender and gray-haired, he introduced himself as Richard Poynter and greeted them graciously. But after a perfunctory glance at Kit, his attention settled upon Hero, his pale blue gaze lingering with interest.

Hero did not flinch under the scrutiny, for she was accustomed to the curiosity of the antiquarian community. Women with aspirations to join the ranks were limited by their lack of education and their inability to travel freely, whether their destination be libraries or ruins. Exceptions, such as Dorothy Richardson and the notable book collector Richardson Currer, were rare, and Hero often had to deal with contemptuous and dismissive colleagues.

But Richard Poynter was not one of those. Gesturing toward the chairs, he took a seat himself, setting aside a pile of papers. "Excuse my haphazard housing here, but I am only providing some aid to the current librarian." He eyed Hero again. "A fact which is not well-known."

"Raven likes to keep well informed."

"I dare say," Poynter said. "I have heard that you

often act for him these days, Miss Ingram. Is he not well?"

"He is fine, but perhaps more reclusive."

"Ah." Poynter nodded, and the simple word implied that he knew far more about Raven than he might say.

"Actually, I'm here on my own," Hero explained. "I was hoping that you might clear up something for me."

Poynter appeared surprised, but he nodded in agreement.

"We've been trying to track some lots from the Cheswick library and have met with a discrepancy. The current earl told us he directed that the volumes go only to certain individuals, yet it appears that Raven possesses at least one."

Hero assumed a suitably puzzled expression. Hopefully, Poynter did not know Raven well enough to suspect he might have obtained the book through questionable means.

Poynter sighed. "Well, you have found me out."

Since Hero had expected him to suggest that Featherstone had sold or gambled away his lots, she tried not to appear shocked at his admission.

"The current earl had some eccentric notions of how to handle the distribution," Poynter said. Though the elderly gentleman maintained his gentle demeanor, Hero suspected he was putting a polite gloss on the experience. However likable the current earl was, he had no respect for books, and a devotee such as Poynter would be appalled, not only by the breaking up of the collection, but by the cavalier instructions.

Pausing, Poynter glanced toward them both. "I

assume you heard of the unfortunate passing of Mr Featherstone."

Hero nodded, as did Kit.

Poynter shook his head. "The earl wanted only those few collectors he liked personally to buy the lots, but I soon came to realize that Featherstone was not in a position to make such a large purchase. Not wanting to go against his lordship's wishes, I suggested to Mr Featherstone that he act as an intermediary, accepting the lot on the behalf of someone else, while taking a small payment for himself to do so."

Poynter paused then, as if assessing his audience. "Naturally, I would not wish to earn the earl's ill will, should he hear of this."

When Hero and Kit both nodded in confirmation of their silence, Poynter eyed Hero with that same look of curiosity she had seen earlier. "Mr Featherstone gladly accepted the commission, handling receipt of the lot that then went to Augustus Raven."

Hero drew in a sharp breath. Did Raven already own the Mallory? She knew that it took time for some buyers to organize and catalogue their purchases, but not Raven, who was meticulous enough to have found the torn scrap of paper that had sent her on this quest.

Was it all some bizarre jest or test, yet another piece of drama orchestrated by Raven? Or had the man finally gone mad, putting her through the paces of a Gothic novel only he envisioned?

"I see you appear baffled," Poynter said. "Isn't that the mystery you were trying to solve? How Raven ended up with the lot that was to go to Featherstone?"

Numbly, Hero nodded.

"Is it possible that someone else might have bought some of the titles?" Kit asked.

Poynter shook his head. "I had dealings with Raven, only, and he is unlikely to have shared his spoils." Poynter then paused as if in thought. "At the time, I was also approached by the Duke of Montford, but too late. The arrangement had already been made with Raven."

Ignoring Kit's startled glance at the mention of the man she so often claimed was pursuing them, Hero kept her attention focused on Poynter, in the hopes that he might reveal something else of interest.

Although Hero had come to think of Montford as a threat, Poynter's expression left no doubt that he would rather have dealt with the duke. He frowned, a look of disapprobation on his face. "I thought perhaps Raven would be willing to concede out of loyalty to his old employer, but he was not."

"Old employer?" Kit echoed, while Hero sat in stunned silence.

"Why, yes," Poynter said, eyeing them curiously. "Your uncle and I once both worked for the duke, years ago when his Grace was first in the thrall of bibliomania. Of course, that was before your uncle was known as Raven."

"What?" Kit blurted out.

Hero was just as stunned, but she was more aware of their roles as niece and nephew to the man and schooled her features accordingly.

"Why, yes," Poynter said, with the faintest of smiles. "He was born Augustus Tovell, or at least that is how I knew him. That was before he became enamored of all things Gothic, changed his name and acquired his castle."

"And when did that happen?" Kit asked. Hero wanted to stop him, to stop her ears, but her own raging curiosity kept her silent and immobile.

Poynter frowned, as though considering dates, then shook his head. "I am not sure when, for it was after I had left the duke's employ myself."

The wry twist of his mouth told Hero that his move probably had not been voluntary. More likely, his fellow staff member had forced him out. Had Raven got his first taste of power and abused it, or was he already orchestrating the fates of others so long ago?

"But it would have been several years later, after he parted ways with the duke, as well," Poynter said.

"Did they have a falling-out?" Kit asked.

"I don't know, but he did not seek another position when he left. It might well have been around that time that his elder brother died. Augustus took over the family fortunes, sold the home in Surrey, bought Raven Hill, and began his retreat from the world at large."

Poynter smiled apologetically. "But you must know all of this. Indeed, you must have changed your name to Raven," he said to Kit.

"He did," Hero answered, before Kit could speak. "We are both distant relatives, and Raven has been kind enough to help establish our futures."

"Ah," Poynter said. "I had wondered at your connections, for I knew of no other siblings besides his brother, and yet here you are." He nodded in approval, for it was not unusual for wealthier members of a family to provide for those less fortunate. Those without heirs might even adopt those they favoured, whether relations or friends.

That was certainly what had driven the real Erasmus to change his name and curry Raven's favor. He wanted Raven Hill and all that went with it. But unless Hero was mistaken, Erasmus had no more love for his uncle than she did. And his position was not secured, which explained his increasingly desperate offers to do Raven's bidding without question.

"Well, Augustus should take great pride in such a fine pair of young people as yourselves," Poynter said with a smile. Hero was hard pressed not to snort a disclaimer, for Raven took no pride in anything except himself and his acquisitions. But then, weren't she and Erasmus little more than puppets, human additions to his growing collection?

"Thank you," Kit said, when Hero did not comment. "Obviously, you harbor no ill feelings toward him."

Poynter's mouth twisted again. "Life is too short, and collecting too cutthroat a passion to carry grudges. Indeed, my path has crossed many times over the years with both Raven and Montford."

He paused to shake his head, his expression sad. "Indeed, I was most grieved to find out that his Grace is gravely ill."

"What?" Again, it was Kit who had the presence of mind to speak, while Hero sat still, stunned.

"Yes, one of the great antiquarians of the age is near death, from what I hear, though I pray God will spare him yet."

"I'm sorry," Kit said. "We had not heard these bad tidings. In fact, when we were at Cheswick, I thought I saw the duke's men or those dressed in his livery."

Poynter shook his head, apparently as puzzled as they by the sighting. "Perhaps they are on some final mission at his behest," the older gentleman finally said with a wistful smile. "I'd like to think his Grace still pursues his final prize, that most rare of volumes, a collector to the end."

# *Chapter Twelve*

Hero was so dazed, she let Kit lead her from the London Institution without thought to who might see them. Her mind was in a whirl, trying to take in all the information that Richard Poynter had imparted and make sense of it.

"Shall we find a place to sit?" Kit asked, ever solicitous.

Hero shook her head. "No, I'd rather walk."

Taking her gloved hand, Kit placed it in the crook of his arm and patted it, as though to comfort her. "Well, that's it," he said. "Obviously, the book was never part of the old earl's library. Martin Cheswick buried it or burned it or somehow disposed of it. The Mallory is lost, and I can't say I'm sorry."

"Maybe," Hero said. "Maybe not."

Kit slanted her a speculative glance. "The only other possibility is that your uncle already possesses the book. And he sent you off on a mission to fetch it from himself?"

Although Hero had considered that possibility, she did not share her thoughts with Kit. But when she did not reply, he eyed her sharply.

"Perhaps you'd like to break into Raven Hill and look for it," he suggested. "That's the only way we'll know for sure."

"You can't break into Raven Hill," Hero said.

"Why not?" Kit asked. "I thought it was possible to tour all the great homes, especially one patterned after Strawberry Hill."

Hero smiled, though not in amusement. "Unlike Walpole, who wrote a guidebook and gave out tickets to view his home, Raven does not open his house to visitors. But his secretive behavior seems to incite more curiosity about the place, causing him to employ several footmen to chase gawkers away from his property." And because of Raven's Gothic fancies, those footmen were armed with swords.

Hero shook her head. "Despite Raven's determination to outdo Walpole, there are few similarities between the two houses. Strawberry Hill is full of innovative designs and wallpapers and original use of colors and light. But Raven is no visionary." He was not interested in creating a showplace, only in feeding his own twisted fantasy.

"While both buildings have vaulted archways and hidden passages, Strawberry Hill is like a fairy castle, with pinnacles, quatrefoil windows and intricately carved staircases. Raven Hill is more an actual castle with battlements and dungeons. It's made of real stone and filigree, not wallpapers that cleverly depict such materials."

Hero never spoke of her household, but once begun, she could not seem to stop herself. "It's like a tomb, cold and dark and uncomfortable. And deliberately frightening," she muttered.

"What?"

Hero nodded. She couldn't begin to count the times she had come across some faux horror, even as a child, that Raven had added for his amusement. "I learned long ago not to scream at the sight of a falling axe or start at some ghoulish sound emanating from nowhere, but to keep on eating my soup in silence."

*"What?"* Kit halted his steps.

"There is not one comfortable chair, not one warm spot in which to read a book, just presses full of protected volumes or cases stocked with medals or other antiquarian follies." Hero drew a breath, intending to go on, only to realize that Kit was standing in front of her, a look of shock upon his face.

"The devil ought to be horsewhipped," he said, making Hero rue her words. She did not want to set Kit against Raven, now or ever. The knowledge that the man had been born an unassuming Tovell did not lessen his power. A Raven by any other name…

Hero shook her head, as though to make light of Kit's charge. "No doubt he deserves such punishment, but for crimes against others far more serious than the lack of desirable furnishings."

"I'm serious," Kit said, with such ferocity that Hero drew in a sharp breath. "I don't want you to go back there. It sounds like you are little more than an unpaid servant at the whim of a madman."

Although Kit was not far from the truth, Hero was

not about to confirm his suspicions. And she certainly did not want his pity, especially if it prompted another proposal. *Because this time she might not have the strength to refuse.*

"Perhaps I won't," Hero simply said. But she couldn't meet his probing gaze. And she did not share with him the desperate scheme she had devised to win her freedom.

Aware of the attention they might be drawing with their public argument, Hero began walking once more, forcing Kit to join her. And she forced a change of topic in the conversation, as well.

"If the Mallory truly is lost, why is Montford searching for it—and us?" she asked.

Kit groaned. "The Mallory *is* lost. And we don't know that the men were Montford's, and we only saw them once."

Hero sent him a questioning look.

"All right, twice, but that's no indication they were chasing us."

"Perhaps Montford heard rumours of the Mallory surfacing," Hero said. "Because of their past connection, the duke might be aware of Raven's interest and had his men follow me as a matter of course."

Kit shook his head. "I still can't imagine a duke's servants trying to kidnap you, and the fellows who did weren't wearing any livery."

"They might have changed their clothes, so we wouldn't be able to identify them," Hero said drily.

Kit snorted. "So what do you suggest we do, march up to Montford's family seat, demanding to see a dying man so we can accuse him of assault?"

Hero frowned at Kit's tone. When he put it that way, the idea did sound absurd, but Poynter understood. He knew that bibliomaniacs were consumed with the madness, whether down to their last coin, last thought, or even last breath.

"If Montford thinks we are on track, perhaps we should continue the search. We could talk to Featherstone's servants and friends and try to discover what happened to his books."

"But the lots went to Raven," Kit said.

Hero paused, struck by a sudden thought. "Yes, but how?" she said, glancing intently at Kit. "Were they delivered directly to Raven or did they pass through Featherstone first? If so, Featherstone might have lifted a few choice gems for himself."

"By cracking open a couple crates and going through every volume?"

"And picking the best for himself? I know I would have," Hero said.

"But Featherstone was sunk too deep in dissipation by then," Kit argued. "He probably was more interested in the money than any of the books."

"Book collecting is as great an addiction as gambling."

Kit shook his head. "You're assuming that Featherstone took delivery of the lots, which more than likely went directly to the purchaser, meaning your uncle."

Hero almost snapped at him not to refer to Raven as any relative of hers, but she caught herself. Instead, she said, "There's only one way to find out."

This time Kit did not groan, and Hero held her breath, for the ties that bound them were tenuous, at best. He had no good reason to continue to help her, and yet…

Finally, he halted again, turning to look at her directly. "You can't give it up, can you?" he asked.

Hero couldn't tell if his expression held dismay or pity, but she shook her head. "No," she answered.

There was too much at stake.

By the time they had returned to the London Institution, Poynter had gone, so they were left with little to do the rest of the day. And Kit refused to return to the inn, which might be for the best, considering what had last happened there. The thought of this man massaging her feet or any other part of her made Hero's face heat and her heart pound.

As long as they didn't draw attention to themselves, she was willing to go along as he dragged her to Madame Tussaud's Wax Museum and Week's Mechanical Museum. Steering clear of stationers, booksellers and circulating libraries, they wandered through a variety of shops, looking at toys and prints and elegant silks. They visited a clockmaker's and a perfumery. And they enjoyed delicate pastries purchased in a bake shop, as well as gingerbread from a street vendor.

For Hero, it was like a dream. After a lifetime of cold duty and a week of masquerading as a young man, the afternoon spent as Miss Marchant, about in London with her attentive brother, was a holiday. But Kit was not her sibling, and though he conducted himself as such, sometimes Hero caught glimpses of a dark glint in his gaze, a sign that his feelings for her were not brotherly. And she felt an answering shift inside, a hot surge of yearning that threatened to rob her of breath, before it faded into the less dangerous manner of easy companionship.

But when they finally approached the inn, the sparkle of the day began to fade into twilight, and Hero's buoyant mood with it. Recalled to reality, she was reminded that she was not Kit's sister. Nor could she ever be anything else to this man whose time with her was rapidly coming to an end.

To add to her distress, Hero was forced to wait in a shadowed corner of the hall while Kit got her greatcoat, bundling her up so she would be unrecognizable before hurrying to her room. The reason for the ruse remained unspoken: she did not want to be taken for a prostitute or sent to jail because of some such misunderstanding.

Once inside the darkened room, Hero shivered while Kit lit a lamp. Her boots were damp, but before they called for a fire, she needed to change. Reaching for her pack, Hero put a hand inside for her shirt, only to realize that it was not on top of the clothing she had placed there, folded and ready for rapid donning.

Drawing in a sharp breath, Hero turned to survey the room. There were few enough of their own belongings about, but her boy's boots were not where she had left them. Although in the same general area, their position was subtly altered, a discovery that made her heart hammer.

"Someone's been in here," Hero said softly.

"What?"

"Someone has searched our room."

Kit looked around at the spare, neat space and sent her a startled glance. "Perhaps the chambermaid…"

Hero shook her head. "She might have moved my boots, but she would not have been inside my pack."

"Unless she's a thief," Kit muttered.

"Try to remember exactly where you put everything and see if it is not slightly changed," Hero said.

Kit must have seen that she hadn't the energy to argue with him, for he turned to look through his own things, then swung round with a grim expression.

"She's not a thief, for I left some money hidden in an old sock. It is still there, but has been shoved farther down into the toe." He paused to shake his head. "Who would go through them only to put them back?"

"Someone looking for the Mallory," Hero said, and, for once, Kit did not argue.

They discussed what to do, then called for the maid to light the fire, conducting themselves as usual. Whoever had been in their room had gone to great lengths to avoid notice, and for now, they would play along. But Kit slept in a chair in front of the door, and Hero tossed and turned in the bed.

The bright, shiny day that she had spent with Kit in carefree excursions had been tarnished. With the coming of the night, Hero's thoughts grew dark, and she wondered at what price she had bought those precious hours.

The next morning Hero was back in her boy's clothing and so quiet that Kit cursed the circumstances that conspired against him. Yesterday she had been delightful company—warm and witty and beautiful in her feminine guise. A strong and independent woman, Hero also possessed a deep well of tenderness just waiting to be tapped. Their silences were comfortable, while their discussions were far ranging, going beyond books to houses, politics and even agriculture. And Kit knew her passion matched his own.

In short, she was everything he might want in a partner. *A wife.* Kit shook his head. He had all but given up hope until yesterday when everything between them was so easy and natural. But it had all gone awry. Hero had turned cold and distant, while they faced unknown threats yet again.

Now, Kit could spare no thoughts for anything except her protection, and he kept his pistol close as he packed his few belongings. Wary of watchers, they were going to slip away before first light, and they spoke in hurried whispers. Kit suggested they look for a place to lease, where they could disappear into the mass of London residents. But Hero shook her head.

"Time is running out," she said in a way that made Kit balk. "Another inn would be better, perhaps a larger one closer to the heart of the city."

Although in the past few days Hero had revealed more of herself, there still was too much missing for Kit to solve the puzzle. "People have been chasing us since we left Oakfield, so why is time running out?" he asked.

Hero hefted her pack. "Because we're on Raven's ground, in his neighborhood, and he will grow impatient for his prize."

"What? Surely you don't think your uncle is the one who searched our rooms?"

"Not Raven himself, but he may well have ordered it," she said.

Despite Hero's earlier revelations about her uncle, Kit was dumbfounded. "Why?"

Hero opened her mouth, then closed it again. Finally, she drew a deep breath. "I don't know," she said. "One never ever knows with Raven."

This was madness. It was an insane way to conduct business, and even more lunatic manner in which to live. There was very little that roused Kit to anger, but his rage toward Augustus Raven had been building for some time.

"Perhaps we should stop haring around town on this fruitless errand and go directly to Raven Hill," he said, giving Hero a hard stare. "I'd like to have a word with your uncle."

Ducking, she shook her head, but Kit was not prepared to let it go. Thus far, he had ceded to Hero's wishes, to her greater knowledge of the situation, but he could be stubborn, too. And he had no intention of letting her return to her uncle's control.

Even if he had misconstrued her interest, even if she would not accept his proposal, he could find somewhere else for her to go. Barto had connections. A post as a companion to a decent gentlewoman had to be preferable. Surely, when Syd met her, she would...

Suddenly, Kit realized just how long it had been since he had been in contact with his sister. Vaguely, he recalled some mention of a Christmas wedding, and he felt a different sort of alarm. Startling as it might seem, the holiday was not that far away, and he had no idea of what the arrangements might be.

Somehow, today he was going to have to get a message to his sister, whether Hero approved or not. The thought of whisking her away to Hawthorne Park was a tantalizing one, but unless he planned to drag her there bodily, Kit was not sure how to accomplish it.

As if sensing his mood, Hero turned toward him, pack in hand. "Perhaps we should separate."

"No." Kit spoke with such deadly vehemence that Hero did not argue. Still, when she moved into the narrow hall, he did not let her out of his sight.

They saw no one but sleepy grooms as they made their exit, taking the most winding route from the inn and sticking to the shadows. For the time being, they left their horses behind, fleeing on foot and climbing into a passing cart before debarking to slip through some alleys, until even Kit was confused over their location.

But in the breaking dawn, Hero pointed out the Maple's Inn, a busy place that was a far cry from their previous small, out-of-the-way lodgings. Since coaches came through at all hours, their appearance would not be marked, and after eating an enormous breakfast, they settled into a more spacious and neat room boasting two beds and a roaring fire.

When Hero made no move to change her costume, Kit looked a question at her. "Are we returning to the London Institution?"

"Not yet," Hero said, without meeting his gaze. "I've an errand first."

"And what might that be?" Kit asked.

When Hero did not immediately reply, Kit planted himself in front of the door with no intention of moving until he got some answers. If time was running out, so was his patience. At one time, he might have returned to his old life without taking action, but those days were gone. Now, he was determined to fight for what he wanted.

Although she had planned to come alone, Hero was grateful for Kit's solid presence as she stepped into Laytham's. She had not admitted as much, but the search of their room had unnerved her. Despite their various escapes, their pursuers had never seemed that close. And somehow, the thought of someone handling her belongings was worse than being threatened with a weapon.

It was more personal. More invasive. In fact, the more she thought about it, the more Hero began to think the secretive manner of the examination was one of Raven's touches. Surely, the kind of men who attacked the carriage or cornered Kit and Hob would engage in haphazard rummaging, not the eerily discreet violation that Hero had discovered.

Did Raven think she already had the Mallory, or was this one of his tricks to make sure she was alert and wary? Hero shook her head, for she knew there was no use trying to determine his motives. But perhaps, she would never have to puzzle over them again...

Heart pounding, Hero approached the counter at Laytham's, knowing full well what was at stake. Yet she managed to keep her face expressionless as she asked to see the owner.

"Mr Laytham is not here," the man said, eyeing her less-than-elegant attire with disdain.

Hero sucked in a breath. She had not anticipated this, but now she saw that Laytham's easy capitulation could have been a ruse. He might be on the Continent by now or, worse, explaining to some magistrate why *she* should be arrested.

"Did he leave anything to be picked up?" Kit asked, while Hero faltered.

"Your name?" the disdainful fellow inquired.

"Marchant," Kit said, taking control with his usual ease, and Hero could only be thankful for his quick command.

"Ah, yes," the man at the counter said. "Just a moment, please." He turned away, opening the door that led to Laytham's office, and Hero waited, her breath caught in her throat.

She wasn't certain what she expected, perhaps authorities swarming from the private area to arrest her or the salesman himself, returning to brandish a weapon. But both outcomes seemed unlikely when there were other customers about. This was a busy shop, a respectable business, in spite of the commission Laytham had agreed to undertake.

When the man returned with a thickly wrapped object, tied with string, Hero simply stared at it for a long moment. For surely none in her long history of acquisitions had carried the importance of this, the least costly.

"Thank you," Hero said, barely restraining herself from snatching up the parcel. Instead, she took it carefully, holding it against her chest as they made their exit. But once outside, she slipped it within her heavy greatcoat, where a large interior pocket was designed to hold all but the largest of volumes.

Now it could not be knocked from her grip or dropped into a puddle. And Hero looked no more than a young man bundled up against the cold, without anyone the wiser as to the prize in her possession. Still, she did not dawdle, and they hurried to the relative safety of Maple's Inn, so that she might take a look at what she had just received.

The walk was long enough for Hero's euphoria to ebb as she considered the contents of her pocket. Despite Kit's influence, hers was a suspicious nature, and she wondered whether she even held a book. The heavily wrapped item could be anything. A piece of wood. A title of no consequence or worth, given to get rid of her, while Laytham covered his tracks, refusing to meet with her ever again.

That fear gnawed at her until panic eroded her good sense, making her careless. And it wasn't until Kit had her halt at their door, in order to check the room, that she became aware of her inattention.

Suddenly nervous, she saw a man down the hall whose stance seemed vaguely familiar, but he stopped in front of another door, and Hero turned back to her own. Still, she was not as wary as usual, and when Kit waved her inside, Hero paid the price as she felt the barrel of a pistol pressed into her back.

"Quietly, now, let's go into your room. I'm sure you don't want any trouble." Hero recognized the voice as one of the two men who had attacked the carriage and threatened Hob, and if that wasn't enough, a poke of the weapon urged her to do as he said.

At the sight of their company, Kit started to reach inside his coat, but the man stopped him with a warning.

"Don't move, or I'll shoot her," he said. "So you just keep your hands were I can see them."

Behind her, Hero heard footsteps, followed by the ominous shutting of the door. A second man came into view, his pistol trained on Kit. It was the tall fellow, so the short one must be behind her, Hero reasoned. What she didn't expect was the appearance of a third man, and she drew in a sharp breath as the vaguely familiar figure from the hallway stepped into her line of sight.

"Erasmus! What are you doing here?" Hero gaped at her so-called cousin. Had Raven put him up to this?

"It has taken some doing, I admit," Erasmus said, his dark eyes birdlike hollows in the whiteness of his face. "You've led a fine chase, but one of Raven's underlings reported you were in town. And luckily for me, he was so startled to see you in that garb that he followed you."

Hero gaped. She'd made sure…

"Or he paid some youth to do some," Erasmus said. "I don't know or care. Nor did your disappearance this morning concern me. For, you see, I had spoken with the dependable Mr Ridealgh at Laytham's, who discovered that you, or rather Mr Marchant as you are now calling yourself," he added with a sneer, "would be back in a day's time. So all I had to do was wait."

Hero spared a moment to regret that all her precautions and wariness had been for naught. Despite her efforts, she could not control those outside her influence, such as Mr Ridealgh, whether he was Laytham's assistant or some lowly salesman eager for a bribe.

"But if you hadn't secreted the parcel inside your

coat, we could have avoided all this," Erasmus said, shaking his head. "A quick knock against you, and I could have been off with the Mallory."

"Why?" Hero asked. "If you plan on stealing from Raven, you've sadly misjudged your opponent."

"Oh, Raven will have his previous volume all right. When I give it to him. While you, after so much time and money, will return a failure."

"And when I tell him what you did to get it?"

Erasmus sneered. "I don't know what you're talking about, cousin."

"It was you who searched my room, wasn't it?" Hero said, and Erasmus's thin smile told her she was right.

"And you sent these brutes to kidnap me, waylay me, and delay me. Dangerous doings, Erasmus," Hero said. "All designed to prevent me from completing my mission, which is not something that Raven will take kindly."

"I don't know what you're talking about," Erasmus repeated, his lips curling in contempt. "I can account for my whereabouts, while you? It seems that you've been traipsing across the country on a romantic fling, spending more time on your lover than your mission, hardly the sort of thing of which Raven will approve."

Hero sucked in a harsh breath. There was no point in arguing, for they both knew the truth. It would be her word against his when they faced Raven, and Erasmus was well aware that those who came bearing gifts were always rewarded.

But just what sort of gift was he intending to present? Hero's knowledge of the parcel was the ace up her sleeve. So instead of the dread she might well have felt, she knew only a cold anger that this inept would-be usurper should ruin her one chance for freedom.

Hero eyed him coolly. "It will do you no good, Erasmus," she said. "Raven doesn't trust you. He knows you're only out to get what you can."

Erasmus's expression turned black with hatred. "Well, then we are two of a kind. While you? I don't know what you are. I've never understood why you're the chosen one when I've done everything to please him, even changing my name to his. I've got his blood. *Do you?*"

Hero did not flinch at the taunt. Nor did she dwell upon the fact that Kit was only a few steps away, listening to it all. Instead, she focused on the skills and experience that had served her well, while Erasmus… As usual, his emotions clouded dealings, which was one of the reasons Raven did not favour him.

She could almost hear Raven in her head. *Cleverness and cunning will out every time, my girl,* he whispered. *No one expects a female to think so cold and clearly.* Lately, Hero had discovered he was wrong about her lack of feelings, but she knew well how to hide them, and she did so now, her lack of reaction spurring Erasmus's rage.

"Everyone knows you're no relation, that you were bought, just like one of his acquisitions, though far more cheaply, I'll warrant."

Hero kept her expression impassive, as though he was discussing the weather, not the most hurtful of truths. But he could not know it all, she told herself. He could not know the worst.

"Where did he get you?" Erasmus said, stepping closer, his pinched face twisted by years of disappointment and jealousy and ill usage. "I've searched through his books, his private correspondence and found nothing," Erasmus spat. "Which proves just how little you are worth."

Erasmus took another step, standing so close now that Hero could see the spittle on his lips. "Did he find you on the streets, a beggar, a thief?" Erasmus demanded. He smiled then. "I don't think so. There's only one place where he could have bought a girl child like you, for the meanest coin. And that was a brothel, where your mother was the lowliest of whores."

Erasmus was staring so fixedly at Hero that he paid no heed to Kit or his hired men, who were gaping wide-eyed at the conversation. And at the word "whore" Kit launched himself. Taking Erasmus unawares, he knocked the smaller man to the ground, while Hero elbowed the fellow who held the pistol at her back. The third man swung his weapon toward them, and a shot rang out, sending Hero dropping to the floor.

"Stop, you idiot! Are you trying to kill me?" The man who had held Hero shouted at his compatriot, whose shot had gone wide, but was sure to draw attention. Hero took advantage of his panic by leaping to the window and pushing up the sash, thankful they had chosen their location for its easy access to a low roof. Whirling, she pulled her own weapon, ready to stop her assailant from following.

But he was busy trying to help his fellow, who was struggling with Kit, while Erasmus lay on the floor, abandoned, his rage replaced by fear. Ignoring him, Hero seized a wooden chair and brought it down hard on the back of the shorter man. With a grunt, he fell, and she retrieved the pistol he dropped.

"Ahhh!" A pained wail rose up from the taller of the two brutes as his pistol, too, dropped to the floor, and he clutched at his sleeve, where a bright spot of red gave evidence of his injury.

In an instant, Kit hurried her to the window, wiping a bloody knife upon the curtain.

"Where did you get that?" Hero demanded.

"My boot."

Hero sent him a startled glance. "And to think you're just a gentleman farmer."

The sound of footsteps alerted them to the imminent arrival of others who had heard the shot, so they clambered over the sill. There was no time to gather their things, only for one last glance at the room, where the two villains lay groaning and the door stood open.

Erasmus was gone.

# Chapter Thirteen

Crouching, they slid, more than walked, along the slippery roof that covered an overhang near the kitchens. Kit dropped to the ground easily, then turned to catch her. Again, Hero was grateful for his quiet strength. But she didn't even have time to savor his touch as he quickly pulled her through the stables and out into the street.

Once among others, Kit slowed his pace to avoid notice, but Hero still had to hurry to keep up. Her mind in a whirl, she could not think where to go, for it seemed that she was watched even more than she suspected. She felt an urgency to get to Raven, but she did not want to appear before him in her current guise. And all her other clothes were gone.

Suddenly, Hero felt as if she had come out the loser in the fight, bruised and battered by the implications of Erasmus's actions. If she could not use the Mallory to her advantage, then her already difficult position would be made worse by Erasmus's enmity. It would be just like Raven to pit them against each other in an endless struggle for his favour.

So caught up was she in these bleak thoughts that Hero barely blinked when Kit hustled her into a hackney coach. He leaned toward the driver to give directions without shouting, then slid in beside her.

"Where are we going?" Hero asked.

"Somewhere safe," Kit said, patting her arm in an automatic gesture of comfort.

At one time, Hero would have viewed his words with suspicion or doubt. But now she simply leaned back her head and closed her eyes, too weary to protest. Her thoughts went round and round, but her lack of sleep and the closeness of Kit's warm body had her nearly nodding off until the coach stopped and he helped her out.

Glancing around, Hero had no idea where they were as they slipped through a shop, exited onto another street, and walked another street before heading up to a neat town house. After a few words from Kit, they were ushered into a cozy parlor, where they were soon greeted by a handsome young man Kit introduced as Charles Armstrong.

"Kit, it's a pleasure to see you!" Armstrong said. He was as fair as Kit was dark, yet he seemed to possess the same friendly nature. "How many times have I invited you to town? But you're a gentleman farmer now, I suppose, with little interest in our doings?"

Hero nearly laughed aloud at that, for among his other skills surely Kit was the only such fellow who kept a knife in his boot and was able to subdue two villains at once. And yet, looking at him, he seemed little different from Armstrong, if a bit disheveled.

He still had that easy grace and untroubled countenance that belied the measure of the man, whose inner strength and abilities made him more formidable than just about anyone. In fact, the juxtaposition of his demeanor and his capability made Christopher Marchant all the more...dangerous.

Swamped by a sudden surge of emotion, Hero swallowed hard and tried to focus on the conversation between the two men.

"And how is that lovely sister of yours?" Armstrong asked, his tone showing more than idle interest.

"She is to be married soon, to our old neighbor, now Viscount Hawthorne."

"Oh, that is...good news, of course. I hope you will tender my heartiest congratulations when you see her."

"Actually, I was hoping that I could post a brief letter to her while here. Pardon our appearance, but we've run into a bit of trouble here in town," Kit said.

He drew his host aside, and they held a whispered conversation punctuated by Armstrong's exclamations and furtive looks her way. At one time, Hero might have distrusted anything she couldn't hear, but Kit appeared to have it all well in hand, while her own mind and body seemed to have reached their limits.

Once they were finished talking, a genial housekeeper led them upstairs, showing Hero to a lovely room before taking Kit on to his. For a long moment, Hero simply stood and stared at the cheery surroundings, decorated with bright chintzes and soft chairs.

Gauzy curtains were drawn back from wide windows, and Hero knew she ought to shut them, but she didn't have the heart.

A low knock heralded Kit's entry, and Hero's weariness was replaced by dread. She had hoped to be gone from his life, without him ever knowing, but Erasmus's accusations made that unlikely. Now it would all come out, Hero thought, her head pounding along with her heart. Although she wanted nothing more than to flee, she could not, and so she walked around the room, admiring the ewer and basin and small comforts that a stranger freely offered her.

"I've explained that you are in disguise," Kit said. Without standing upon ceremony, he sank into one of the upholstered chairs. "He's going to have a maid bring you some of his sisters' clothes. In case you'd like to change," Kit added.

Hero choked back a laugh. Now that they were in Kit's world, she felt her own lack. A strange female who dressed in boy's garb, she did not fit in here. It was just as well…

"Shall we have a look at it?" he asked.

For a moment, Hero had no idea what he was talking about. And she nearly laughed again when she realized how far her thoughts were from her singular purpose. It didn't seemed possible that she had forgotten the Mallory, the most important thing in her life. Or so she told herself.

Unbuttoning the heavy greatcoat, Hero reached inside and pulled the parcel from her pocket. "It's not real," she said. "I had it made up."

"What?"

"It's a forgery," Hero explained as she walked across the room. "Raven always hinted at the authenticity of Laytham's pamphlets, so I gambled on him being right." She did not mince words, for what could it matter now? "I blackmailed Laytham into creating an edition that might fool Raven, at first glance, at least."

"Clever," Kit said. Startled, Hero glanced toward him, but his expression held no hint of the disapproval she'd expected. A bit dumbfounded, she set the parcel upon a drum table that stood near his chair.

"We'll see," Hero said, for her success remained to be seen. Raven was far more clever, and she was still uncertain what she would find beneath the wrappings. Putting shaking fingers to the string, she was confounded until Kit reached into his boot for the knife, slicing clean through it. And suddenly, her whole body seemed to shake as she moved the paper aside to reveal what was nestled inside.

It was a book, and Hero let out a low sound of relief. The bindings were old, a hundred years at least, and the title barely legible. Whether accidental or deliberate, that was a nice touch, Hero thought as she gently tipped open the cover with one finger. Inside, the title page looked just as old, and Kit rose to his feet to stand behind her.

"It looks real enough," he said.

"Believe me, it isn't," Hero said. "Or else Laytham would never have parted with it."

A knock on the door made Hero start, and she quickly rewrapped the volume as a pert little maid entered the room, carrying several garments.

"Mr Armstrong said you'd be needing these, uh, sirs," the girl said.

"Yes, thank you," Kit said.

She laid the items on the bed. "And I'll be bringing up a tray for you. Will there be anything else?"

"A bath?" Kit suggested.

"Of course, sir," she said, with a nod, and was soon shutting the door behind her.

A bath. And clean clothes. And some good food, not purchased at an inn. Thinking of the pleasures that Kit so valued allowed Hero to avoid the inevitable.

But she knew it could not be staved off for long. Wrapping the book as neatly as possible, she slipped it into the bottom of a heavy wardrobe, beneath a chamber pot, which she would never have cause to use, just as she would never use the pretty bed with its thick coverings.

"Will your uncle be fooled?" Kit asked.

"Don't call him my uncle." The words were out before Hero could call them back.

For a long moment, Kit was silent. "Surely you don't believe any of that rot your cousin was spouting, vitriol that was born of jealousy?"

"No," Hero said softly. "It's worse than that." She turned to face him. He was seated again in the upholstered chair, looking so at home in such surroundings that she felt an interloper. She *was* an interloper.

"Raven bought me at an asylum. My mother was a madwoman."

Although Hero braced herself, the horror and judgement that she knew Kit would be unable to hide did not appear. In fact, he simply shook his head. "I don't believe it. From what you've told me, that's just the sort of tale he would concoct to frighten you and keep you tethered to him."

Kit paused to eye her directly. "Maybe he's your father."

Hero shuddered at the possibility, which would still make her the offspring of a lunatic. *Perhaps two lunatics.* But the idea that Raven had engaged in intimacy of any sort with anyone seemed highly unlikely.

Hero shook her head. "I can't imagine him having a child with anyone. Ever."

"Even in a fit of passion?"

"Raven's fits of passion aren't the kind that would result in childbirth."

"Have you ever asked him about it?"

Hero laughed humorlessly. "Question his word? You don't understand. Conversation with him devolves into hints and mysterious intrigues, while disputes are met with stony silence."

Kit lifted his dark brows as if she had just proven his point for him. "If he talks in riddles and is known for his intrigues, why would you take his word about this?"

*Because Raven appeared to revel in her origins, subtly hinting that her own eventual madness was a foregone conclusion.*

When Hero didn't answer, Kit pressed her. "Why would he go to an asylum to shop for children to adopt?" Kit asked. "That makes no sense."

"I assumed he wanted someone no one else knew about, with no connections, who would be grateful…"

"He could do that anywhere on any street, without

the possibility of spending his time and money on someone who might not be grateful or useful."

"Maybe the idea appealed to him," Hero said. "It would certainly fit into his sense of Gothic melo-drama. He could use me until I went mad, then lock me in the tower, where my shrieking and wailing would only add to the atmosphere of Raven Hill," Hero said, shivering at the very real possibility.

"The idea might appeal to him, but would a recluse actually visit such a place, inviting into his private home someone who might not be as easily governed as he might wish?" Kit shook his head. "I think he's concocted the tale out of whole cloth."

Hero opened her mouth to argue, then shut it again as she stared at Kit's open expression. He spoke with such absolute certainty that for the first time in her life, doubt crept into her mind.

Raven had never talked of her antecedents outright, but in a cryptic manner that left Hero to divine the truth. Not even Erasmus had guessed the real story, and Hero had kept it hidden, dark and festering, from everyone until this very moment. Yet, now she wondered if, in his own twisted way, Raven hadn't dropped the hints purposefully so that she might draw the wrong conclusions.

But if her entire history was a lie, then where had she come from? And who were her parents?

As Kit dressed in fresh clothes, he silently thanked Charlie for his generosity. A cousin of the Armstrongs who had once been Kit's neighbors, Charlie wasn't a close friend, but he had provided the two who had showed up on his doorstep with good food and the luxury of an enormous copper tub, in which Kit had enjoyed a good long soak.

He also provided them with a safe haven, for Kit couldn't envision Erasmus and his hired thugs venturing into this genteel neighborhood. Kit loosed a low sigh, relieved that the villain harrying them had turned out to be nothing more than a disgruntled relative, not deadly followers of Mallory's writings.

Kit had no doubt that Hero's cousin was dangerous, for his ranting smacked of someone with a tenuous hold on his wits. And the men he'd hired had brandished their pistols alarmingly. But once Hero was removed from Erasmus's orbit, he would have no further reason to threaten her.

And Kit had all intention of removing Hero from his reach, as well as from Raven's. He'd had no chance to say as much when the maid had appeared with her bath water, but he hoped to receive a different answer when next he tendered his proposal. For, at last, the final piece of the puzzle that was Hero had fallen into place. And the deep, dark secret she had so zealously guarded seemed nothing more than a Gothic tale from the master of Raven Hill.

Although Kit was fairly certain Hero had not come from an asylum, he was just as certain that Raven had wanted her to think so. What better way to keep her tied to him? He permitted her no friends, no social life, no interaction with other women or potential suitors. And if, by chance, she should form an attachment, his ugly lie would keep her from pursuing it.

Kit shook his head as he closed the door behind

him. Although many women had few choices in life, this man had made sure that Hero had none. With a combination of threats and lies and virtual imprisonment, he had maintained a stranglehold upon her, body and mind. It was a measure of Hero's strength that he had not broken her spirit, as well.

As he walked toward Hero's room, Kit's steps slowed, but the sight of a passing maid spurred him onward. Now that they were at Charlie's, it wasn't prudent to make himself a frequent visitor to a bedroom occupied by a young, unmarried miss. Ruefully, Kit realized that circumstances had forced them into behavior that had become habit, but that society would not condone.

Although, by necessity, Charlie had been apprised of Hero's disguise, he had been told little else. Kit had kept to himself the fact that the two had been traveling alone together. The servants might suspect something odd, but they had all been told that a woman was to occupy that room.

Charlie had even contacted his dowager aunt to come serve as chaperone, a gesture Kit much appreciated. For Hero's sake, he did not want her reputation tarnished in any way in the eyes of the world. Barto and Syd wouldn't put stock in gossip, but it had a way of following one, even to the farthest corners of the countryside, and preventing acceptance into genteel society.

In fact, Charlie's aunt might already have arrived and be meeting with Hero, so Kit hurried down the curving stair to the floor below, where he found Charlie seated at a writing desk in the parlor.

"Oh, hello! You said you wanted to post a letter to your sister," Charlie said, rising to his feet.

"So I did," Kit answered. "Thank you for the reminder, as well as all else you've done for us."

Charlie waved away the gratitude. "Next time I need rustication in the country, you shall simply have to open your new home to me."

Kit laughed. "I'm afraid you won't find the place as entertaining as your cousins'."

"I'm sure it would be less taxing than London," Charlie said. "Rest and relaxation amongst nature, eh?"

Kit smiled in reply, and for the first time since the fire, he began to think about the landscape that had been denuded behind the house. He certainly did not want to revive the hedge maze that had burned down, but he would like a garden, the kind of area that would be a welcome refuge, such as Charlie mentioned. With walkways and trees and plantings bright with flowers. Perhaps he could call in a designer…

But he was getting ahead of himself. There was business to be taken care of first, and one of the matters that most required his attention was Syd. Taking the place that Charlie had vacated, he wrote her and Barto a brief assurance that he was safe and would like to introduce someone to them. Unwilling to get ahead of himself again, Kit did not explain why, but promised to head to Hawthorne Park as soon as he tied up a few loose ends in London. That one of those consisted of Augustus Raven, Kit kept to himself.

He had barely given the missive to a footman when Charlie's aunt arrived. Short, pudgy and wearing a variety of shawls and fur muffs, she was ushered into the parlour in an endless stream of chatter, involving her conveyance from her own town house to Charlie's. As the butler helped her from her heavy cloak and various fur pieces, Charlie shot Kit a glance that spoke volumes.

Kit realized he was even more beholden to his friend, for he suspected that Charlie's aunt was not a frequent visitor, for reasons that were rapidly becoming obvious. Once relieved of her heaviest garments, she snatched back a brightly colored shawl.

"And then, it began a cold drizzle, which at my age is the very worst of conditions," she was saying. "I admit, Charles, that I would only have ventured out for you and the most urgent summons."

Having finally situated her garments to her apparent satisfaction, the stout female turned to survey the room. "Ah, there are you are, Charles," she said, acknowledging her nephew with the fluttering handkerchief.

Squinting in Kit's direction, she paused to pat her enormous bosom, from which general area she produced a pair of spectacles. "And who is this?"

"This is Mr Marchant," Charles said, throwing Kit another glance of apology. "He's a friend of mine, a former neighbor of William and Elizabeth's."

"William and Elizabeth! That brood," she said, heaving herself on to a chaise longue. "I've told her time and time again of the need to rein in those children. And how often has that youngest scamp of theirs gotten into trouble, I ask you?"

Although Kit knew the family well, it wasn't long

before he had lost all track of the conversation, if one could call it that. Charlie tried to look attentive, while Mrs Armstrong kept up her ceaseless prattle. She didn't seem mean-spirited, simply eager for a chance to give her opinions on all and sundry.

Kit realized that she would probably drive Hero to distraction, but he had often been trapped with his father and his father's scholarly friends, so he had developed the skill of judicious nodding when listening to long-winded discourse. In fact, he had practically nodded off when a sharp change in the pitch of Mrs Armstrong's voice had him jerking to attention.

"Mr Marchant! I say, this young woman you wish me to accompany, where is she?"

"She's resting, Aunt," Charlie said. "She requested not to be disturbed."

The combination of Charlie's last words and the lengthening shadows outside made Kit surge to his feet, abruptly alert. "I'll go check on her."

At Mrs Armstrong's horrified gasp, Charlie stood and summoned a maid for the task, but it was all Kit could do to remain where he was.

"Really, young man, you cannot expect me to act as a chaperone when you make such outrageous remarks. Why are you looking so pale?" the older woman demanded, lifting her spectacles, the better to peer at Kit. "She isn't ill, is she?"

Having discovered a new topic for discussion, she launched into a long, detailed account of a young lady who had suffered most violently from what they claimed was gout. "But that hardly seems likely, now, does it?" she asked no one in particular.

The maid, who had been urged to hurry by Charlie, soon reappeared, shaking her head. "No one's in the room, sir," she reported.

"But I don't understand," Charlie said. "Did anyone see her go out?"

"No, sir," the maid said. "I can ask the kitchen staff, but I'm sure they would have told the housekeeper, if the young lady had gone that way."

"But then, how?" Charlie asked to the room at large. Swinging toward Kit, he sputtered a protest. "You don't think someone managed to gain entrance to the house and…make off with her, do you?"

At Charlie's horrified expression, Kit shook his head. "She probably climbed out the window."

"Climbed out the window? In winter?" Mrs Armstrong's voice rang out as she looked from her nephew to Kit, her eyes wide behind her spectacles and her jaw slack with astonishment.

Without answering, Kit rushed past her, but he heard her speak to Charlie in a scolding tone. "My dear boy, I can see that this charge is going to be more difficult than you let on."

Bounding up the stairs, Kit headed to Hero's room, where a quick check confirmed that she had made her escape in her borrowed female clothing. But why? Kit threw open the doors of the wardrobe, searching for the book she had hidden there, only to find it gone, as well.

The doubts that Kit had once entertained came surging back, fuelled by the memory of his poor judgement at Oakfield. That experience had made him distrust his own instincts, and now he wondered whether he had been wrong about Hero, as well. Perhaps she had been playing him all along, and, having found the real Mallory, was off to collect the huge price it would bring.

But even as such thoughts flashed through his mind, Kit dismissed them. Whether right or wrong, his heart held sway over his head, and he was not about to let Hero go until things were settled between them, once and for all.

Swearing under his breath, Kit realized he should never have left her alone. In the future, he might consider tethering her to him with a chain. With a lock. *If there was a future.*

The thought spurred Kit to action. He needed to borrow a horse from Charlie and head…where? Kit could only guess that she had gone home, which meant he would have to do the impossible: break into Raven Hill.

# Chapter Fourteen

⁓⁓⁓⁓⁓

The cold drizzle Mrs Armstrong complained about had stopped, leaving only a few slick patches in its wake. But as twilight descended, a mist appeared, making Kit's first sight of Raven Hill enough to give anyone pause.

He had barely turned onto the long lane when he saw Hero's home ahead, an old castle rising out of the fog as night gathered around it like a cloak. The size of the place was not imposing, for it looked to be a keep that had been added to in an odd fashion. But a high stone wall surrounded it, culminating in a massive iron gate and a gatehouse whose window blinked in the coming darkness.

At least there wasn't a moat.

But the gatehouse light might indicate a presence, and just in case Raven's defences included keeping a lookout atop the battlements, Kit veered off the lane, though he was still far away. Tall trees added further gloom to the setting, and Kit headed toward them, hoping to avoid being seen.

Too late, he wished that he had pressed Hero for more information about the home she claimed no one could breach, patrolled by guards and perhaps even filled with traps for the unwary. Hadn't she said something about falling axes?

Tethering Charlie's horse to a tall sycamore, Kit stood at the edge of the stand of trees and studied his target. As he surveyed the daunting stone structure looming before him, he took a good, long look past the obvious. And he realized that Raven's fortress was designed to intimidate, to convey a Gothic atmosphere, a melodramatic mystique nurtured by its owner and intended to keep the curious at bay.

Like the facade that Augustus Tovell had assumed, it was based more upon perception than reality. For no matter how wealthy Raven was, he could not afford an army to patrol the grounds or workmen to repair the ancient structure. Raven Hill was showing its age, and while that might add to its eerie impression, the cracks in the walls and crumbling stone would provide Kit the footholds he needed to gain entry to the grounds.

What he would find inside was anyone's guess.

It was better this way.

That's what Hero had told herself all the way from the Armstrong town house to the massive great room of Raven Hill. Although she hadn't wanted to leave Kit without a word, she needed to face Raven alone, to try to bargain for her future with the book she carried with her. She did not need the distraction Kit would bring to herself—or to Raven.

The owner of Raven Hill would have been outraged by the presence of an outsider in his sanctum, hardly a good beginning to any dealings, let alone the most important of Hero's life. And he would have been in no mood to give her what she wanted.

Although that consideration had been the deciding factor, Hero had another, more selfish reason for coming here without Kit. He was from a different world, where there were such things as gentlemen and kind strangers and welcome refuges, a world that Hero wanted to keep separate from the one ruled by Raven.

And here, Hero did not need the protection Kit had so ably provided. Raven would easily handle Erasmus, should he arrive to make trouble for her. In fact, her only fear lay in the chance that she would not succeed in buying her way out of this place for ever. But she kept that concern well hidden behind an impassive countenance, lest it be marked.

For Raven was here. Hero could feel it. He was probably in one of the upper galleries, spying upon her during the long wait that was intended to shake her composure. But Hero did not bother looking for him. She could see little in the perpetual gloom, for only one torch had been lit, and its feeble glow did not reach far beyond its placement at the rear of the hall, near the dais where Raven liked to hold court.

Even though she could see little of her surroundings, Hero knew them well. The tiles stretched out on all sides to walls hung with threadbare tapestries and ancient hauberks. Swords, axes and other weapons were displayed, although Raven did not keep any valuable collections here. *Too public*, he said, though he rarely allowed anyone to enter, let alone members of the general population.

Alongside the armaments stood the trappings of war, whole suits of armour assembled to stand freely upon unseen frames. They were placed in the shadows, so that at first glance, they might be mistaken for menacing figures. Long ago, when Hero had become inured to their presence, Raven had arranged for someone to don the old metal and step toward her from the darkness.

Hero had been hard pressed not to react. But after that, she came to expect most anything, including the rising of the dead from Raven's prized effigies, which occupied an alcove added for their presentation. That had never happened, and Raven claimed that the tombs were empty, probably because trading in the dead might be illegal.

Although the effigy alcove was the largest, there were many smaller ones that the odd piece of furniture or marble statue occupied. And some dark recesses contained a curtain or a hidden door that Raven had added over the years. Even Hero didn't know all of the castle's secrets.

Above, there were hiding places, as well, where Raven could look down, unobserved, upon all he had wrought. A wooden panel, carved in an open pattern, rose from the floor behind his dais nearly to the ceiling and could easily obscure him, while allowing him to see the pool of light below. And there were other spots behind cleverly designed walls, along galleries, or under decorative bays.

Waiting below, Hero expected him to send some wisp of silk flying down or sound a boom of cannon-like proportions by way of twisted welcome. And to see her reaction. But nothing fell from the darkness or broke the silence except for the ticking of the massive old-fashioned clock that marked the time.

And just when she wondered when he would show himself, Raven suddenly appeared, stepping from the shadows as if a part of them. He certainly did his best to be indistinguishable, his tall, thin figure cloaked in black, his eyes and cheeks unseen hollows, his ebony cane ever present. "You've taken your time," he said, by way of greeting.

*Hello to you, too.* "I ran into some difficulty," Hero said.

"I take it Marchant did not have the book?"

"That copy was destroyed."

"Unfortunate."

"But the letter spoke of another, and that's the one I found," Hero said, evenly.

"Did you, now? Clever girl."

Was there some inflection in his voice that hinted otherwise? Hero's pulse picked up its pace at the thought. She did not trust herself to speak, but she had to take her chance. "I-i-it was a treacherous errand, and since the book is worth so much, I would like something in return."

Now that she was here before him, eyeing his pale, gaunt face, Hero felt her determination weaken.

"And what would that be?" His back was to the light, so Hero could not discern his expression, and his tone gave nothing away, not anger or annoyance or amusement. "A new hair ribbon? A gown? Perhaps a new boy's costume?"

Hero winced at that, but she could hardly have conducted all of his business the way she was dressed, especially after what had happened to her coach. The memory of that, and the circumstances that had thrown her upon the mercy of a stranger, made her stand up straighter.

"I want more than that," Hero said. "Not only did I have to hunt down the missing volume myself, but I was delayed and threatened throughout by Erasmus."

"An annoyance," Raven said, in dismissal.

"He hired men to shoot at me, more than once," Hero said, her voice rising. "I could have been killed. And for that I should have my freedom."

The word hung in the air like some kind of obscenity. But before Raven could react, Hero went on. "I ask only for a small stipend, a settlement that would allow me to live elsewhere while troubling you little," she added, lifting her arm to take in Raven Hill and the valuable collections he had amassed, often with her aid.

"If I wanted to be robbed, I could have Erasmus handle it with more delicacy—and venality," Raven said. His voice was low, his anger obvious. "At least he is not an ingrate. Do you remember where you came from? Or perhaps you would care to go back there."

"Back where?" Hero asked. "You've lied about so much, why should I believe your innuendos about my origins?"

The stillness that followed vibrated with his rage,

and he took a step forward. "Make no mistake about my power," he said. "I can arrange to have you put away in such a place, and no one will ever find you again."

"I don't think so." The sound of that familiar voice, calling down from above, bolstered Hero's wavering strength and made Raven start in surprise.

Against all odds, her gentleman farmer had managed what no one else had ever accomplished. He had made his way unchallenged—and unnoticed—into the heart of Raven's realm. Although she had spent a lifetime cowed by Raven's seemingly otherworldly powers, they faded in comparison to Kit's very real skills. And at the moment, Hero was convinced there was nothing the man couldn't do.

But before she could gloat, Raven called to his guards, and one soon appeared in costume, complete with sword and helm. "We have an intruder. See to him," Raven said.

"That's not an intruder. He's my guest," Hero said. But the guard did not obey her, and Raven told the other who appeared to light the torches in the upper gallery, where Kit was hiding. Hero called out a warning, and she heard Kit's footsteps running lightly above, followed by a thud.

Hero cursed the darkness as she craned her neck. Then light blazed forth from one of the torches set into the wall, illuminating two silhouettes armed with swords, one of which Hero easily recognized. It appeared that Raven's personal protectors were more decorative than effective, for Kit must have got his weapon by overpowering the first guard.

And now he harried the other. As Hero watched in awe, Kit thrust and parried, driving the second guard back along the gallery and up against the wall. It was no surprise to Hero that, in addition to all his other skills, Christopher Marchant was an excellent swordsman.

Since Kit obviously had the upper hand, Raven needed no prescience to predict the outcome. "Close him off," Raven shouted to his startled butler. "Shut him up there!" While the elderly servant hurried to do Raven's bidding, there was a grunt and a clatter from above, as Kit disarmed the guard.

Kicking the fellow's weapon aside, Kit knocked him to the floor, where he disappeared from view. Then, rather than find the exits bolted against him, Kit leapt on to the carved railing, tugged at one of the fading tapestries, and swung from the gallery to the floor in one fell swoop.

Hero squeaked out a protest, for fear the old material would crumble in his hands, dropping him to the hard tiles below, but he landed on his feet, ever graceful, like some latter-day Robin Hood. Hero didn't know whether to laugh in delight or swoon at the arrival of her champion, who turned to Raven, weapon in hand.

But Raven ignored him, as though he were no more than a pesky gnat, and fixed Hero with his hooded gaze. "You are mine, and I won't be handing you over, now or ever."

Hero shuddered at the statement, but it was too late and the taste of freedom too strong. "I'm not part of your collection, Raven," she murmured.

"I acquired you, didn't I?"

Hero flinched, but Kit stepped forward. "If you did, she has repaid your investment many times over. Now, she's of age and marrying me, so you will just have to find someone else to handle your dealings for you."

Hero didn't dispute Kit's claim of betrothal, though she had no more desire for his pity than she ever had. She simply could spare no thought for the future when the present was so precarious.

"She's not going anywhere with anyone, least of all a penniless, upstart intruder," Raven snapped, visibly angered.

But the lapse was a brief one, and when he spoke again, it was to Hero, his tone low and derisive. "Perhaps this young man, Mr Marchant, I presume, is unaware of your family…legacy."

Before Hero could respond, Kit stepped forward. "I don't care where Hero came from, and I'm certainly not going to believe your version of events, *Mr Tovell*." Swinging the sword in the air, he spoke over his shoulder to Hero. "He never struck you, did he? Because if he did, I'll run him through right now."

"No, Kit," Hero said. At one time, she might have enjoyed the sight of someone toying with the great Raven as he had toyed with so many others. But Kit was too much the gentleman to employ Raven's tactics. "I don't want any trouble."

*"You already have it,"* Raven said, his voice harsh with promise. "Trespassing, menacing, assault, at the very least. Mr Marchant will enjoy a long stay in jail."

Hero's heart pounded at the threat, which Raven,

with all his seeming resources, might well make good. And for once in her life, Hero felt faint. All the childhood terrors and horrors of this place were as nothing to the frightening power Raven now wielded: power over the man she loved.

It was an admission she had failed to make, even to herself, but one that Hero could not deny, and she stood, trembling and uncertain. Such was her fear that she might have thrown herself at Raven's feet, begging for a mercy she knew he would not grant. But Kit must have sensed she was wavering, for he put himself between them.

"And what about imprisonment of a young woman not related to you?" he asked, no hint of his own courage faltering. "There are laws in this land against slavery."

Raven laughed, a chilling sound in the hollowness of the hall. "You can't touch me. I'm above the law."

And then, as though to prove his claim, footsteps sounded from one of the passageways. Whirling, Hero was not sure what she expected, at the very least additional guards summoned from outside. But the lone figure that appeared made her loose a shaky breath of relief.

"Erasmus, rid the hall of this intruder," Raven said, lifting an arm to extend a bony finger toward Kit.

Obviously startled by the directive, Erasmus stopped to gape at Kit, armed with the sword, but made no effort to evict him. He had tangled once with the gentleman farmer and had come out the worst for it.

"He's of no consequence to me," Erasmus said dismissively. "All I want is the Mallory."

Raven laughed. "Ah, the Mallory. It seems to have been an ill chance that set me lusting after it." He paused dramatically, as though to make certain he had the attention of his audience before continuing.

"I admit to being ruled by my passion for the arcane, the unusual, the singular, so I could hardly resist the lure of a missing book, especially one with— what shall I call it?—a Gothic tone."

"Not Gothic. Druidic," Kit said, his expression tense.

"Yes, so I heard," Raven said.

Knowing Raven as she did, Hero was wary of his sudden desire for speech. She opened her mouth to warn Kit not to listen, but Raven was already talking again. "I found the scrap of letter as soon as I purchased the lot, of course. I knew the significance of such a find, so I sent out some discreet inquiries."

Raven paused to fix Kit with his hooded gaze. "I even wrote to the woman who owned Mallory's old home, to no avail. Oakfield, I believe it is called? But then she must have been a relative of yours?"

Raven's words had their intended effect, and before Hero could intervene, he lifted his cane and knocked the sword from Kit's hand to clatter upon the tiles. Although Raven's cane had always seemed an unnecessary affection, now Hero wondered if it held a blade. And she slipped her hand into her reticule.

It was Erasmus, however, who proved to be the greater threat, for he retrieved the sword before either Raven or Kit could move. "Now, if you will just hand over the Mallory," he said, backing toward Hero.

Raven laughed, and Erasmus swung toward him.

Waving the blade wildly, he was all the more dangerous for his lack of skill. "I've wasted enough years
toiling for no reward, kicking my heels at your beck
and call," he said, his pinched features twisted with
anger. "It's time I established my own reputation. And
the Mallory will do it."

Hero swallowed a gasp of surprise at Erasmus's unexpected defection. His previous plot having been
thwarted, he was gambling everything, his present and
his future, on a book that was not even genuine. But
Hero was not about to enlighten him, and she held out
the volume she had carefully rewrapped.

Erasmus snatched it from her, his beady eyes alight
with avarice, yet his triumph was short-lived.

"Go ahead and take joy of it," Raven said. "It's a
fraud."

The flush of victory faded from Erasmus's pale
face. "You lie."

Raven laughed. "This is why I put my faith in the
girl, you fool. You were always too stupid to understand the intricacies that came so easily to her."

Wanting only to be left out of this, Hero took a step
back, and she was relieved when Erasmus turned the
sword toward Raven.

"Put that thing down," Raven ordered. "You don't
know how to use it, any more than you know how to
use the information at your fingertips." He paused to
point his cane toward Hero, and she tightened her hold
upon the pistol she kept hidden.

"She was seen getting the book from Laytham's,"
Raven said. "Not from Oakfield or Cheswick or
Featherstone or even Poynter. From Laytham."

"So?"

"So," Raven said, sneering, "if Laytham had such a rare book, he would be crowing to the skies like the rooster he is. Your precious edition is as authentic as one of his pamphlets, a fake, a forgery fit only to fool an idiot like you."

At Raven's words, Erasmus whirled toward Hero, the sword slicing violently through the air. "Is this true?" he demanded, turning the full force of his hatred upon her.

If he hadn't been so dangerously volatile, Hero might have found amusement in the reversal of their roles. For right now, Erasmus seemed far more likely to carry the taint of madness. But out of the corner of her eye, she saw Kit move closer, and she was not about to lose him.

"Stop right there," Hero said, raising her hand inside its silken covering. "Don't make me ruin a perfectly good reticule."

Erasmus halted, as if frozen, and in the ensuing silence, Hero noticed an odd crackling noise. She cocked her head to listen, but it was soon drowned out by Erasmus's shouts.

"This is all your doing! You played with me, toyed with me," he screamed, lunging at Raven. Hero sucked in a sharp breath, certain he would draw blood, but Raven lifted his cane to ward off the blow.

"Stop! Look!" Kit called. At first Hero thought he was trying to put an end to the struggle, but he was pointing to the corner of the vast room, and what Hero saw there made her blanch.

The tapestry that Kit had used to swing from the

gallery had fallen against the lighted torch, and fire chased up the old material, catching the other tapestries ablaze, as well as the carved wooden screen that covered most of the rear of great hall. The smoke that drifted upward in the huge space, now could be seen—and smelled.

It took a couple more shouts to capture the attention of both Erasmus and Raven, who were grappling upon the tiles. But when they fell apart, they both gaped at the blaze that was racing through the furnishings.

"My books!" Raven screamed, rising to his feet. "We must save my collections!" He turned to run toward one of the alcoves, Erasmus not far behind.

"No! Save yourselves!" Kit called.

But they paid him no heed, and Hero had one last look at the two men who had so ill used her before they disappeared into a shadowy passage, fire at their heels. Hero knew that their mania and greed would surely be their death, but she took no joy in it. When she lifted her hand to her mouth, she wasn't certain whether she was stifling a cough or a sob.

"Hurry!" Having given up on the others, Kit grasped her arm and pulled her toward the entrance. The heavy bolt was slid home, and as he wrestled with it, Hero wondered what other exit they might seek among the maze of passages, for already the smoke hung thick in the air, and she heard something crash to the floor behind them.

"Kit, through the back," Hero said, trying to judge how swiftly the blaze was traveling and in what directions. But at that moment, Kit managed to push the massive wood aside and to fling open the door.

They raced through the opening, gulping in great breaths of the chilly air that met them. Outside in the foggy darkness, Hero caught a glimpse of eerie figures dashing into the night, and for an instant, she wondered whether Raven had made his escape, after all. But she realized that, like rats abandoning a sinking ship, his meagre staff were fleeing their master and his Gothic nightmare.

## Chapter Fifteen

Kit dragged Hero away from Raven Hill, but the eerie landscape that met them firmly reflected its owner. The rising moon lent a pale glow to the expanse of open ground ahead, illuminating tendrils of fog that veiled any path—or trap—that might be there. Kit could only hope that Hero would alert him to pitfalls.

But they made their way without incident to the gatehouse, which stood unmanned, its door hanging open. Either the guard had hurried to aid Raven or he had fled at the first sign of trouble. Kit halted to catch his breath, and as though she could go no further, Hero stepped inside, sinking wearily on to the heavy wooden bench.

She probably was in a state of shock, for despite everything, Raven Hill had been her home, and the people inside the closest she had to a family. Glancing back at the castle, Kit saw the tall windows gleaming brightly, like some kind of leering pumpkin, consumed from the inside out. And he was struck with a sense of the past repeating itself.

Kit didn't know whether Raven's interest in the Mallory had roused the attention of Malet and his followers or simply coincided with their own search. But the end was the same. Just as the maze went up in flames, taking those who would kill with it, now Raven Hill was burning, claiming its victims.

Kit shook his head, unwilling to believe in some kind of curse that could follow even a forgery, but his surroundings did not lend themselves to coherent thought. The sooner they left here the better, he realized, but Hero had reached the end of her resources, and the empty building was as good a landmark as any in the mist.

Kit knelt before her. "I've got to fetch Charlie's horse, so I want you to stay here until I come back."

Hero lifted her head. "Where would I go? I have n-n-nothing."

"You've got me," Kit said. He took her face in his hands, forcing her wide eyes to focus on his own. "I love you, and I think you love me, too."

She did not deny it, and for once, all that she felt was visible on her face. The outpouring of emotion was nearly Kit's undoing, and he kissed her with all the force of a claim laid. She clung to him, and when Kit stepped back it was because he knew they could not linger.

"Stay here," he repeated. Exiting the gatehouse, Kit ran round the wall that enclosed Raven Hill's inner court, glad that he had not been forced to climb it again. He was heading for the woods, trying to get his bearings, when a sudden crashing in the brush had him backing against a black trunk.

But it was only a deer, scared up by the smoke, and Kit went on, though his pace slowed considerably as he groped through the trees, the mist rising to obscure his way. Finally, he heard a whinny nearby. No doubt, Charlie's animal had smelled the smoke, too, and was restless.

Still, Kit approached slowly, wary that someone else might have come across the horse, someone fleeing the fire. But the animal was tethered where he had left it, and he led it out of the woods toward the wall. The looming gray curtain was the only solid marker in an increasingly misty world, and he followed it, even though the massive stone seemed to disappear into the distance.

So thick was the fog now that Kit was upon the gatehouse before he realized it. Breathing a sigh of relief, he led Charlie's horse right up to the open door and called softly to Hero. When she did not appear, he wondered whether she could even stand, considering the state she'd been in when he left her.

Dragging the reins, Kit stepped inside, only to bite back a cry of alarm. For even in the near darkness, it was obvious that the seat was vacant, and a search of the shadows revealed the small gatehouse was empty of all life, Hero having vanished into thin air.

Kit shook his head to clear it. As tempting as it was to blame the ghoulish atmosphere in which he found himself, Kit knew that this was no Gothic trickery. There was a logical explanation for Hero's disappearance, and he quickly dismissed the most obvious one—that she had fled from him yet again.

And then he heard it.

Stepping outside the gatehouse, Kit laid a calming hand upon Charlie's animal to still it, then cocked his head to one side, listening. Now that the horse was quiet, there was no mistaking the creak of wheels and muffled hooves. Looking down the long lane, Kit could see nothing in the fog, and he realized the noise could be coming from anywhere, a path back to the stables or along the acres of property that surrounded Raven Hill.

Raven or Erasmus could have come to their senses, left the burning building and come upon Hero. A servant might have offered rescue—or taken her back toward the blaze. Kit only had moments to decide, to make the gamble of a lifetime as he swung into the saddle.

In the end, he chose to move forward, heading down the lane and putting Raven Hill behind him.

Hero sat back in the luxurious coach, so tired that she felt as though she might lose consciousness. Weeks of tension and danger, lack of sleep and the events of the last hour had robbed her of her strength. And her wits. They had left her completely, or else she would not be here now.

The wariness that had served her well for so long had deserted Hero as she sat slumped in Raven Hill's gatehouse, trying to make sense of all that had happened. Even if she hadn't been distraught, Hero would have seen little need for caution, with Erasmus and Raven both…gone.

So when some dark figures appeared, gently urging her from her seat, Hero thought them servants or neighbors who had seen the fire. Dazed, she had let them lead her to the coach. At some point, she'd had the presence of mind to ask about Kit, and the vague assurance she received belatedly roused her suspicions. But by that time, it was too late. She was inside a vehicle far too comfortable to be Raven's, the door firmly shut behind her.

Hero could only think Erasmus responsible, but he was dead, wasn't he? Or had he left his mentor to burn in order to claim the inheritance? If so, he would have no qualms about doing away with her, as well. But Hero's last sight of him, fire close behind, was too fresh in her mind to imagine any other outcome for the man she had called cousin.

For a moment, Hero wondered whether Kit had been right all along and some black-caped Druids were kidnapping her. But even that possibility could not rouse her to action. She was too tired to keep up the carefully cultivated facade that Raven had insisted upon, let alone muster her waning resources. All she wanted to do was to crawl into Kit's arms and stay there.

But even the thought of the man she loved filled Hero with despair, for Raven had taken the facts of her birth with him to the grave. Now she would never know whether her parents had been insane, eager to sell their child to a passing stranger.

Although Kit claimed that he didn't care, Hero did. How could she marry him, knowing that she might turn on him? Christopher Marchant, gentleman and scholar, deserved the best of everything, and that did not include becoming caretaker to a madwoman.

Hero closed her stinging eyes and choked back a moan. She could not take the chance that she might make him miserable or turn violent. And worst of all, loomed the possibility that she might some day sell her own child in a lunatic act, repeating her sordid history.

Swallowing hard, Hero realized that she should be grateful that fate had spirited her away from Kit and the temptation he presented. If Raven had given her a stipend, some kind of future, she could have tried to make a life for herself. But now, with Kit all that was left to her, she might have given in.

It was better this way, Hero told herself, though she had no idea how she would make her way in the world. But perhaps that would not be a concern for long, she thought, as she peered out into the night with no knowledge of her whereabouts.

Yet Hero soon recognized the lights in the distance as those of the great estates that Raven had so coveted. Raven Hill was as close as he could get to the homes of the country's nobles and most wealthy, and though they had done business with him, they had never welcomed him into their ranks.

The darkness and fog made it difficult to determine her exact location, but once the coach passed through gates and turned toward a stylish facade, where rows of windows appeared out of the mist to wink with light, Hero realized her destination. And she laughed.

Although she had never been here, Hero knew that the elegant residence was built during the last century in the classical mode, with four stories of cream-colored stone and slender marble columns marking the entrance. When the horses drew up before the stairs, Hero did not even bother to seize her pistol or try to escape. She simply stared as a footman appeared and hurried toward the coach.

Upon opening the door, he bowed and held out a gloved hand to assist her descent, a treatment so different from her arrival at Raven Hill that Hero stifled another laugh. Unlike her old home, which was sadly neglected in favour of Raven's collections, this place was neat and well kept and well staffed. But then the owner was wealthy beyond even Raven's dreams.

Inside, the marbled foyer was ablaze with light, in stark contrast to Raven Hill's miserly darkness, but the mood was sombre. The footman handed her off to a grim-faced butler, who showed her into the study, an enormous circular room with carved ceilings and a door that seemed to disappear into the woodwork. The walls were hung with pale silk and the accents all painted, which made the space bright and airy even at this hour.

Several lamps were set about, chasing away any shadows, and the furnishings were white and gilt, probably French collectibles worth more than some libraries. But Hero didn't know much about furniture. Instead of inspecting it further, she walked to the pier glass to have a look at herself.

Even to her jaundiced eye, she did not appear as though she had but recently escaped a conflagration. Thankfully, she had kept on her cloak at Raven Hill, and she kept it on now, as well, not knowing what was in store. Her boots were wet from her run through the grass, and she settled into a delicate chair near the marbled fireplace, where a roaring blaze warmed her cold feet.

Compared to Raven Hill, with its petty horrors and perpetual discomforts, this home was the epitome of fine taste and opulence. And yet, her very presence here confirmed that the owner could be no better than Raven himself.

However, as a prison, this place was preferable, and the absence of any guards made escape a simple option. In fact, Hero was tempted to go to a tall window and check the drop to the ground below, but she could not rouse herself. Besides, she was too interested in what her host intended.

She did not have long to wait. Soon, the subtle door opened, and a slender older gentleman entered. He was dressed all in black, and although there was nothing lacking in his costume, it was not of the quality Hero expected. It took her a moment to realize that he was not the master of this house.

"Miss Ingram," he said, with a polite bow. "I apologize for the abrupt manner of your arrival. I understand it was quite the hurried undertaking, but I assure you there was cause for haste." He turned away, walking toward a large ormolu desk that sat in the center of the room.

He made a careful show of pulling out his chair, taking a seat at the desk and folding his hands in front of him. In the light, Hero could see that his face was pale, the shadows under his eyes attesting to some strain. When he spoke, his voice cracked under it, and he was forced to clear his throat.

"You see, we had hoped, but…" He paused, as though to gather his composure. "Again, I apologize for my erratic behavior. My name is Fiskerton, and I'm the secretary to the…late Duke of Montford."

"Late?" Hero asked.

Fiskerton nodded. "His Grace passed away earlier today."

Hero shook her head. "I'm sorry." Although she had never met the man, he was a fine collector whose presence would be missed in the book world. And despite his liveried servants harrying her over the past weeks and practically forcing her into his coach, Hero forgave him. As Poynter had said, he appeared to be in pursuit of one last, great find. And how could she begrudge him that?

Fiskerton cleared his throat again. "The timing is most unfortunate because his last wish was that he speak to you." He drew a deep breath. "But you are a difficult young lady to find."

Hero blinked in surprise.

"When his Grace made his intentions clear, we wrote repeatedly to you at your home, I believe it is called Raven Hill?"

Hero felt a cold chill dance up her spine. She nodded, then shook her head. "But I never received any messages."

"Yes," Fiskerton said, frowning. "I suspected as much. I even sent one of my representatives there in the hopes of speaking with you in person, but he was denied admittance." He sighed. "As his Grace grew more ill, my queries became more insistent, but then Mr Raven claimed that you were no longer living with him."

Hero drew in a sharp breath.

"Unfortunately, a great deal of time was wasted before we came to the conclusion that Mr Raven might not be forthcoming to us." Fiskerton frowned. "That's when we were forced to make some alternative inquiries, and we discovered that you were traveling, but your whereabouts, again, were difficult to determine. During this time, we also set a, ahem, watch upon Raven Hill, should you return at some point."

Hero could only gape in astonishment at this revelation, which explained why the coach had been so quick to retrieve her.

"Unfortunately, since time was of the essence, they might have been a bit abrupt. Indeed, I believe they were prepared to enter the house, if need be," Fiskerton said, with obvious disapproval. "Thankfully, that was not necessary, though I understand that a fire was reported?"

Hero nodded numbly.

"In that case, their abruptness may be excused, for their intention was to get you safely away, and to bring you here, of course."

It was the "of course" that finally prompted Hero to speak. "But why?" she asked, in confusion.

At her question, Fiskerton assumed a more businesslike expression. "That was for his Grace to explain, but when it became clear that we might not be able to locate you, he did empower me to notify you as to the, uh, circumstances."

Looking down at a sheaf of papers on the desk, Fiskerton began shuffling through them, as though he was not eager to explain further. "And from your curiosity, it appears that Mr Tovell…er, Raven, kept his part of the bargain in that you are unaware of your relation to his Grace."

Hero blinked, uncomprehending.

Fiskerton cleared his throat. "You are, ahem, the duke's natural child," he said. "Of course, inheritance laws and entailments apply, so that his Grace did not intend to, uh, formerly recognize you. A cousin will inherit the title and estates, but his Grace did want to make certain that you received something."

Hero felt as though someone had struck her. She tried to draw in air, but her stomach roiled, and her lungs did not seem to be working.

"Miss Ingram? Are you all right?"

Fiskerton rose from his desk to come round to her chair. "Put your head down," he advised, obviously agitated. "Perhaps I should send for a maid or Mrs Ferguson. She will know… Shall I call for smelling salts?"

Hero shook her head and swallowed a hysterical laugh. She had seen and heard it all, Gothic horrors that would set any sane woman to screaming, yet now she threatened to swoon at something that was not even frightening.

"Are you certain?" Mr Fiskerton asked. When she nodded, he awkwardly patted her arm. "I wish you could have spoken to his Grace directly, for…I know that when he neared the end of his life, he rued his earlier decision."

Hero's head shot up so quickly that she almost knocked the older man aside. "He gave me to Raven!" she said, as the realization struck.

Fiskerton frowned. "Actually, the man was then Augustus Tovell, and he served the duke's library well. It was only, uh, afterward that he assumed his, uh, new character."

"Why?" Hero asked numbly. Although legitimacy counted for much in society, many fathers, including the royal heirs, provided for their natural offspring, setting them up in households without acknowledging them officially.

Fiskerton shook his head. "Again, that was for his Grace to say. I was not privy to the decision."

Hero looked at the man long and hard until he finally glanced away. "I believe pressure from the dowager duchess was involved."

Pressure from his mother, Hero thought dismally, then she drew in a sharp breath. "Who was *my* mother?"

Fiskerton shook his head. "His Grace never named her."

Again, Hero gave him a hard look, for servants knew everything that took place in their households and were privy to every bit of rumour and gossip. She knew it, and Fiskerton knew it.

Frowning, he finally spoke, with obvious reluctance. "There was talk that she was a princess royal. But I know nothing for certain, and you will find little to gain should you pursue that avenue."

Hero reared back in outrage at such a suggestion.

As if fearing he had said too much, Fiskerton returned to his seat at the desk, put the massive piece of furniture between them, and resumed his business-like manner.

Shuffling through the papers, he did not look up when next he spoke. "As I said, his Grace's final wish was to talk with you, but he made arrangements on your behalf, should he be unable. He was most pleased that your interests echoed his own, so his bequest reflects that shared appreciation."

Hero felt like her weary head was spinning. What was he saying?

As if she had spoken aloud, Fiskerton lifted his head to eye her sombrely. "His Grace left you his library."

Again, Hero reeled as though from a blow, unable to comprehend what she had just heard. "Wh-what?"

"You have inherited his Grace's collection of books, which is worth a great deal of money—" Fiskerton began, but he was interrupted by the sound of a commotion beyond the confines of the quiet room.

Hero heard muffled shouts before the discreet door burst open to reveal a familiar figure, followed by the butler and assorted footman, who appeared to have been shaken off in some sort of altercation.

"What's going on here? Hero, are you all right?"

But by the time Kit spoke, Hero had already leapt to her feet, intent upon throwing herself into his arms. They were a haven that she would never have to leave, she realized, as she cried out in relief.

"Oh, Kit, my parents weren't lunatics."

# *Chapter Sixteen*

Once Hero identified Kit as her betrothed, the footmen trooped out, leaving the two of them alone with Fiskerton. However, the duke's secretary eyed Kit up and down with some disfavour, as though the new arrival did not quite meet his approval.

Hero swallowed a bubble of hysterical laughter at the suspicion that Kit might be after her money. Not long ago she had been homeless, penniless and of dubious parentage, and still he had pressed his suit. At the memory, she wanted nothing more than to throw herself back into his arms.

However, Fiskerton frowned upon such displays, so Hero restrained herself, for the time being, and tried to appear impassive. But the facade that had served her so well in the past was unattainable. Despite her best efforts, Hero felt her lips curving and her cheeks flushing. Happiness, long denied, filled her so completely that it threatened to spill out.

Of course, Fiskerton could not know that her joy

came from his news, not of her inheritance, but of her ancestry, and with it, her ability to accept Kit's proposal without reservation. She had kept him at arm's length for his own sake, as well as her own, and now she would close any distance between them.

"Perhaps you don't realize, Miss Ingram, the value of your bequest," Fiskerton said, frowning at her seeming giddiness. "His Grace's library is a great responsibility and will make you a wealthy woman, should you choose to break it up."

"I can well imagine members of the Roxburghe Club salivating at such an opportunity, but I don't intend to put the collection up for auction," Hero said. She nodded toward Kit. "Mr Marchant is planning some improvements to his estate, and perhaps that will just have to include the library."

Although he had not been privy to the earlier discussion, Kit took her cue, as usual, and nodded in agreement, while Fiskerton looked dubious.

"Oh, yes, Mr Fiskerton," Hero insisted, her smile wide. "Perhaps his entrance here gave the wrong impression, but I can assure you that Mr Marchant is both a gentleman and a scholar."

If Fiskerton still was not convinced, he kept his opinion to himself and included Kit in the ensuing conversation. There were details that had to be seen to and papers to sign, as well as questions about the fire at Raven Hill to be answered. But Raven's reputation for being reclusive and eccentric made for little inquiry, as did the statements from the Duke of Montford's liveried servants and Hero's presence in his Grace's home.

\* \* \*

It was late by the time all the business was concluded, and rather than see them off into the cold at
that hour, Fiskerton offered them accommodations for
the night in the dowager's residence tucked into the
woods nearby.

"It's not staffed at this time, since her Grace passed
away some time ago, but I had the housekeeper prepare some rooms and light fires," Fiskerton said, giving his papers a final shuffle.

Although Hero would have liked to see more of her
father's home, the true heir would be arriving soon,
and, understandably, Fiskerton wanted to avoid any
awkwardness. When presented with the prospect of
setting out for Charlie's in her current state of exhaus-
tion, Hero was eager to bed down anywhere.

Still, she was hardly prepared for the lavishness of
her destination. Although not built on the grand scale
of the main residence, the dowager's house was larger
than Oakfield and beautifully appointed. While the
fires were being lit, Hero wandered around, running
a finger over the dusty surface of a gilt writing desk
and a medallion-backed chair.

Her presence here, in the home of the woman seemingly responsible for her life, made Hero feel oddly
off balance. Although the dowager duchess might not
have arranged Hero's placement with Raven, she had
made sure the duke never knew his daughter. And she
had been Hero's *grandmother*. That thought was startling enough, but then Hero considered just who her
other grandparents might be, and she had to stifle
another hysterical laugh.

Wasn't the king himself rumoured to be mad? It seemed that Hero could not escape that taint, but it was enough that she had not be purchased from asylum inmates—and that she was not related in any way to Raven. Although Hero regretted his stewardship, she found it difficult to envision any other existence, especially one as the illegitimate daughter of a duke, and her steps faltered.

On the surface, the idea seemed ideal—the dream of every orphan who ever pondered her ancestry. But upon reflection, Hero felt an uneasiness far different from that engendered by Raven and his Gothic home.

In truth, Hero was not sure she would have liked the stigma of natural birth, even with such an exalted pedigree. And what kind of world would she have inhabited? She could not have lived with either parent, and would never have known her mother, for though there were rumours, the royal princesses did not acknowledge any scandals.

Would her caretaker have been any better than Raven? Probably. But who would have made up her circle? Would she have been pursued for connections, her influence? Hero could not imagine anyone like Kit in that setting, someone kind and decent, who wanted her only for herself, without name or coin attached.

And suddenly her parents seemed poor, despite their wealth, concerned only with their position, with no thought for love or what was right. Glancing up to where Kit was speaking softly with the housekeeper, Hero realized that her gentleman farmer was worth more than the lot of them.

As if sensing her attention, Kit looked up and

flashed Hero a smile that chased away the chill in the air. The house was cold in more ways than one, she realized, hugging her cloak close. For all its luxury, it held no life or hospitality, and the expensive furnishings were as brittle and meaningless as Raven's elaborate collections.

"You're cold, miss," the housekeeper said. "Here, let me show you to your room, and you, too, sir, then I'll be off. If you need anything else, just give a ring, for I'll have one of the maids stay in the quarters here."

Ushering Hero into a bedroom where a fire burned brightly, the woman closed the door, leaving her to stand in the middle of a vast space, occupied by an elaborate bed decorated with heavy hangings. As in the other rooms, the dowager's taste tended toward French furnishings and gilt, taken to extremes.

Although elegant, the place had none of the appeal of the Armstrong town house or even the Smallpeace farmhouse. But it would do for tonight, Hero thought, bone tired as she removed her cloak. She had barely laid it upon a painted couch when the door burst open and Kit strode in unceremoniously, a determined look upon his face.

"What?" Hero asked, as he made a point of eyeing the curtained windows. For a moment, she fell into her old habit of wariness, but who could be after them now?

"I just wanted to make sure you weren't planning your escape," Kit said, slanting her a speculative glance.

Hero smiled, and the odd mood that had settled upon her since entering the dowager's domain lifted. "I'm not going anywhere."

"Well, I'm here to make sure of that," Kit said, advancing upon her, his lips curved in a devilish fashion.

Hero took a step back, her weariness forgotten as a frisson of excitement danced up her spine. Suddenly, she realized just how alone they were in this strange house, without even a staff of servants to gossip. "You'll just have to learn to trust me, even though it may take a lifetime."

"I'm counting on that, but in the meantime I was thinking about a chain to tether you to me. With a lock," Kit added, coming so close that Hero found herself up against the curtained bed.

Had she thought the house cold and dead? Kit brought warmth and life with such force that the very air around her crackled and her body roused itself in response.

Kit gave her a jaundiced look as he inched nearer, his hard frame almost touching her own. "But by the time I find one, you might be gone."

When Hero opened her mouth to protest that he needed nothing to keep her to him, Kit put a finger to her lips. And the sensation was so powerful that she lost all train of thought.

"I could try to get a special licence, so we might be married immediately, but again, I don't have enough time, especially since we need to leave for Hawthorne Park as soon as possible to attend my sister's wedding," Kit said.

A subtle nudge from him had Hero falling back upon the soft bedding, and he leaned forward. "So I'm going to have to do something else to make sure you never leave me again."

"And what's that?" Hero whispered, even though she recognized the dark intent in his eyes.

Kit grinned as he moved over her. "I'm going to thoroughly compromise you."

Hero felt her pulse leap at the warning, but instead of protesting, she sighed in anticipation. "Well, in that case, I'm definitely not going anywhere."

Hero arrived at Charlie's town house in far more elegant fashion than before, in the Duke of Montford's coach, his liveried footmen in attendance, and Kit riding Charlie's horse alongside. Although Charlie was out, they were shown to their rooms and settled in for an overnight stay before leaving London.

This time, Kit threatened to remain in Hero's bedroom during her bath, but when she invited him to join her, he left, muttering something about Charlie's aunt. While Hero lingered, enjoying a perfumed toilette for the first time in her life, he arranged for their horses to be retrieved from one inn and their packs from another.

It was all over, and yet, Hero felt like her life was just beginning. Although she was inclined to toss out her boy's clothing, Kit insisted she keep it in case she wanted to muck about with the new landscaping that he planned for Oakfield. Hero smiled to herself, certain that his reasons had less to do with work than play. Hadn't he whispered something to that effect last night, about the look of her legs, clad in breeches?

Hero flushed as the memories rushed back of his long, slow seduction, intent yet playful, sweet yet fierce, a tangle of limbs and smooth skin, and Kit's mouth moving upon her. He had whispered of his love over and over until Hero had haltingly spoken herself, stuttering at first, as she choked with the force of her emotion. It returned now, and she had to swallow hard as she packed away her boy's clothes for some future romp with her future husband.

Although Hero insisted that quid pro quo demanded Kit keep his Harlequin costume, he balked, claiming that he had already arranged for the earl's purloined masquerades to be returned to Cheswick. However, when pressed, he reluctantly agreed to wear something similar should Hero devise it—as long as no one else was involved in its construction.

Hero's cheeks grew heated at the thought, and she realized the project would be as good a reason as any to perfect her meagre sewing skills. But she said nothing to Kit as he escorted her to the parlour for some biscuits and chocolate. The hot drink was a delight that Hero had never known before, and she finished her own cup and then half of Kit's, while he complained about the missing Mrs Armstrong.

"It appears your would-be chaperone has fled," Kit said, leaning back in a chair near the fire. "So we'll have to see about obtaining another." Putting his feet up on a nearby hassock, he looked as though he might nod off, which was not surprising, considering how little sleep either of them had got the night before.

That memory not only made Hero flush, but seemed to negate her need for a chaperone, and they were in the midst of arguing the point when a commotion erupted in the foyer. Charlie's butler arrived one step ahead of a pair of guests, but he did not have a chance to announce them before the woman rushed forward.

"Kit!" she called out. He rose to his feet in response, and Hero felt a stab of alarm. But as the lady flung herself toward Kit, the uncanny resemblance between them became apparent, and Hero realized this must be his sister, Sydony. At the discovery, Hero's alarm turned into a kind of queasy feeling that had nothing to do with the chocolate she'd consumed.

"Where the devil have you been?" Sydony demanded, and for a moment, Hero didn't know whether she was going to strike her brother or throw herself into his arms. "I've been worried sick!"

"As I wrote in my letter, we had a bit of adventure," Kit said, ruefully.

"A bit of adventure!" The woman scoffed. She nodded toward the dark, silent man, who stood distant from the siblings. "Barto and Hob have been out searching London for you! They stopped short of storming Raven Hill only to learn it burned to a hollow shell last night!"

Kit looked apologetic. "I'd forgotten about Hob."

"Yes, Hob! He came to us with tales of knife-wielding assailants, kidnappers, warrants…" Sydony paused as though to catch her breath. "I didn't know whether to go on with the wedding, or if you'd be there, or even where you were or if you were hurt…" She trailed off, a stricken look on her beautiful face, and Kit soon was patting her back in awkward comfort.

Although Hero could understand the woman's agitation, it did little to ease her own queasiness. For it was she, a total stranger, who had put Kit in danger and wrought havoc in all their lives. Would they hold her responsible?

As if sensing Hero's thoughts, the woman turned from Kit to look at Hero, her dark eyes missing nothing. "And you must be Hero," she said. "Are you all right?"

The question was not what Hero expected, and it took a moment to respond. When she nodded warily, Sydony moved to take both her hands. "Well, then, welcome to the family."

"What?" Kit asked, looking startled. "How did you know?"

"Perhaps it was the undertone of your letter." The dark man stepped forward, his tone wry. "I'm Viscount Hawthorne."

"Just call him Barto," Sydony said, pulling Hero down into a chair and taking a seat beside her. Now that she had found her brother in good health, she appeared more composed and less daunting.

Yet Hero remained uncertain. Her stomach seemed to have settled, but she was not accustomed to being the center of such attention and her dealings with women, especially those near her own age, had been few. Her anxiety was not eased by her sudden realization that she was destined to call the future viscountess her sister.

Although Sydony leaned forward, as if expectant, Hero had no idea what to say. She knew nothing of the traditional female occupations and could not watercolor or play the pianoforte. Nor did she even trust herself to conduct a proper conversation on feminine topics until Sydony put her at ease with a smile and a single demand.

"Now, tell me everything."

# Epilogue

Kit stood on the threshold of the barn from which he and Hero had once made their escape and smiled, for the view before him was much changed. Then, it had been cold and dark, an eerie fog veiling the bleak landscape devastated by the fire behind his home. But now, the summer sun shown upon neat lawns that stretched up to Oakfield's rebuilt terrace.

The property was a far cry from the one Kit had inherited. The lands that had lain fallow were tilled, the formerly empty tenant farms bustling with life. Sheep grazed not far away, and he could see a horse and plough off in the distance, growing crops that had made the estate a success and bounty that made his table groan with good food.

The house that had seemed cursed now glowed in the afternoon light, its stone stripped of dark growth. The stables had been rebuilt, bigger and better than before, and the blackened remains of the maze had been cleared away, replaced by clipped grass and new trees and plantings. Kit had helped in the design himself, disdaining the old formal beds for bright spots of colorful flowers scattered among gravel paths.

It was a place to walk and linger and sit upon benches tucked in the shade, and sometimes Kit couldn't believe his good fortune. Immediately after the fire, he would have never imagined this outcome, and he knew who to thank for it all. But for the arrival of Hero, he might still be stuck in the dismals, drinking and brooding, while his holdings further deteriorated around him.

Now, he could look back without flinching. The fire had changed him, but it had not scarred him, becoming nothing more than a bad memory. Afterward, he had matured from a careless boy into a responsible man, shedding the guilt and tension, with Hero's help, until he felt like himself again, at home in his own skin.

Although she claimed that all he needed was to pummel someone insensible, it was more than that. By protecting Hero, Kit had redeemed himself, and now he felt he could handle just about anything. Although he had stopped looking over his shoulder for Druids, he stayed alert, intent upon guarding his own.

Those experiences had also taught him to savor every moment, and Kit did so now, taking a deep breath scented with grass and flowers. Ahead, on one of the gravel walks, he could see the figures of Sydony, Barto and their son Max gamboling with the dogs, carefree and happy, and he felt the same.

Behind him, he heard Hero's light footfalls, and as she moved to stand beside him, Kit slipped an arm around her. His hand immediately moved to rest upon the swelling that marked the child who would be coming soon.

"How are George and Harold?" he asked.

"And Missy and Clyde and Thomas and Toby...." Hero's recitation trailed off into a laugh. "All the cats and kittens are well. In fact, I've another who wishes to come to the house with me."

Kit groaned as she lifted her hand to reveal a tiny, orange ball of fur, purring contentedly. "It's not sleeping in our bed," he said.

"I love you," she whispered, knowing full well that the admission, so long in coming, was bound to bend him to her will.

"I love you, too," Kit said, because he knew she never got tired of hearing it. Turning his head to nuzzle her silken hair, he resigned himself, with a smile, to yet another cat.

But how could he deny his wife anything when she continued to surprise and delight him? Once distant and secretive, she had proven to be warm and giving, and laughter filled their days. She had made their home welcoming and comfortable, a haven for all who came to visit, not just Syd and Barto. Why, the last time Charlie had been here, he threatened never to leave.

The library was filled to overflowing with her inheritance, and she had been named Raven's heir, as well. Although Hero had sold off what little was left of Raven Hill as quickly as possible, she had decorated Oakfield with the "blood money" that her father must have paid her caretaker over the years.

But after updating the catalogue and parting with

some volumes, Hero had shown little interest in the books that had once been such a part of her life, and Kit sometimes wondered… He slanted her a speculative glance. "Do you ever miss your adventures?"

She blinked at the unexpected question. "I never had any until I met you."

"What about all your book dealings?"

Hero shook her head as she put the kitten to her cheek. "Those were usually boring transactions made with dull antiquarians, hardly something I enjoyed." She looked up at him, her lips curving. "Are you saying life with you isn't an adventure?

Kit shrugged. "Well, I am just a gentleman farmer."

Hero laughed. "I don't think so," she said, slipping an arm around his waist. "You might have the rest of the world convinced, but you can't fool me, Kit Marchant." Her eyes shining, she gave him a teasing smile.

"You're a gentleman and a scholar."

\* \* \* \* \*

*Rancher Ramsey Westmoreland's temporary cook
is way too attractive for his liking.
Little does he know Chloe Burton came to his ranch
with another agenda entirely....*

That man across the street had to be, without a doubt, the most handsome man she'd ever seen.

Chloe Burton's pulse beat rhythmically as he stopped to talk to another man in front of a feed store. He was tall, dark and every inch of sexy—from his Stetson to the well-worn leather boots on his feet. And from the way his jeans and Western shirt fit his broad muscular shoulders, it was quite obvious he had everything it took to separate the men from the boys. The combination was enough to corrupt any woman's mind and had her weakening even from a distance. Her body felt flushed. It was hot. Unsettled.

Over the past year the only male who had gotten her time and attention had been the e-mail. That was simply pathetic, especially since now she was practically drooling simply at the sight of a man. Even his stance—both hands in his jeans pockets, legs braced apart, was a pose she would carry to her dreams.

And he was smiling, evidently enjoying the conversation being exchanged. He had dimples, incredibly sexy dimples in not one but both cheeks.

"What are you staring at, Clo?"

Chloe nearly jumped. She'd forgotten she had a

lunch date. She glanced over the table at her best friend from college, Lucia Conyers.

"Take a look at that man across the street in the blue shirt, Lucia. Will he not be perfect for Denver's first issue of *Simply Irresistible* or what?" Chloe asked with so much excitement she almost couldn't stand it.

She was the owner of *Simply Irresistible*, a magazine for today's up-and-coming woman. Their once-a-year Irresistible Man cover, which highlighted a man the magazine felt deserved the honor, had increased sales enough for Chloe to open a Denver office.

When Lucia didn't say anything but kept staring, Chloe's smile widened. "Well?"

Lucia glanced across the booth at her. "Since you asked, I'll tell you what I see. One of the Westmorelands—Ramsey Westmoreland. And yes, he'd be perfect for the cover, but he won't do it."

Chloe raised a brow. "He'd get paid for his services, of course."

Lucia laughed and shook her head. "Getting paid won't be the issue, Clo—Ramsey is one of the wealthiest sheep ranchers in this part of Colorado. But everyone knows what a private person he is. Trust me—he won't do it."

Chloe couldn't help but smile. The man was the epitome of what she was looking for in a magazine cover and she was determined that whatever it took, he would be it.

"Umm, I don't like that look on your face, Chloe. I've seen it before and know exactly what it means."

She watched as Ramsey Westmoreland entered the store with a swagger that made her almost breathless. She *would* be seeing him again.

*Look for Silhouette Desire's*
*HOT WESTMORELAND NIGHTS*
*by Brenda Jackson,*
*available March 9 wherever books are sold.*

# HARLEQUIN® HISTORICAL:
Where love is timeless

# *The Horseman's Bride*
## ELIZABETH LANE

After taking the blame for his brother-in-law's murder, Jace Denby is on the run. He must leave the ranch, though the beauty and fierce courage of Clara Seavers entice him to stay....

Clara doesn't trust this farm hand, but the rugged and unexpectedly caring man ignites her spirit...and heart. The more Jace fights their mounting passion, the more she'll risk to make him hers forever.

*Available March 2010*
*wherever you buy books.*

# *Miss Winthorpe's Elopement*
## CHRISTINE MERRILL

Shy heiress Miss Penelope Winthorpe never meant
to wed a noble lord over a blacksmith's anvil.

The Duke of Bellston had no intention of taking
a wife. Now the notorious rake has a new aim—
to shock and seduce his prim and proper bride.

But the gorgeous duke will be taught a lesson
of his own as scholarly Miss Winthorpe becomes
his seductive duchess!

*Available March 2010
wherever you buy books.*

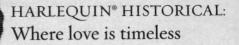

HARLEQUIN® HISTORICAL:
Where love is timeless

# The Earl's Forbidden Ward
## BRONWYN SCOTT

Innocent debutante Tessa Branscombe senses that
underneath her handsome guardian's cool demeanor
there is an intensely passionate nature. The arrogant
earl infuriates her—yet makes her want to explore
those hidden depths....

The Earl of Dursley has no time for girls!
Miss Tessa Branscombe, in particular, is trouble.
She tempts this very proper earl to misbehave—and
forbidden fruit always tastes that much sweeter....

*Available March 2010*
*wherever you buy books.*

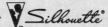

# SPECIAL EDITION

## FROM *USA TODAY* BESTSELLING AUTHOR
# CHRISTINE RIMMER

# A BRIDE FOR JERICHO BRAVO

Marnie Jones had long ago buried her wild-child
impulses and opted to be "safe," romantically
speaking. But one look at born rebel Jericho Bravo
and she began to wonder if her thrill-seeking side
was about to be revived. Because if ever there was
a man worth taking a chance on, there he was,
right within her grasp....

*Available in March*
*wherever books are sold.*

---

# REQUEST YOUR FREE BOOKS!

 HARLEQUIN® HISTORICAL:
Where love is timeless

## 2 FREE NOVELS PLUS 2 FREE GIFTS!

**YES!** Please send me 2 FREE Harlequin® Historical novels and my 2 FREE gifts (gifts are worth about $10). After receiving them, if I don't wish to receive any more books, I can return the shipping statement marked "cancel." If I don't cancel, I will receive 6 brand-new novels every month and be billed just $4.94 per book in the U.S. or $5.49 per book in Canada. That's a saving of 20% off the cover price! It's quite a bargain! Shipping and handling is just 50¢ per book in the U.S. and 75¢ per book in Canada.* I understand that accepting the 2 free books and gifts places me under no obligation to buy anything. I can always return a shipment and cancel at any time. Even if I never buy another book from Harlequin, the two free books and gifts are mine to keep forever.

246 HDN E4DN   349 HDN E4DY

| | |
|---|---|
| Name | (PLEASE PRINT) |

| | |
|---|---|
| Address | Apt. # |

| | | |
|---|---|---|
| City | State/Prov. | Zip/Postal Code |

Signature (if under 18, a parent or guardian must sign)

### Mail to the Harlequin Reader Service:
**IN U.S.A.:** P.O. Box 1867, Buffalo, NY 14240-1867
**IN CANADA:** P.O. Box 609, Fort Erie, Ontario L2A 5X3
Not valid for current subscribers to Harlequin Historical books.

**Want to try two free books from another line?**
**Call 1-800-873-8635 or visit www.morefreebooks.com.**

* Terms and prices subject to change without notice. Prices do not include applicable taxes. N.Y. residents add applicable sales tax. Canadian residents will be charged applicable provincial taxes and GST. Offer not valid in Quebec. This offer is limited to one order per household. All orders subject to approval. Credit or debit balances in a customer's account(s) may be offset by any other outstanding balance owed by or to the customer. Please allow 4 to 6 weeks for delivery. Offer available while quantities last.

**Your Privacy:** Harlequin Books is committed to protecting your privacy. Our Privacy Policy is available online at www.eHarlequin.com or upon request from the Reader Service. From time to time we make our lists of customers available to reputable third parties who may have a product or service of interest to you. ☐ If you would prefer we not share your name and address, please check here.

**Help us get it right**—We strive for accurate, respectful and relevant communications. To clarify or modify your communication preferences, visit us at www.ReaderService.com/consumerschoice.

HH10